"Why now, Miss Bell? This is what puzzles us. Police Constable Powell came to see you after Mr. Bell's death, but you made no reference to murder then."

"You're upset by your brother's death, of course," Quantrill said, practicing kindness. "But if you'd gone to the inquest and seen how thoroughly the matter was dealt with, I'm sure it would have set your mind at rest. As it is, you're probably imagining—"

She snapped back at him, proudly. "Please don't humour me, Mr. Quantrill. I know quite well what you think. My brother was a figure of fun in Breckham Market: poor old Clanger—yes, I know what you all called him—poor old Clanger Bell, the town drunk. None of you took him seriously in life, and you're not prepared to take his death seriously either."

WHO SAW HIM DIE?
by Sheila Radley

Bantam offers the finest in classic and modern British murder mysteries.
Ask your bookseller for the books you have missed.

Agatha Christie

Death on the Nile
A Holiday for Murder
The Mousetrap and Other Plays
The Mysterious Affair at Styles
Poirot Investigates
Postern of Fate
The Secret Adversary
The Seven Dials Mystery
Sleeping Murder

Dorothy Simpson

Last Seen Alive
The Night She Died
Puppet for a Corpse
Six Feet Under
Close Her Eyes

Sheila Radley

The Chief Inspector's Daughter
Death in the Morning
Fate Worse Than Death
Who Saw Him Die?

Elizabeth George

A Great Deliverance

Colin Dexter

The Riddle of the Third Mile
The Lost World of Nicholas Quinn
Service of All the Dead
The Dead of Jericho
The Secret of Annexe 3
Coming Soon: Last Seen Wearing

John Greenwood

The Mind of Mr. Mosley
The Missing Mr. Mosley
Mosley By Moonlight
Murder, Mr. Mosley
Mists Over Mosley
Coming Soon: What, Me, Mr. Mosley?

Ruth Rendell

The Face of Trespass
The Lake of Darkness
No More Dying Then
One Across, Two Down
Shake Hands Forever
A Sleeping Life
A Dark-Adapted Eye
    (writing as Barbara Vine)
A Fatal Inversion
    (writing as Barbara Vine)

Marian Babson

Death in Fashion
Reel Murder
Murder, Murder Little Star
Murder Sails at Midnight

Christianna Brand

Suddenly at His Residence
Heads You Lose

Dorothy Cannell

The Widows Club
Coming Soon: Down the Garden Path

Who Saw Him Die?

Sheila Radley

BANTAM BOOKS
TORONTO · NEW YORK · LONDON · SYDNEY · AUCKLAND

This is a work of fiction. Names, characters, places, and
incidents either are the product of the author's
imagination or are used fictitiously. Any resemblance to
actual events or persons, living or dead, is entirely
coincidental.

*This edition contains the complete text
of the original hardcover edition.*
NOT ONE WORD HAS BEEN OMITTED.

WHO SAW HIM DIE?
*A Bantam Book / published by arrangement with
Charles Scribner's Sons*

PRINTING HISTORY
Scribner's edition published January 1988
Bantam edition / December 1988

John Betjeman's poem, "In a Bath Teashop," from
his *Collected Poems*, is reproduced by permission of
John Murray Ltd.

ISBN 0-553-27607-7

*Bantam Books are published by Bantam Books, a division of Bantam
Doubleday Dell Publishing Group, Inc. Its trademark, consisting of
the words "Bantam Books" and the portrayal of a rooster, is
Registered in U.S. Patent and Trademark Office and in other
countries. Marca Registrada. Bantam Books, 666 Fifth Avenue, New
York, New York 10103.*

PRINTED IN THE UNITED STATES OF AMERICA
O   0 9 8 7 6 5 4 3 2 1

For Margaret

In a Bath Teashop

"Let us not speak, for the love we bear one another—
   Let us hold hands and look."
She, such a very ordinary little woman;
   He, such a thumping crook;
But both, for a moment, little lower than the angels
   In the teashop's ingle-nook.

                John Betjeman

1

His name was Cuthbert Redvers Fullerton Bell, but everyone in Breckham Market knew him as Clanger. He was fifty-two years old, and a bachelor. For most of his adult life he had been acknowledged and respected as the town's principal drunk. And now he was dead.

There was no mystery about his death. It occurred in public, in the soft damp light of early afternoon on a mild day in November. Three eye-witnesses saw him emerge unsteadily from the Boot, his favourite pub, at closing time and stand swaying at the edge of the pavement for a few moments before stepping out in the path of an oncoming vehicle. The driver, who was travelling down the one-way street at a lawful twenty-seven miles an hour, hadn't a chance of avoiding him. Bell sustained multiple injuries, and he was dead by the time the ambulance arrived.

The manner of Clanger Bell's death caused no surprise to anyone in Beckham Market. The wonder was that it hadn't happened sooner. Clanger—a shambling, uncommunicative man, always either badly in need of a shave or badly shaven, habitually dressed in a homburg hat and a rumpled city suit, and carrying a bulging briefcase—had for years been a hazard to motorists in the centre of the town. It was his custom, when crossing the narrow streets on his meandering route from one pub to another, to play a solitary game of chicken: to stand on the pavement deliberately waiting for a vehicle to approach, and then to stagger across at the very last moment.

He had of course been given many a talking-to by the police, without effect. But he was such a well-known figure that every local driver kept an eye open for him, particularly when passing the pubs he was known to frequent, and slowed to a walking pace when he wavered into sight. It was Clanger's misfortune that John Reuben Goodrum, the driver of the Range Rover that hit him, was—although a Suffolk man—a newcomer to Breckham Market.

There were few to mourn Clanger Bell. His only near

relative was his unmarried elder sister Eunice, with whom he
shared the large Victorian house that had been their family
home. Although he had lived in Breckham Market all his life,
no one considered him as a friend. As a boy, he had been away
at boarding school; as a young man he had spent four hours a
day commuting by train to and from London, where he
worked for a time in a city bank; as the town drunk, he drank
alone.

His passing was, however, regarded with a widespread
sense of regret. Eunice and Cuthbert Bell were the last
representatives of one of the town's most respected families,
property owners and civic leaders for a hundred years and
more. Cuthbert had spoiled the family's reputation, but in
doing so he had endeared himself to the local people who took
pride in the fact that their town drunk was a gentleman. In the
quarter of a century during which he had held the office, he
had become an institution. Breckham Market wouldn't be the
same without him.

Even the local police were sorry, despite the fact that
Clanger had been a thundering nuisance for longer than the
most long-serving of them could remember. They had always
known that there was nothing to be done with him, and so the
coppers had treated him with a patience and a tolerance that
amounted almost to affection.

For most of the time he had wandered about the town in a
dazed silence, doing no harm to anyone. When he became
fuddled and began muttering aloud in the streets, the police
had steered him in the direction of his home. When his
mutterings turned to incoherent shouts, they had driven him
there. When he fell down, legless, they had given him a night
in the cells for his own protection. They had taken him into
custody only on those occasions when, shouting wildly in an
incomprehensible climax of frustration or anger, he had begun
swinging his heavy, newspaper-crammed briefcase and had
inadvertently smashed a shop window.

At his subsequent appearance in the magistrates' court, on
average once every six weeks, the police would ensure that
Clanger was not only sober but tidy and shaven. He would
plead guilty, in his little-heard, well-bred voice, to having
been drunk and disorderly, and would make courteous apology
for the trouble he had caused. But as to why he had caused it—
what memory, what hurt or fear had driven him to make his
outburst—he refused to enlighten anyone. He had always paid

the fine, costs and compensation, accepted a lift home in a police car, and immediately walked back to the nearest pub to begin the cycle over again.

The police were going to miss him. As soon as the news of his death reached the headquarters of the Breckham Market division of the county force, the station sergeant organised a whip-round for a wreath. The sergeant also requested permission for himself and a senior police constable to attend the funeral, as a mark of respect for their most regular client. And in view of the status of the Bell family, the divisional superintendent decided that he too might put in an official appearance and help to send Clanger off in style.

There was a good deal of sympathy—respectful rather than affectionate—from all quarters of the old town for the dead man's sister. Reserved, upright and fastidious, Eunice Bell was unmistakably a gentlewoman. Her brother's behaviour must have been a considerable embarrassment to her, and it was understandable that she had avoided involving herself in the public life of Breckham Market. She had always been a regular worshipper at the parish church, St. Botolph's, but apart from that she had chosen to spend most of her time fifteen miles away in Saintsbury, where she did voluntary work for the Red Cross.

Miss Bell took the news of her brother's death with well-bred stoicism. She preferred not to attend the inquest, where a police officer provided formal evidence of the dead man's identity. The Coroner recorded the expected verdict of accidental death.

But the following day, Eunice Bell telephoned divisional police headquarters and demanded to speak to the superintendent as a matter of urgency. She told him that, having read the report of the inquest in the local newspaper, she had come to the conclusion that her brother's death was no accident. She had, she said, good reason to believe that Cuthbert had been murdered.

2

John Reuben Goodrum, the driver of the Range Rover in the path of which Clanger Bell had played his terminal game of chicken, was a lucky man. He told himself so as he stood in front of his dressing room mirror, in the big Georgian house he had recently acquired in Breckham Market, giving his massive slab of a chin a very close wet shave. ("Desperate Dan" his wife had just teased him as she tried to avoid contact with his bristles during their customary final cuddle before getting up.)

"By God, Jack, you're a lucky man!" he said aloud in the warm slow voice that, rising slightly at the end of each sentence, had an authentic Suffolk sing to it. He peered more closely into the mirror, parting his lips and crimping his mouth into temporary toothlessness, and contrived to scythe an outcrop of bramble from the tricky area just below his nostrils without flecking the shaving soap with a single drop of blood. He was making an expert job of it, these days, he reckoned, considering that he hadn't given a damn about his appearance until a couple of years ago.

Not that shaving himself cleanly had anything to do with luck. He'd put skill and judgement into it, as he had into the business enterprise by which, starting from nothing, he had made his fortune. But luck had always seemed to run his way, and evidently was still running. His first wife Doreen must have been right when she told him that the devil would always look after his own.

Satisfactorily shaven, Jack Goodrum turned his head from side to side and studied his profile. Yes, he was much less heavily jowled, now that he'd cut down on food and alcohol and taken up regular exercise. He was still well-thatched with brown hair, and he reckoned that having it tamed by a good barber, and getting rid of his shabby old sideburns, had improved his appearance no end. He looked younger and much fitter—and felt it, too, by God . . . He thumped his knuckles on his broad chest and gave his reflection a nod of vigourous approval.

Whistling, he stepped into the shower cubicle and began to

soap his body, enjoying the feel of rediscovered muscles under the thickets of greying hair. Soaped clean, he turned the shower to full volume and gasped with satisfaction as the water sluiced over him, running in streams down his strong, full thighs. Then, on an impulse of happiness, he inflated his lungs, flung back his head, and shouted his pleasure aloud. He had finally got rid of every trace of his former existence. At fifty-one years old, and thanks to his new wife Felicity, he felt that his life was just beginning.

Jack Goodrum knew enough now to acknowledge that for the past twenty-five years he had been a slob. For most of that time he'd been working so hard to build up his poultry products business that he hadn't cared what he looked like. Life had been nothing but work—hard physical, messy, smelly work—and fried meals and exhausted sleep. His only form of relaxation had been beer-drinking, and if that gave him—as it did—a sagging gut, what had that mattered?

Even when his business had prospered and expanded, he had taken no care of his appearance. He had the height to carry his weight, and his opinion at the time was that his size helped to establish him as a man to be reckoned with. He'd demanded rock-bottom prices from his suppliers, and as much work from his employees as from himself. To achieve these aims he had cultivated a loud voice, an aggressive manner and a menacing presence. He'd frightened the living daylights out of some of the cheating, idle bastards, but by God he'd got what he wanted out of 'em!

By the time he'd finally made his pile, two years ago, by selling out to a national food manufacturer for a cool three-quarters of a million, it had seemed too late to bother about his appearance. Why should he? He was hobbies proud of being what he was, a self-made man. He had no hobbies other than propping up the bar of his local pub, in the village near Ipswich where he had lived all his life and had established his chicken-meat empire, and after his early retirement he began to do that for much of his time. The only difference in his habits was that he started buying drinks all round, to provide himself with companionship; and the fist that held his beer mug was newly bedecked with heavy gold rings.

But then he'd met Felicity Napier. That really was a piece of luck, the best thing that had happened to him in the whole of his life.

Towelling himself dry, revelling in cleanliness, he wondered

with wry disgust what she'd thought of him at that first
meeting. He must have stunk of beer—and probably of sweat,
too, because in those days he'd thought himself clean if he
wallowed in a bath and changed his underclothes once a week.
It was still difficult to believe that a woman like Felicity could
have entrusted herself and her teenage son to him with so little
hesitation.

He'd asked her about it, as soon as they were safely married,
but her answer had baffled him. "All I could see, when you
came to our rescue," she had said in her light, precise, middle-
class voice, "was the shining armour." Then she had added, by
way of explanation: "Half a dozen cars had swished straight
past us. You were the only driver who was kind enough to
stop."

It had been a filthy night, he remembered. The pub had just
closed, and he was driving—as he always did, whatever the
weather, because he was too fat and lazy to walk—the half-mile
to his outlying home. He had seen ahead of him the flashing
warning lights of a stationary car, and then his headlights had
picked up two white, wet, scared faces . . .

" 'Course I stopped," he had replied gallantly. "The minute I
clapped eyes on you, I could see that you were special."

"Nonsense, you did it because you were kind. That was why
I trusted you, Jack. No one but a truly kind man would have
stopped in all that rain to help a bedraggled middle-aged
woman and her great tall son. I felt secure with you. And when
I blurted out my problem and you realised I had good reason
to be panic-stricken, you took charge of us completely—even
to the extent of driving us to a hotel and registering us in your
own name, so that if my husband was following he wouldn't be
able to find us. Then you had our car towed away and repaired,
and you brought it to the hotel next day and stayed to enquire
whether we were all right . . . I thought then that you were
the kindest man I'd ever met in my whole life. I still think so."

That had astonished Jack Goodrum when he heard it. He
didn't believe in kindness. He'd always considered it a form of
weakness, and he certainly hadn't made his fortune by showing
that to anyone.

But he had been able to relax, since selling his business.
There was no longer any need for him to hustle and be
aggressive, and for that reason he'd felt he could afford to stop
and help the stranded motorist. The reason *why* he'd stopped,

though, was simply that he'd been in no hurry to return home. There was nothing to go home for.

It wasn't kindness that had taken him back to the hotel the next day, either. He'd felt sorry for Mrs. Napier and her son, but he'd never before gone out of his way to help anyone. She wasn't even much of a looker—thin, pale, jumpy, her eyes smudged round with weariness and big with fright. But she'd fascinated him, all the same. What she had was something that Jack Goodrum admired above all else in a woman: class.

His first girl friend had had class too. Not by a long way the first he'd mucked about with, experimenting behind the hedges on the way home from village school on summer afternoons, but the first girl he'd badly wanted. For a long time she had held herself aloof . . . but then he'd caught her looking at him from under speculative virgin eyelids, and he'd known that he could have her if he made the right approach.

Eventually he'd manoeuvred her into a secluded spot, with her back to a tree. Hot and urgent, he'd pressed himself against her. But her look of desire had changed abruptly to one of disgust, and she'd pushed him away. "You smell!" she had said.

After that, Jack Goodrum had stuck to his own class of girl. He'd thought he had completely forgotten that early incident. But something about Mrs. Napier—her voice, her behaviour—had drawn him strongly. And this time he intended to make no mistakes.

On the morning after he had rescued the fugitives he'd astonished his wife by taking a bath and demanding clean socks and a clean white shirt. He'd then put on a new, sharply tailored light grey suit that he had purchased to celebrate the sale of his business. Before presenting himself at the hotel where he had established Mrs. Napier and her son, he had bought and used a mouthwash, and had his hair shampooed and blow-dried.

He'd still looked all wrong, he knew it now. That suit was the wrong colour, the wrong cloth, the wrong cut. His tie was gaudy, his gold rings were flashy, his sideburns were ridiculous. He must have ponged of aftershave. But thankfully, none of this had seemed to put Felicity Napier off when he'd asked if he could see her again; and over the next twelve months, with her help, he had transformed his whole appearance.

The pleasure that could be derived from being permanently clean had come to Jack Goodrum as a revelation. Now, there was nothing he enjoyed more after his morning shower than putting on clean boxer shorts (how could he ever have endured the grottiness of those sagging grey underpants that Doreen had provided for him?), a fresh shirt and socks, soft cord trousers, soft woollen sweater. He felt right, good, on top of the world at last.

It had taken a long time. Felicity's divorce had been very difficult, and his own hadn't been as simple as he'd expected. Then, though he had bought the old house in April with the intention of having it renovated so that they could move in as soon as they were free to marry, it hadn't been ready until early October. They had been married for three weeks before they were able to take up residence. And even then, when they finally moved into The Mount nearly a month ago, an unexpected problem—more accurately, a little local difficulty—had cropped up.

Perhaps the problem ought not to have been so unexpected. Perhaps he should have anticipated it, and taken the precaution of buying a house elsewhere. But Felicity had so much liked Breckham Market, when he had driven her through the town on one of their house-hunting expeditions, and had fallen so irreversibly in love with The Mount, that even if the difficulty had occurred to him at the time he wouldn't have had the heart to disappoint her.

It wasn't until after they had settled in that the problem had come to his notice. Perhaps he had let it worry him unnecessarily, but he saw it as a potential threat to his new-found happiness and he couldn't ignore it. His luck had held, though—as his dreary first wife had prophesied it would—and the problem had been resolved. Now everything *was* perfect.

Whistling triumphantly, Jack Goodrum hurried downstairs to join his beloved second wife in the breakfast room.

"G'morning, my dear."

It had seemed odd to him at first to give a formal daily greeting to his wife when they'd been snuggled in bed together not half an hour before; but Felicity seemed to set store by it, and he loved and respected her so much that he would do anything to please her.

She looked up from the letter she was reading. "Good morning, Jack."

She had a lovely smile, and happy eyes. Her new husband's chest expanded with pride as he saw the transformation he had brought about in her. When they'd first met her face was so deeply lined and her fair hair so prematurely grey that he'd assumed her to be his own age, or older. But that was what twenty years of marriage to that bastard Austin Napier—a gentleman born and bred, a London barrister, no less—had done to her. In fact she was just forty. And now that she had escaped from the man and had survived a bitterly contested divorce, her face had become almost miraculously smooth and untroubled.

She lifted it as Jack passed her chair. He bent to her and they kissed on the lips, frankly, almost like children, and yet with a tiny cross-current of sensuality that sent him to his own chair with a grin on his face. He sat down at the pretty breakfast table (sunshine coloured cloth; earthenware with a botanic garden design; a small bowl of late flowers from their own garden; and at his place a glass of fresh grapefruit juice, a rack of toast and a boiled egg) and unfolded his napkin. Felicity, as neat in her Liberty housecoat as she would be during the day in skirt and lambswool sweater, poured freshly ground, freshly made coffee. As she passed his cup, their eyes met. Smiling, they both shook their heads in mock bewilderment, dazzled by the good fortune that had brought them together.

For both of them their second marriage was a complete beginning again. Their courtship had been that of a shyly respectable Edwardian couple, with decorous friendship blossoming into affection. They had no expectation of love and no requirement of it, because neither of them had cause to set much store by that emotion.

Nor was there any sexual element in their relationship before they married. Felicity, who equated sex with indignity and pain, could hardly bear, in the early days of their marriage, to be touched. Jack had hoped for marital intimacy—his first wife had shut up shop after their second daughter was born, and he'd never had the time or spare energy for girl friends—but he wasn't sure whether he'd still be up to it. He didn't want the humiliation of trying with Felicity and failing; and he certainly didn't want to distress or hurt her.

But because their affection was genuine, they found that they enjoyed being close. When they set up home in The Mount they agreed to have separate bedrooms, but they soon discovered that there was comfort and reassurance in sharing a bed for at least part of the night. Gradually, Felicity learned to

trust her new husband's embraces. Gradually, Jack learned to
be considerate with his new wife. Together, they found the
experience of sex more pleasurable than either of them had
ever thought possible. They also found, on occasions when
they chose to abstain, that an exchange of tenderness could be
just as satisfactory, in its way, as conjugation; every bit as
soporific, and even more conducive to love.

What finally brought them to the realisation that they had
fallen in love was the fun they began to share in bed. Being
playful and absurd was a new experience for both of them. Jack
loved to make Felicity giggle. He considered it another
achievement, all the more unexpected because, in company,
she always looked and sounded so precise, almost prudish.
The knowledge that when they were cosy together she could
be both funny and sweetly silly endeared her to him completely. And because she could relax so unhesitatingly in his arms he
knew without doubt—and with considerable pride—that his
love was returned.

"You seem particularly happy this morning, Mr. Goodrum,"
she observed as he began his breakfast.

He grinned at her. "I've got good reason to be, haven't I?"

"*Apart* from that, I mean." She looked at him with quizzical
affection. "There's an air of relief about you, as though you've
just sorted out some kind of problem. Have you?"

"D'you wonder I'm relieved?" he parried. "It hasn't been
comfortable, having the inquest on that drunk who fell in front
of the Range Rover hanging over me. But we can forget about
it now, thank God." He gave his egg a casual thump with the
back of his spoon, crushing the shell. The egg was cooked just
as he liked it, the white firm, the yolk slightly runny. He
dipped in a finger of toast—no butter, he was a reformed
character now—and munched with contentment.

"Yes, of course the accident's been a worry for you," his wife
agreed sympathetically, "even though everyone knows it
wasn't your fault. But your problem went back further than
that, didn't it? Something's been bothering you almost from
the day we came here."

He looked up from his egg, surprised and slightly on guard.
He hadn't realised that she was so observant. "D'you reckon
so?"

"Oh yes." Felicity smiled at him. "Feminine intuition," she
explained. "Or perhaps it's simply because I love you . . ."

That made him grin again. "You're a marvel, Mrs. Goodrum.

And I love you too. *That's* why I was worried when we moved in. I want to make you happy, and I wasn't sure we'd done the right thing by coming to live in Breckham Market. You'd taken such a liking to this house and garden, but I was afraid that after living in London you'd find a small country town too dull. Now I've seen how well you've settled, though, I've stopped worrying."

Jack turned his empty egg shell upside down in the cup, and bashed the other end for good measure. "So there's your answer, my dear," he concluded cheerfully. "Is that a letter from young Matthew you've got there? How's he settling down?"

"Very well, by the sound of things. He seems so much happier than when he was a day boy at the City of London School, with all that pressure from his father to do as well as *he* did when he was there. Matthew always longed to go to boarding school, and it was such a good suggestion of yours to let him finish his education at Saxted."

"I could just as easily have afforded Eton, if that was what you'd wanted," her husband reminded her. His knowledge of public schools was confined to the names of Eton and the one nearest to Breckham Market, Saxted College. In his opinion, they were of equal standing.

Felicity smiled at him fondly. "I know, Jack. You're so very generous. But Saxted was a better idea. I prefer Matthew to be no more than twenty miles away from us, and out of reach of his father. You know how bitterly Austin resented my being given custody . . ." She shuddered at the recollection of her divorce proceedings, then looked again at her son's letter. "He asks after you, by the way."

"Does he?" said Jack eagerly. He was anxious to be liked by the boy because he knew that Felicity adored her only child.

She passed her husband the page of hasty scrawl and indicated the final paragraph: *How's Jack? Don't let him forget that he promised to take me shooting in the Christmas holidays!*

"I haven't forgotten," said Matthew's stepfather with pleasure. He'd always wanted a son to pass on his skills to. "And, let's see, won't he soon be seventeen?"

"Next March."

"Right, then it's time he learned to drive. Tell you what, my dear, I'll buy him a car for Christmas—"

"*Jack!*"

"Only a banger, but a reliable one. I know a farmer who's got some private roads on his land, and I can teach the boy how to handle the car there before he's officially old enough to drive. Then he can take the test and get his full licence as soon as he's seventeen."

"Oh Jack—and you've only just bought him a computer! You really mustn't spoil him." Felicity paused, then looked anxiously apologetic. "He didn't *ask* you for a car, I hope? I heard him telling you, when he was here at half-term, that he'd already applied for a provisional licence."

"Ah, that was so's he could take part in a course on motor bike riding. He certainly didn't ask me for any transport—but I can remember well enough what it was like to be young! A boy of his age needs some wheels of his own, and a car's a lot safer than a motor bike."

Her eyes bright with affection, Felicity stretched her hand across the table. "You *are* so kind."

"'s not kindness," Jack said. "I reckon it must be love." He reached out and took her hand, clasping it warmly and sighing with happiness. "By God, I'm a lucky man . . ."

3

In Jack Goodrum's former marital home, not far from Ipswich, breakfast was a more mobile occasion.

The residents of Factory Bungalow saw no point in getting up at any particular time. There was nothing to get up for. Doreen Goodrum and her daughters Sharon and Tracey had had no occupation in the two years since the family business was sold. Ever since Jack had left them, they had spent their mornings wandering aimlessly about the bungalow in their nightwear, eating and drinking as they went.

They felt no inclination to do more than a scant minimum of housework. Factory Bungalow had never been much of a place to live in. It was a small, immediately-post-war prefabricated building that had been given an extended lease of life by the application of a brick and tile skin. Its rural position, on a wired-in half-acre of rough grass and scrub at the side of the old wartime airfield road that led to the factory site, was solitary and unattractive.

Inside, the bungalow was packed with showy furniture and expensive electrical appliances. Nothing was more than two years old, and some of the more attention-demanding items of equipment—the microwave oven, the dish-washer—were so evenly covered with unfingermarked dust that they were clearly never used. Jack Goodrum's original family had, it seemed, enjoyed one enormous shopping expedition and then lost interest in their acquisitions.

Their present lethargy was understandable. They had all worked so hard in the poultry-meat business—the girls, now twenty-three and twenty-one, since their earliest teens—that the abrupt ending of their jobs had disoriented them. Spare time was such a foreign commodity to Mrs. Goodrum and her daughters that they had no idea what to do with it.

It was not that they had wanted to continue with the business. Doreen had been exhausted by it at the end of the first ten years. Slaving all hours in the factory, as well as looking after her husband and children and the home, was wearing her out and she had begged Jack to sell up.

"We can't *afford* to, woman!" was all he had shouted by way of reply. And whenever she had renewed her plea, as she struggled through another ten years of unremitting hard labour, he had given her the same answer.

"Good God, I've just bought you a refrigerator" (and later, a washing machine; later still, a tumble-dryer), he had added with a bellow of exasperation. "I'm doing as much for you as I can, woman! What *more* do you want?"

Even when Jack did at last decide to put the business on the market, there had been a further eighteen months of work and worry before the sale was completed. Productivity had to be not only maintained but improved on, he insisted, if they were to sell the business for what it was worth.

And so Doreen and the girls had buckled-to again, standing as usual on the production line because they were none of them confident enough with figures to ask for a sitting-down job in the office. But at least, during those final eighteen months, Doreen had had time to accustom herself to the idea that her long hard slog was nearly over. The prospect of being able, shortly, to stop working in the factory *for good* entranced her. She longed for that wonderful moment.

But when it actually did come, on the day when the business was officially transferred from J.R. Goodrum Ltd. to the new owners, and Doreen was able to hang up her overalls for the last time, she had sat down in Jack's office and burst into tears.

"*Now* what's the matter?" he had hissed. The room was occupied by smooth legal and financial men, assembled to celebrate the satisfactory outcome of months of negotiation, and Jack was wrestling with the unfamiliar wiring of a champagne cork. "For God's sake stop blubbing, woman, and fetch over the glasses!"

"Let me help you, Mrs. Goodrum," one of the smooth men had said. And everyone, it seemed, had turned to look at her.

It was too much. All those posh voices, all those smart suits and crisp shirts, all those closely shaven chins and clean hands . . . Doreen had struggled to fit into her best mail-order dress for the occasion, but she knew that her body looked ungainly and her yellow-grey hair was a mess. She gasped for air as a hot flush suffused what she knew to be her homely face. Over-wrought, humiliated, she had run bawling out of the office and away from the factory and back to the grimy familiarity of her home.

"I dunno what you're goin' on about!" Jack had said when he eventually rolled in. His new light grey suit couldn't disguise the fact that he was as ungainly as she was, but he had always been satisfied with his appearance. Now, awash with champagne and toweringly pleased with his business achievement, he was mystified by his wife's lack of gratitude.

"I've given you everythin' you ever wanted, haven't I?" he pointed out, tipsily aggrieved. "*Haven*' I? I've worked and provided for you all these years, and bought you everythin' I could think of to make your life easy. *Everythin*'. You *an*' the girls. An' now I've done what you wanted an' sold the business, jus' so's you can do absolu'ly nothin' for the rest o' your lives . . . So what are you still blubbin' for, you schupid woman?"

Doreen didn't really know.

She was accustomed to think of herself as being stupid. Jack had often enough told her so, in the course of their married life. She knew the production side of the business—the transformation of cheap, prematurely worn-out battery hens into valuable soup and pie-meat—inside out, but she had been content to leave the administration to her husband.

She didn't even know how much the business was eventually sold for. It hadn't mattered to her. She had had so little opportunity to spend money, in the whole of her life, that she

hardly knew at first what to do with the housekeeping increase
Jack gave her.

The girls had had plenty of ideas, of course. They wanted
clothes, to begin with; then holidays. Sharon, who was
engaged to the firm's sales manager, had set about planning the
slap-up wedding that her father had promised her. Her
younger sister Tracey, who had no intention of tying herself to
any one man, preferred to talk her father into giving her the
money for a car so that she could racket about Ipswich having a
good time.

Doreen, too, had thought about having a holiday. She
collected brochures by the armful, but couldn't make up her
mind where to go. And anyway, Jack wouldn't consider going
with her and she was unnerved by the thought of staying in a
hotel on her own. So she settled, instead, for having the
bungalow redecorated inside and out.

She would really have liked to move. Preferably to the
seaside, Lowestoft or Felixstowe. Even Jack had spoken about
the possibility of moving, though all he'd wanted was to be
nearer the village pub.

But then a change had come over him. He had started
taking frequent baths, and wanting clean underclothes and
shirts. Doreen was puzzled. One thing about Jack, he'd never
before bothered with girl friends; and if he had just acquired
one, why had he immediately given up wearing his new gold
rings and his dazzling new ties?

His attitude towards her had altered, too. He began to be
much kinder. And although he said no more about moving
house, it was at this time that he had offered to have Factory
Bungalow redecorated. The new owners of the poultry-meat
business had decided to transfer the operation to one of their
more modern plants, and close down the old site. This would
put an end to the flow of heavy lorries past the bungalow which
would then, as Jack pointed out, become nice and quiet, and
easier to keep clean.

"You can buy new furniture, an' all," he'd said generously.
"Might as well do the job properly while you're about it. No, I
don't mind what you buy, you please yourself entirely. Take the
car and go to Ipswich for the day. Order whatever you like, and
tell 'em to send the bill to me!"

If only she'd had the sense to realise what the crafty devil
was up to . . . But then, though she hadn't loved him for
years, and had never much liked him, it simply hadn't

occurred to her that Jack would cheat her out of the fortune she had helped him to accumulate.

The first Mrs. Goodrum was an angry woman.

Physically, she was in rather worse condition than she had been on the day, two years previously, when the business was sold. Then she had neglected her appearance because she had no time to spare. Now, she neglected it because she couldn't be bothered with it. She was fatter, greyer, far more unkempt.

But emotionally she was much stronger. She had recovered from the exhaustion that had caused her to weep on the day of the sale.

If Jack had remained loyal, she might well have been plunged into depression by the wealthy purposelessness of her life. But his defection, possessed of everything except the refurbished marital home, the five-year-old Ford Granada and a lump sum that barely provided her with enough to live on, had given her a grim sense of purpose.

Not only grim, but righteous. It wasn't just her own interests she had to look out for; there were her daughters—*Jack's* daughters—to be cared for, too. Because old as they were, it now seemed that she was going to remain responsible for the pair of them for the rest of their lives.

What had happened to her daughters might have happened anyway, of course. Even if Jack had stayed with them, and they'd had all that money—or if he'd persuaded her into the divorce but had had the decency to treat her fairly—the girls' lives might still have gone wrong. But that was no reason to let her ex-husband get away with his crime.

Besides, it wasn't just his own family that Jack had cheated. He'd done down his one-time partner, Dave Wheeler, too. And there were others who'd been after him, calling at the bungalow, telephoning day and night, all wanting to know where the old bastard had got to . . .

It was finding Jack that had been the problem, for all of them. Doreen hadn't seen him—at least not close enough to speak to—since he'd announced his intention of getting out of the way while the bungalow was being refurbished. Women's affairs, he'd said; no point in their having *him* hanging round. Thought he might buy a new car and travel about for a week or two, see what he could do in the way of business. If she needed to get in touch, his solicitor would know where he was.

Since then, their only communication had been through

Jack's lawyers. And although Doreen had eventually engaged a local solicitor to handle the divorce her husband asked for, Jack's sharp city advisers had run rings round them both. Doreen's subsequent attempts to trace her ex-husband and demand her rights had been a failure.

But now, unexpectedly, she had had a breakthrough. This morning, glittering-eyed and fortified by gulps of strong tea and mouthfuls of bacon sandwich, she was trying urgently to make a telephone call.

"Where *is* the fool?" she stormed, slamming down the unanswered receiver for the third or fourth time. Her patience with people other than her daughters had become shorter as her emotional strength increased.

A wail came from the bathroom, where Sharon was closeted. "I'm *here*," Doreen's elder daughter protested tearfully. Since the sales manager had dumped her, Sharon had reverted to a childhood unhappier than her own had ever been. "Don't shout at me, Mum," she sobbed, "I'm being as quick as I can . . ."

Doreen clasped the edges of her dressing gown across her protruding nightie and shuffled hurriedly towards the bathroom. "It's all right, my lovey, Mum's not cross with you," she called through the door in an affectionate but absent tone. "Don't strain yourself, you've got all day . . ."

Thinking hard, Doreen returned to the telephone. She took another bite of sandwich and then riffled through the directory with greasy fingers.

"Who're you ringing?" said her younger daughter huskily. Tracey, in brief pyjamas, skinny, white-faced, hollow-eyed, spiky-haired, was leaning against the open door between the kitchen and the living room. She wore a gold stud in the side of her left nostril. In one of her hands was a mug of coffee, in the other a cigarette. Both mug and cigarette were shaking.

"Never you mind who I'm ringing," snapped her mother. "It's not about you. Go back to your room, Trace, and shut the door. Go on. Yes, all right, I'll give you some money to go out with—just as soon as I've made this call."

Tracey dragged on her cigarette and went, coughing and shuddering.

Doreen dialled another number. This time the telephone was answered.

"Dave? Dave Wheeler? It's me, Doreen Goodrum. Where the hell have you been, I've been trying to get hold of you ever since last night . . . No, don't tell me, just listen. *I know where Jack is!*

"Yes, still in Suffolk! Only forty miles away. But his number's ex-directory, so we'd never have found him through the phone book. He was so cunning about covering his tracks, the devil, but now he's had his name and address published! A report on an inquest. Seems he ran over a drunk.

"No, I don't s'pose it was deliberate. One thing I'll say for Jack, he wasn't violent. Never lifted a finger against me or the kids. Anyway, the Coroner said it was an accident.

"Where? Ah, that'd be telling! We'd better meet, and come to some arrangement . . . Yes, I know how badly you want him, but so do I, Dave—me *and* my girls. Jack Goodrum's got a hell of a lot to answer for . . ."

4

In his semi-detached house at number 5 Benidorm Avenue, Breckham Market, Detective Chief Inspector Douglas Quantrill came down to breakfast in a bad temper.

For one thing, he had a thick head. He didn't usually drink much more than the odd pint, in deference to the drink-driving laws; but he'd just spent two days at county police headquarters, in company with his fellow divisional CID chiefs, on a computer familiarisation course that had been enough to turn any non-technical man to drink.

He couldn't deny that he'd made the most of the after-course get-together, in the knowledge that a police driver would give him a lift home and that he could have a long lie-in next morning. Today should have been his day off. But he'd been hauled out of his morning sleep by a telephone call from the divisional superintendent, who wanted him to investigate an unlikely-sounding allegation of murder. And he was so bleary-eyed that he'd cut himself while shaving and was now decorated about the jowls with bloodstained scraps of green Andrex.

Quantrill—over six feet tall, and broad with it—sat down at the kitchen table and stared without enthusiasm at his breakfast. The one pleasure of going on the course had been the opportunity it gave him to spend a night of depravity at a good Yarchester hotel. He'd really enjoyed that. Having a bed to himself, sitting up in it drinking beer out of a tooth glass while watching a late-night Western on television, then breakfasting extravagantly on porridge, egg-bacon-tomato-and-sausage, and several slices of toast with lashings of butter and marmalade . . .

His wife Molly hadn't fed him as well as that for years. She believed in watching his weight, and he resented it, even though he knew (because she wouldn't let him forget) that it was for his own good. Despite the fact that nature had obviously intended her to be a plump woman, and that she was never going to win her long-running battle against two surplus stones of weight, she would regularly engage in a determined attempt to get rid of at least half of it. And when Molly went seriously on a diet (as distinct from reading *Slimming* magazine while absent-mindedly nibbling biscuits) she made quite sure that her husband dieted seriously too.

Quantrill sighed, and embarked glumly on his single slice of brown bread, moistened by a dab of low-fat spread and smear of Marmite. Thank God she'd made him a pot of strong tea, even though the milk was skimmed and she kept the sugar permanently hidden.

"Did you enjoy your computer course, dear?" Molly enquired. Douglas never talked to her about his work, but she felt that this was one question she could safely ask him. He rarely listened when she told him about her own job, as a part-time receptionist at the local health centre, and he took no interest at all in her back-stage work with the Breckham Market and District Amateur Operatic Society; but she tried hard to keep her marriage in what she thought of as good repair, and she'd recently read an article in *Woman and Home* on the importance of talking to your husband. Unfortunately she had never noticed, in twenty-eight years of marriage, that Douglas—even when he was in a good temper—hated making bright conversation at breakfast.

"No, I didn't enjoy the course," he answered. "I never expected to." He could see that the newly installed computer system would be invaluable for storing and retrieving the mass of information collected in the investigation of major crimes, but he himself could make neither head nor tail of the new technology and he resented being made to feel like an old-fashioned copper, even if he was one. "Computers," he added, "are for the bright boys—the Martin Taits of this world, blast them."

"Was Martin there too?" asked Molly eagerly.

"Oh yes, *he* was there. Detective Chief Inspector Martin Tait, Bachelor of Science . . . Knowing everything, as usual."

"Well, he *is* very clever, Douggie. When you think that he came here only four years ago as your sergeant, and now he's the same rank as you! And he's still only twenty-seven . . ."

Molly had hopes of an eventual marriage between Martin Tait and her younger daughter Alison. They seemed well suited, and Martin—who had just been appointed head of Saintsbury divisional CID—was definitely a good catch. But young people these days were so casual about getting married . . . "He's got a brilliant career ahead of him, hasn't he?" she said a little wistfully.

"Do you wonder, with his advantages! University degree, special course at police college, accelerated promotion guaranteed—" Quantrill grumbled away, sore with envy. It had taken him twenty years' hard slog to attain the rank that had been bestowed on his former sergeant. "It's all right for *him*. The rest of us, the real coppers, have to do it the hard way."

Douglas wasn't usually so bitter about Martin, Molly reflected. Peevish, yes; but fair-minded enough to concede that what really annoyed him was that the younger man was in fact as good a detective as he imagined himself to be. She might have spoken up in favour of her son-in-law elect, if it wasn't that she had a more personal subject on her mind.

"And what about Sergeant Lloyd?" she asked with an overelaborate attempt at casualness. "Was she on the course, too?"

"No, she wasn't."

Molly relaxed. She didn't really think her husband was having an affair with his present CID sergeant; but he was only forty-nine, still good-looking, and he had always been susceptible to women he met in the course of his work. When he'd been so keen to spend Monday night at an hotel in Yarchester, and again when he'd stayed on in the city so late last night, she couldn't help being suspicious. But happily, it seemed that her worries had been groundless.

"I just wondered, Douggie," she said, and hurried out to the hall to answer the telephone. After all, this was supposed to be her husband's rest day, and she liked to save him from outside interruptions whenever possible.

Quantrill, who hated being called Douggie, stared morosely after her matronly back. If only Hilary Lloyd *had* been on the course! Not that anything would have come of it . . . She'd never given him a word or a look that he could safely interpret as encouragement, and he didn't think he'd have dared to risk a direct approach. Better to keep on dreaming than to be rebuffed.

But he valued Hilary's company and her conversation. Just to be with her, off duty, would have been almost enough. She didn't appear to be attached to anyone else, and if only they'd had the opportunity to get to know each other better there might have been something to hope for in the future.

As things were, his outlook was dreary. There wasn't, he supposed, anything drastically wrong with his marriage; they didn't have rows, that wasn't Molly's way. But their life together was completely humdrum. He and his wife had had nothing to say to each other for years, and her persistent attempts at conversation bored and irritated him.

Worst of all—though Molly tried hard, experimenting with eye-shadow, having her hair done regularly, spending pounds in Marks and Spencer's on clothes—she no longer attracted him physically. It wasn't that he minded her plumpness. When they'd first met he had been captivated by the curves above and blow her slim waist, and she'd put on the weight so gradually that he'd hardly noticed it. But that was the trouble, now: he hardly noticed her at all.

And there ought to be more to life than this. He felt a dissatisfaction, a restlessness, a sense of time slipping away, wasted . . .

His wife was chattering excitedly on the telephone, almost shrieking into it. Quantrill scowled, clutched his pounding head, and went upstairs to the bathroom in search of aspirin. He'd been a fool to drink so much last night. He'd stayed out, trying to enjoy himself, simply because he was in no hurry to return home; and the reason for *that* was that there was precious little for him to come home for.

"Douggie! Oh, Douggie, the most wonderful news—you'll never guess!"

"I don't intend to try." Quantrill emerged from the bathroom sore-chinned, having stayed there long enough to ease the blood-caked scraps of tissue from his shaving cuts. "No doubt you'll tell me anyway."

"Oh, it's so exciting!" Molly was half-way upstairs, laughing, delighted, sounding—her husband suddenly realised—years younger. As she looked up at him, the happiness in her soft brown eyes and the engaging tilt of her nose gave him an unexpected reminder of the pretty girl she had been not all that long ago.

"What's so exciting?" he said in a kinder voice.

Molly paused dramatically. "Would you believe it? Our daughter is going to have a baby!"

"She's *what*?" Quantrill's kindly impulse was swamped by a surge of anger that reddened his face and swelled the veins in his temples. If that upstart Martin Tait had impregnated Alison—

And then he remembered something.

"*Who* is?" he said uncertainly.

"Why, Jennifer, of course! Jennifer and Nigel, after all these years . . . Isn't it marvellous?"

Quantrill simmered down. "Oh, yes—marvellous," he agreed dutifully. His elder daughter had lived away from home for so long that there were times when he almost forgot her existence. She'd always wanted to be a nurse, and at eighteen she had chosen to go to London—possibly because, at the time, he and Molly were going through a bad patch and she'd wanted to get away from them—to train at Guy's Hospital. And there, now a ward sister, she had remained ever since.

His wife had hoped, of course, that Jennifer would marry a doctor. He knew that it had been a great disappointment to Molly that her daughter had fallen in love, instead, with a medical technician, though Nigel had turned out to be a good steady husband, keen on do-it-yourself jobs about the home and a steam railway enthusiast in what remained of his spare time. They'd been married for seven years and had seemed to show no interest at all in starting a family, to Molly's further disappointment.

But now some of his wife's hopes were going to be fulfilled, and Quantrill felt glad for her. Come to think of it, Molly must have been finding her life a bit dull, too . . . She'd always doted on babies, and enjoyed nothing better than knitting small garments, so perhaps the newcomer would help to keep her happy.

And, thinking about it further as he followed his excitedly chattering wife downstairs, he felt genuinely glad for Jennifer and Nigel. A marriage needed children. That was what had justified his own, and provided the adhesive that had kept it together for so long. He hadn't much cared for the nappy stage, but he had to admit that he'd thought the world of all three of their children when they were small. Still did think it of Alison—she'd always been Dad's special girl. If only their useless layabout of a son would show some indication of turning out half as well as either of his sisters . . .

"It's time that boy got up," he stated crossly.

"Oh, but it's a free morning for him, Douggie. And he needs his sleep."

But their son was already up. Nearly seventeen years old, and well on the way to being as tall and as broad-shouldered as his father (and in Molly's eyes as darkly handsome as Douggie had been when he was young), Peter came tottering dozily out of his bedroom wearing only a sweatshirt and a pair of briefs.

"I say, Mum," he croaked from the top of the stairs, ignoring his father. "Where're my new jeans?"

Molly, who had reached the hall, turned back instantly to face her favourite child. Peter was her hope, her sun, even though he had lately been growing increasingly uncommunicative and unresponsive. He had been such a nice boy when he was younger; not as clever or as interested in school work as his sisters had been, but bright and open and affectionate.

It was inevitable, Molly supposed, that he should have changed as he grew towards manhood. He was bound to lose his boyish hobbies. But unlike most of her friends' sons, he seemed to have found no other interests to take their place. He had become secretive and moody, and his mother was extremely worried about him. She would have liked to discuss the problem with Douglas, but she knew that he would only tell her to stop fussing over the boy.

Meanwhile, any communication with Peter was better than none: "I haven't seen your jeans since you brought them home, dear. Aren't they where you put them?"

"I can't find them anywhere . . ."

"All right, I'll come and look."

"Oh no you won't!" said her husband, barring her way. "You do too much for him, Molly. Let him learn to take care of his own clothes." He raised his voice: "Look a bit harder," he instructed his son sarcastically. "Try moving things with your hands."

Peter scowled, muttered something inaudible, and began to mooch back to his room.

"Did you hear the news?" Molly cried after him. "Jennifer's going to have a baby!"

The boy returned to the top of the stairs, scratching his hair. "A what?" he said, bemused.

"A *baby*. Isn't it wonderful?"

Peter blinked and knuckled his eyes. "Jennifer and *Nigel*? Sounds like a miracle . . ." Then, newly awake, he let out a sudden guffaw and raised his voice as though in the hope of conveying a message across the ether to his brother-in-law in Streatham. "Well done, Nige . . . you finally managed to get it up, then!"

Quantrill took exception to the expression, on his wife's behalf. Nice girls of Molly's generation weren't accustomed to verbal crudity. "Don't you speak like that in front of your mother!"

"Why not?" asked Peter, seizing the opportunity to return his father's sarcasm. "Can't she remember how you used to do it?"

"Why, you young devil—" Intolerably galled, Quantrill charged the stairs two at a time.

"Joke!" Peter pleaded, back-pedalling. "*Joke*, Dad." But he took the precaution of nipping smartly into the bathroom and shooting the bolt.

While her husband thumped the bathroom door and shouted to Peter to come out and apologise to his mother, Molly hovered wretchedly on the stairs not knowing whether to go up or come down. She'd been embarrassed, as Douglas knew she would be, by the vulgar expression her son had used, and it had sorrowed her to hear him use it. But the simplest and most dignified response would have been for her to pretend she hadn't heard it and to walk away.

Douglas had been unusually considerate in speaking up on her behalf, but she wished he hadn't. The apology that he was now demanding was solely on account of his own hurt pride. It must be very hard for him, Molly acknowledged, to have his non-existent sex life commented on by his son. Not that Peter really meant anything by it, his mother was sure; his father was always grumbling at him and making pointed remarks, and the boy had just been trying to get his own back.

Keeping her head down, busying herself by picking fluff off the stair carpet, Molly reflected that it was perfectly true that Douggie hadn't made love to her for a long time. But that was largely her own fault—she'd made so many excuses, for so long, that he'd finally given up trying. She had been glad, of course. She'd never really enjoyed sex. All she'd wanted was the closeness, the affection, the cuddles that usually went with it. And now she had nothing from him at all.

She really must give this stair carpet a good hoovering, as soon as he'd gone off to work.

Outside the bathroom door, Quantrill was about to issue an ultimatum. "Peter! I'll give you just ten seconds to come out of your own accord—"

He paused, recognising the counter-productivity of breaking down his own door and thereby putting himself in the even more vexatious situation of having to buy a new one. Fortunately, the door began to edge open. Peter's hand appeared, flapping a white towel.

"Don't wave it," snarled his father, "wear it! I won't have you wandering about the house half-naked, at your age."

The door opened wider. Peter sidled out, modestly kilted. "Sorry, Dad," he muttered.

"All right. Now apologise to your mother."

Peter shuffled to the head of the stairs, clutching the towel round his waist and looking contrite. Molly, of course, had forgiven him already. She'd been quite amused and relieved by the way he'd waved the white flag, acting up in the lovably naughty way the old Peter used to do. She might have smiled, except that that would have made Douglas even crosser.

"Sorry, Mum," said Peter. And then, knowing exactly how to get round her, he beamed and added meaningfully, "Or should I say—*Granny*?"

The effect on Molly was instantaneous. She'd been so embarrassed, so depressed by the whole incident that for a minute or two she had quite forgotten the wonderful news about Jennifer's baby. Her cheeks coloured again, but this time with the pink of pleasure.

"Oh, go on with you," she said, and bustled, exulting, to the kitchen to grill some bacon for her son's breakfast.

Pleased with himself, Peter turned to his father and gave the old man a wink. "OK, Grandad?" he said.

5

It had been a mild autumn. With no frosts to sharpen their colours and no gales to blow them from the trees, the leaves had hung on, limp and pale, until early November. Now they were coming off all at once. As the overnight fog began to lift, the morning seemed to be dripping with yellow leaves.

Eunice Bell stood in the window of her gloomy drawing room at Tower House, Breckham Market, watching the last of the sodden foliage detach itself from the pollarded lime trees that lined the short gravelled drive leading from her front door to Victoria Road. The road itself, and much of the daylight, was blocked from the window by the dark spines of a monkey puzzle tree that dominated the front garden.

Miss Bell was breakfasting as she stood, saucer in one hand, cup in the other, drinking rich black coffee from Coalport china. Her appetite was small, her tastes fastidious.

She was a small stiff woman whose severely drawn-back hair, still dark except for a few threads of grey, emphasised her bony features. She wore a discreetly expensive navy blue dress, touched with white; not because the muted colour was an appropriate acknowledgement of her brother's death, but because she invariably wore navy blue, in cotton lawn or fine wool or silk according to the season and the occasion. She was not greatly interested in clothes, but she liked to know that she was always impeccably dressed.

Her expression, as she waited for the arrival of a senior detective from the county CID to discuss Cuthbert's alleged accident, was impassive. She was quite alone, in the seven-bedroomed mid-Victorian house—built by her great-grand-father in the Italianate style, complete with shallow-roofed campanile—but she had long ago trained herself never to betray her emotions either in public or in private. In fact, she was excited. She felt an eager anticipation such as she had not experienced since she was a child.

As she stood, uncompromisingly erect, sipping her coffee, she knew again the *frisson* of pleasure with which she had approached all her childhood birthdays; a pleasure intensified by the necessity of pretending not to feel it, for fear of her parents' displeasure. She had learned at an early age that she must never mention her forthcoming birthday, or her present would be withheld. She must never draw attention to herself in any way, or she would be punished.

But that parental tyranny had never prevented her from feeling a natural excitement as each birthday drew near. *I'm going to be nine* (or ten or eleven or twelve), she had whispered to herself, inwardly exulting. *Next week* (not-the-day-after-tomorrow-but-the-next-day; the-day-after-tomorrow; *tomorrow!*) *I shall be in my teens*.

It was this secret anticipation that, in those childhood days, had been her major source of pleasure. Her birthday itself had always been an ordeal. First there had been the opening of her present—one only, because she had no near relatives, though some among the succession of cook-housekeepers had occasionally made her a surreptitious gift of a bar of forbidden chocolate.

She had been required to receive and open the plainly wrapped parcel in a tense little ceremony in her mother's sitting room. This was a room that she had not been allowed—had never wanted—to enter without a specific summons. Her mother, who had not married until she was nearing forty, had been a cool, withdrawn woman, apparently indifferent to her children except in the matter of their good behaviour and obedience.

Eunice, summoned on the morning of each birthday, had unwrapped her annual parcel in the knowledge that its contents, though probably expensive, were certain to be more useful than interesting. She could particularly recall the year of the new school overcoat, in good dark grey melton cloth cut long to allow for growth. She had already had two fittings for the coat, without realising that it was going to be her birthday present. But as soon as she saw what the box contained she had performed the required ritual: expressed her surprise and pleasure, kissed her mother's cool cheek, and then, bracing herself to hide her fear of her irascible father, had gone to his study to give her dutiful thanks to him . . .

But that had been a very long time ago. Now she could savour the pleasure of anticipation, secure in the knowledge that there would be no anti-climax. With Cuthbert unexpectedly dead she was, for the first time in fifty-four years, completely free.

Free to leave Tower House: she had always hated it for its ugliness, its coldness, its gloom, above all for the unhappiness it had contained.

Free to leave Breckham Market: she had never liked the town because of the weight of all the family associations, the long memories of the older inhabitants. She would have moved to Saintsbury years ago, after her widowed mother's death, but for the duty of looking after her brother. As a child she had given all her love to the small boy she had called Cub, and he to her. Cub had never learned to protect himself from their parents, and so she had done her best to shield him. At times she had even taken the blame; and the punishment, for his misdemeanours. When he grew into difficult, unstable manhood her love had waned, but her sense of duty had remained strong. To remove him from his familiar surroundings would, she knew, have disoriented him completely.

It would also, of course, have spoiled what she had of a life of her own. Eunice had no close friends, but many valued acquaintances living in and near Saintsbury; and she had her absorbing voluntary work there as a vice president of the county branch of the Red Cross society and the organiser of its local centre. She intended to keep her social life immaculate, and this would have been impossible with Cuthbert wandering drunkenly in her vicinity, physically as well as mentally lost. And in the larger, busier town, the police would have been less tolerant than they were in Breckham Market. Better, she had concluded, to go on living with her brother at Tower House, but to put herself at a discreet distance by spending most of her time well out of his way in Saintsbury.

But now, suddenly, she was free to leave. She had thought at first that she might simply pack a trunk, lock the house up, and take a room at the Angel Hotel in Saintsbury while she settled her affairs. But Victoria Road was no longer the most select part of Breckham Market, and her solicitor had advised her against leaving Tower House empty and at the mercy of vandals. Both he and her estate agent—she had instructed the senior partner of the most reputable firm of auctioneers and valuers in the town to handle the sale for her—had advised her not to expect the property to sell quickly.

Eunice Bell was neither surprised nor disappointed by their advice. The estate agent had of course been positive, using the tactful adjective "substantial" to describe the unattractive property and asserting that it would be eminently suitable for

conversion to flats, or offices, or an old people's home, subject
to planning approval. But Eunice, hating every aspect of the
house, found it difficult to imagine that anyone would be
prepared to buy it at the price she was determined to ask. She
had investments that provided her with a comfortable private
income, but she knew that the type of property she proposed
to buy (one of Saintsbury's Georgian town houses that she
could set about modernising with taste and discretion) would
take all the capital she could raise from the sale.

And so she prepared herself for a long wait. There was,
anyway, a good deal to do before Tower House could be sold:
the unused rooms to be opened, the heavy furniture to be
unswathed from its dustsheets and sent for auction, the family
effects to be sorted. It was not a task that she relished. In fact
she had been avoiding it—but then, everything had happened
so quickly and so recently that she had not, until now, had a
moment to stand still and think. Once Cuthbert was buried,
on Friday afternoon, she must set to work in earnest.

The clock in the hall, mid-Victorian mahogany and brass,
undistinguished except for its excessive size, struck the half-
hour. Eunice Bell looked at her watch. Half past nine, high
time the detective arrived.

She began a restless walk through the house. Her great-
grandfather, who had been more concerned with ostentation
than with comfort, had sited it so that its principal rooms faced
towards the town, regardless of the fact that this was due
north. After her mother's death, Eunice had established
herself in two small first-floor rooms that caught the sun, and
had shut up most of the others. She would have liked to use
her mother's former sitting room, the only agreeable ground-
floor room in the house, but its associations were too unpleasant. Fortunately it had been possible for her to avoid even
walking past the door, because the room was on its own in a
passage that led only to the stairway to the tower where her
father had had his study . . . and nothing would have
induced her to re-visit *that*.

But this morning, as she opened the doors of the ground-
floor rooms to survey all that needed to be done, she steeled
herself to confront her memories. She was no longer a
frightened child, or a quaking adolescent. Her mother and
father were long dead, safely buried in the family plot where
Cuthbert would soon join them. She was free of them all.

Or so she tried to convince herself. But as soon as she set
foot in that dreaded corridor, where she had gone only when

summoned for her birthday ordeal or, more frequently, to explain some minor breach of conduct to her mother who had then referred her to her father for sentence, the years of independent adulthood might never have been. Everything— the cold black and white tiles on the floor, the dark brown paintwork, the stained-glass window that provided the corridor with such dismal light, the heavy silence, the pervasive smell of rising damp—reminded her of her youthful unhappiness. As she forced herself to walk past that former sitting room, Eunice recalled how her mother had been accustomed to sit there for hours with the door ajar, playing patience. And how, as she had passed the doorway, trembling, on her way to the tower, the *slap slap slap* of her mother's cards had presaged the punishment she was about to receive at her father's hands.

No. She had not been up in the tower for years, and there was no need for her to go there now. Before she could put her mind to clearing the house, she had to complete her family duty by burying Cuthbert. And she could not feel free to bury him until the police had properly investigated the suspicious circumstances of his death.

6

Douglas Quantrill left home to go to work in a state of domestic shock. He didn't *want* to be a grandfather. He wasn't ready for it yet. He was too young!

He had said as much to Molly, but there was no sympathy to be had from that quarter. She had merely told him not to be so selfish; and as for being too young, she declared, that was nonsense. "Think yourself lucky, Doug Quantrill, that Jennifer and Nigel didn't get married and start a family at the age we did, or you'd have been a grandfather at forty-one."

It wasn't the most tactful of reminders. Starting a family had been the last thing he intended, as he had lain with his girl friend on a river bank one pre-pill summer's evening and persuaded her—just this once—to allow him a special twenty-first birthday privilege. Molly had been a most attractive girl, and he'd certainly wanted her; but not as a wife! Marriage hadn't entered his head. He was too young for it, he'd protested a few weeks later, when she told him tearfully that once had been enough to make her pregnant. But that hadn't stopped her parents from organising a very rapid wedding.

And now he was trapped again, pushed unprepared into a role that was even more ageing. He himself was certainly not going to tell anyone, but in a small town like Breckham (and with Molly tickled pink) the news would get out soon enough. So he might as well abandon all hope of ever furthering his relationship with Hilary Lloyd, because the fact that he was almost a grandfather was bound to put him, in her estimation, completely out of the running.

Quantrill's route to Tower House from Benidorm Avenue (a 1960s development by a local builder who had named it after his favourite holiday resort) took him past the school that Peter still attended. Built as the Alderman Thirkettle Secondary Modern School it was not Breckham Market Comprehensive, with a sixth form centre where, as far as Quantrill could make out, his son was passing his final year in ignorance and idleness.

Peter had been a great disappointment to his father. Much as he had loved his young daughters, Douglas Quantrill had naturally hoped for a son; and just as naturally he had hoped that the boy would do as well at school, if not better, than his sisters.

But Peter (as Molly, who had not been very clever but whose Church of England parents had sent her to a convent high school so that she could learn French and Art in the company of other nice girls, was sometimes provoked into pointing out) took educationally after his father. Douglas Quantrill had found his schooldays insufferably boring, and had thankfully bolted from the classroom at what was then the standard leaving age of fourteen.

He'd regretted it subsequently, of course. He was always conscious, particularly in the company of up-and-coming younger colleagues, of his lack of secondary education. But at least there'd been some excuse for his dislike of his village school, where an elderly headmistress had been in sole charge of the cavernous Big Room, filled with children between the ages of eight and fourteen, with a blackboard, a map of the world, a wireless set and a cane as her only teaching aids. No wonder he'd been bored, he told himself defensively, suppres-

sing the shame that accompanied the remembrance of the way
he and the other boys had teased and harried the poor woman.

For Peter, though, it ought to have been different. His
school was modern, properly staffed, fully equipped, surrounded by playing fields. From the age of eleven the boy had
been given the opportunity to learn any subject, to pursue any
hobby, to take up any sport. His father had constantly urged
him to make the most of his chances, but the more Quantrill
urged, the less his son had been inclined to do.

Perhaps, Quantrill admitted to himself, that was where he'd
gone wrong. Molly had always said that he tried to push Peter
too hard; but it had seemed to him that unless he pushed, the
boy would have done nothing at all. The unfortunate result
was that he'd managed to put a barrier of ill-feeling between
himself and his son—a barrier that was strengthened by the
nature of his own job.

Everyone in Breckham Market associated the name Quantrill with the police, and there was no doubt that Peter must
have taken a lot of stick on account of it. A copper's son was
bound to feel that he had to prove himself to his mates, and
Peter had gone out of his way to do so. When he was fifteen he
had appeared, to the shame of his parents, before a juvenile
court on a charge of causing malicious damage to the church
hall where the youth club met. A fine way for a chief inspector's
son to behave . . . and God knew, now, what the wretched
boy got up to in the wasteland of his spare time.

Quantrill was very worried about his son, though he tried
not to let his wife know it. She doted so uncritically on Peter
that there was no point in attempting to discuss him with her.
Besides, knowing what he did about the darker side of life,
Quantrill had always made a point of trying not to alarm Molly.
It had seemed best to let her issue the necessary parental
cautions about road safety, and later about smoking and
alcohol, while he took secretively upon himself the tightrope
tasks of warning the children against strangers without making
them afraid of people, and forbidding them to experiment with
drugs without arousing their curiosity.

Well, it least none of his three had been molested, thank
God. And the two girls had grown up thoroughly wholesome.
But Peter . . .

After his court appearance, the boy had become sullen and
uncommunicative. The magistrates had given him a condition-
al discharge, and Quantrill had tried to impress upon his son

the need to change his friends and to take up a healthy sport or hobby. Peter had certainly kept out of any further public mischief, but the nature of his current activities was a mystery to his parents. He treated the house as a hotel, and—apart from the occasions when his father hollered at him to answer when he was spoken to—withdrew from any participation in family life.

Naturally, Quantrill had begun to fear the worst. He had searched Peter's room and found neither smell nor sign of drugs or solvents—but if the boy was using them he would know better than to do so at home. Whenever he could get within reach of his son Quantrill peered suspiciously for tell-tale physical signs, but the only result of this policy was that Peter now kept out of his father's way as much as possible.

This morning's incident, when he had chased the boy upstairs to demand an apology from him, was in fact the first direct communication that they had had for months. Irritated as he had been at the time, Quantrill had begun on reflection to take heart from the episode. For a few moments Peter had looked and sounded like the cheerful young rascal of old. He'd been quite funny about Jennifer's weedy husband Nigel . . . probably right, too . . . If only Molly hadn't been there, looking embarrassed, they could have had a father-and-son laugh about it. Still, if it meant that Peter was beginning to come out of his self-imposed exile, that was something to be thankful for.

Quantrill felt almost light-hearted, until he recalled his son's cheeky punch-line. *Grandad* . . . What a humiliation to have to come to terms with! And there, as he drove along Victoria Road towards Tower House, was Hilary Lloyd waiting for him in her car . . . She was just thirty-one, only eighteen years younger than he was, but she would be bound to think of him as irretrievably middle-aged, once she knew.

Once she knew. Quantrill's spirits began to lift again. Hilary didn't know, yet; almost certainly wouldn't, for some time. For the next few weeks, or months, he still had some credibility as a youngish man—so why not try to make the most of it?

He accelerated towards her, indulging in a moment's fantasy until he heard—faint but clear, and coming unmistakably from the direction of Benidorm Avenue—the voice of common sense telling him not to go making a silly fool of himself.

Quantrill brought his Maestro smartly to a halt at the kerb, nose to nose with Sergeant Lloyd's Metro. He got out of his car as athletically as possible, and went to speak to her through her open window.

" 'Morning, Hilary!" And then, because he hadn't seen her for several days, and because she looked in some way different, he added impulsively, "How are you?"

"Peeved," said Sergeant Lloyd. She spoke pleasantly enough, but the smile he had hoped for—the rare whole-hearted smile that lit up her strong-boned face in a way that invariably dazzled him—failed to appear. "This allegation of murder sounds a time-waster, but I'd have liked to handle it myself. There was no need for you to give up your rest day to come and take charge."

"Not my idea," Quantrill assured her hastily. "And it's certainly no reflection on you, Hilary. Apparently Miss Bell went over all our heads to the Super—and you know how he jumps when he's spoken to by anyone who's likely to be acquainted with the Chief Constable. I suppose he promised her that he'd put his senior CID officer onto the inquiry, so here I am whether I like it or not."

Liking it—or at least this part of it—he opened her car door. Reassured by his explanation, Hilary Lloyd gave him a workaday smile of thanks and got out. As she stood up—tallish, gracefully straight-backed, but regrettably thin for his taste—he widened his eyes and stared at her. The difference in her appearance that he had noticed while she was still in her car was now fully revealed.

"You've had your hair cut!" he accused her.

This time she laughed. "I don't deny it. Though I can't imagine which section of what act you're proposing to charge me under."

"No, no, I'm not objecting!" He continued to stare, fascinated by the change in her appearance. She had previously worn her dark hair with a sideswept fringe that was obviously designed to hide a scar on her forehead. But the scar—the result of an attack made on her when she was a uniformed policewoman by a Yarchester villain wielding a broken bottle—had always been impossible to conceal. The lower end of it, just missing the inner side of her left eye, puckered her eyebrow in what appeared from a distance to be a permanent frown.

But the irregular line of the scar above her nose had now faded and she had, it seemed, stopped trying to hide it. Her hair was now smoother, brushed well clear of her forehead, shaped more closely to her head. Quantrill thought he might approve, once he had a chance to get used to it.

"No, I'm not complaining at all," he assured her. "It looks—"

"It looks a monstrosity of a house, doesn't it?" Hilary said, turning his attention firmly to the place they had come to visit. "So this is where Clanger Bell lived . . . It's like a scaled-down version of the Town Hall—almost as big, twice as ornate, and probably even more uncomfortable."

Quantrill pulled himself together and gave his attention to his job. For the first time ever, he took a good look at Tower House. Whenever he had driven past it along Victoria Road he had seen nothing but the stiffly aggressive monkey puzzle tree in the front garden, and the foreign-looking shallow-roofed tower—as Hilary said, a smaller version of the Town Hall's—rising behind it.

Now, from the iron-gated entrance to the drive, he could see that she was right about the rest of the house. It was every bit as narrow-windowed and uncosy as the Town Hall, but whereas the public building had been constructed in good plain local grey brick, Tower House was built in yellow brick decorated with bands and lozenges of red and blue. There was nothing about the house that was typical of Suffolk; nothing that fitted in with the rest of Breckham Market. But then, the same could have been said of poor old Clanger.

"The Bell family were builders, so I've heard," he said. "One of them was responsible for building the Town Hall in the middle of the last century. Then he became Mayor, and proceeded to show off by building himself a new house in the same style, but with more elaborate brickwork. Mind you, they've always been a very public-spirited family by all accounts, doing a lot of voluntary work in the town. I daresay Miss Bell would have been a town councillor and a magistrate, and taken her own turn as Mayor, if it hadn't been for her brother."

"Are you acquainted with her?" asked Hilary.

"Only by sight. My wife does some Red Cross work, lending out walking frames and wheelchairs, and she knows her to say good morning to. Miss Bell's one of the top Red Cross people in the county, though, and Molly finds her a bit awe-inspiring. But then, I believe Eunice Bell's like that. It was typical of her to make a direct approach to the Super about her brother's accident. We'll probably find that she thinks she's summoned us to an interview with *her*."

Quantrill held the gate for his sergeant to walk through. Hilary took a closer look at Tower House, gloomy behind the last few damp yellow leaves on the branches of the trees beside the drive. "It's such a depressing place," she said. "No wonder poor Clanger Bell lost his wits. Is there anything eccentric about his sister, do you know?"

"Nothing I've ever heard mentioned. This allegation of murder sounds so far-fetched, though, that I'm wondering whether the shock of her brother's death, on top of the strain of looking after him for so many years, has tipped her off balance. Who dealt with the accident, by the way?"

"PC Powell, sir."

"Hmm. Tim Powell's a bright lad. If there was anything suspicious about that accident, he'd have spotted it. On the other hand, he hasn't yet developed into what you might call a sympathetic listener—and that may be all Miss Bell really needs. Let's be patient and hear what she has to say, and with a bit of luck we'll be able to talk her out of the idea that her brother was murdered."

7

Eunice Bell, stiff and uncommunicative, led her visitors through the chill gloom of the hall to the equally unwelcoming drawing room, heavy with Victorian furniture and the cold silence of disuse. As the two detectives followed her into the room she took her stand beside the empty marble fireplace and looked severely at the Chief Inspector.

"Quantrill," she said. Her voice was as strong and spiny as the evergreen foliage of the monkey puzzle tree that blocked most of the light from the north-facing window. "Do I know your wife?"

Chief Inspector Quantrill was aware that he spoke with a slow Suffolk accent, and he was not normally well disposed to witnesses who addressed him as though he were one of several applicants for the post of jobbing gardener. But having decided that this enquiry could best be cleared up by kindness, he answered her peaceably. "Quite probably. My wife works as a receptionist at the health centre, and I believe she helps with the Red Cross medical loan service."

Miss Bell ducked her head in what was clearly intended to be a gracious nod. "Ah yes. I thought I'd heard the name in that connection. As well as in connection with Breckham Market CID, of course. But I don't believe—" she turned, stiff-necked, to look hard at Hilary Lloyd "—that I've heard *your* name mentioned before."

"Probably not." Hilary, suspecting that Eunice Bell's formidable manner was a protective façade, answered her with a pleasant smile. She too liked to keep her private life private, but she achieved it by being apparently outgoing, doing so much lively talking that people could spend hours in her company without realising that she was giving away nothing about herself at all. Miss Bell's method of keeping people at bay was no doubt extremely effective but it did run the risk, Hilary thought, of needlessly putting their backs up.

"But I would like to say," the sergeant went on sincerely, after explaining that she had come to Breckham Market only the previous year, "how saddened my colleagues and I were by your brother's death."

"Thank you." Eunice Bell ducked her head in acknowledgement. "Superintendent Roydon was kind enough to say much the same thing. I'm well aware that my brother was often a nuisance. As I told Mr. Roydon, I very much appreciate the kindness and forbearance shown to Cuthbert by the police. However—" she directed her penetrating, dark-eyed gaze back to the Chief Inspector "—I am not at all satisfied with the investigation into the circumstances of his death."

"So Mr. Roydon tells me," said Quantrill in a soothing tone. "May we sit down while we talk about it?"

"Please do."

Quantrill remained on his feet until after both women had seated themselves. They were so very different, he thought, watching them: Eunice Bell sitting ramrod-straight on a hard chair, severe in navy blue; and Hilary, almost as thin, almost as straight-backed, but gracefully at ease and looking very attractive in a dusky pink suède jacket that, come to think of it, he didn't remember having seen before . . .

But he could see similarities between the women, too. They were both independent, strong-minded, self-contained. And considering that he had spent eighteen months working with Hilary but was no closer to her now than when he started, he foresaw little chance of finding out much about Eunice Bell during the course of the next ten minutes.

There was one thing he could tell about her, though. In whatever way she had been affected by her brother's death, Miss Bell had not been knocked off balance by it. During the course of twenty-five years of detective work, Quantrill had interviewed thousands of witnesses; he was accustomed to talking to people who were under extreme emotional or mental stress. He could recognise the rigidity of fear, the sweat and shake of nervous tension, the inward stare of the mentally disturbed, the gleam in the eye of the obsessed.

But Eunice Bell showed none of these signs. Her stiff posture was clearly a long-established habit, an indication of nothing more than reserve and fastidious self-control. She sat with a practised composure, her hands and feet neatly placed, calmly motionless. And he knew that—much as he would like to discount what she was about to say to him, on the grounds of emotional imbalance—he was obliged to accept that fact that he was dealing with a rational woman.

"Why *now*, Miss Bell? This is what puzzles us. Police Constable Powell came to see you after Mr. Bell's death, but you made no reference to murder then. In fact you told the constable that your only surprise was that your brother hadn't been run over years ago. All the evidence pointed to accidental death, and that was the Coroner's verdict. So why are you now suggesting murder?"

Eunice Bell looked at him from under dark, level eyebrows. "I expressed no surprise at the time, Mr. Quantrill, because I was well aware of my brother's habits. It was stupid and wrong of him to make a practice of crossing the road quite deliberately in the path of oncoming vehicles. Unfortunately, I could do or say nothing to stop him. He was a menace to local drivers, and I'm only thankful that he wasn't the cause of anyone else's injury or death."

"We're all thankful for that," said Quantrill bluntly. "But—"

"I didn't at first realise that Cuthbert had been murdered," Miss Bell continued, ignoring the interruption, "because I decided long ago that when the inevitable collision occurred, I would prefer not to know the identity of the driver. I thought it would be unjust of me to hold anyone other than Cuthbert himself responsible for his death. And so I didn't read the local newspaper report of what happened, and I didn't attend the inquest.

"But for some reason—curiosity, I suppose—I *did* read the report of the inquest in yesterday's newspaper. And when I saw the name of the driver, and realised who he was, I knew that he must have lied about himself at the inquest. And because he had gone to the length of lying—or at least of deliberately misleading the police and the Coroner—I now believe that he drove at my brother with the intention of killing him."

"Now hold you hard," said Chief Inspector Quantrill, making the Suffolk idiom sound magisterial. "This driver—"

"John Reuben Goodrum," supplied Sergeant Lloyd, consulting her notebook. "Known as Jack Goodrum."

"Ah. Right, then, Miss Bell: do I understand that you're personally acquainted with this Jack Goodrum?"

"No, Mr. Quantrill, I am not. But despite the impression he gave at the inquest, Goodrum is no stranger to Breckham Market. And he would have known full well who Cuthbert was."

Quantrill looked to Sergeant Lloyd for information. She flicked through her notes again. "Until a month ago, Mr. Goodrum had always lived and worked in the Ipswich area. He bought The Mount in April, but wasn't able to take up residence before October 5th. The Coroner saw that fact as significant. He said that Mr. Bell had undoubtedly survived so long because his habits were well known—all the local drivers slowed right down when they saw him.

"But Mr. Goodrum, as a newcomer to the town, didn't know Mr. Bell and couldn't be expected to keep an eye open for him. That was why the Coroner found that no blame for the accident could attach to Mr. Goodrum."

"So I read, in the newspaper report," said Eunice Bell drily. "But Goodrum spent several weeks of each year in Breckham Market when he was a boy. He got to know Cuthbert well. What's more, he had good reason to harbour a grudge against my brother. And that's why I believe that when Goodrum returned to the town and learned that the man who wandered the streets was Cuthbert, he seized the opportunity to take his revenge."

Miss Bell presented the story in crisp detail. When she and her brother were in their early teens, there had been a butcher's shop just off Victoria Road, on a site now occupied by the Shell filling station. The butcher, who had supplied meat to the Bell household, was a man named Reuben Goodrum. Reuben had a grandson, Jack, who came up from the Ipswich area every summer during the school holidays to help in the shop and with the deliveries.

Reuben Goodrum owned a piece of grazing land which adjoined the far end of the grounds of Tower House. The Bell children were forbidden to play outside their own garden, or to mix with the local children; but Cuthbert had always liked to sit on the high garden wall watching the animals in the butcher's field, and in doing so he had struck up a summer acquaintance with the butcher's grandson. Cuthbert was a year older than Jack Goodrum, but smaller and weaker, and he had soon come to hero-worship the bigger boy.

"One could hardly call it friendship," reflected Eunice Bell. "I imagine that Goodrum merely tolerated my brother. The association had to be kept secret from our parents, of course, but Cuthbert was always talking to me about the boy: it was *Jack Jack Jack* all the time. My brother must have followed him about like a puppy—and of course that meant going out of the garden, and no doubt getting into all kinds of mischief."

"You say, *no doubt*, Miss Bell," commented Quantrill. "You didn't know what they actually got up to, then?"

"No, and I didn't wish to. I was older than Cuthbert and I felt responsible for him. I knew there would be trouble enough if our parents found out that he was roaming about with the butcher's boy, regardless of what the two of them were doing. But even in those days," she added wryly, "I had very little control over my brother."

The unauthorised holiday relationship between Cuthbert Bell and Jack Goodrum had continued until Cuthbert was about seventeen. Then, at last, it had been discovered by his father. Something had been done that enraged Mr. Bell; he had summoned his son to his study in the tower, demanding to know the identity of the culprit; and Cuthbert, terrified by his father's threat to beat him, had revealed that Jack was to blame.

"And what was the incident?" asked Sergeant Lloyd. "What had been done to enrage your father?"

"The subject was never discussed with me," said Eunice Bell. "All Cuthbert would tell me was what had happened to his friend. My father was a magistrate, but that hadn't stopped him from taking the law into his own hands and thrashing Jack Goodrum. We none of us ever saw the boy again.

"And this is my point: my late father was a quick-tempered, violent man. A thrashing from him would be something that any culprit would remember for the rest of his life. It is my belief that Jack Goodrum *has* remembered it, and that when Cuthbert crossed his path he quite deliberately ran him down."

Both detectives sat back in their chairs. They looked sceptical.

"It's a very interesting story, Miss Bell," said Sergeant Lloyd, "but—"

"But where's your evidence?" said Chief Inspector Quantrill.

Eunice Bell looked stiffly from one to the other. "I beg your pardon?"

"Evidence," repeated the Chief Inspector patiently. "You've put forward a theory that sounds plausible, Miss Bell. But what we must have, if we're to pursue it, is good hard evidence that will stand up in a court of law. There's already been an investigation into your brother's death, and all the available evidence points to an accident. So if you want the case reopened, you'll have to provide us with more than a theory to work on."

Eunice Bell stood up, looking—for the first time—disconcerted. "I have no 'hard evidence,' as you call it, to give you. I had imagined that *you* would search for evidence, once you had grounds for suspicion. I thought that was how detectives worked. Am I mistaken?"

Quantrill too got to his feet. "Well, no," he said apologetically. "You're not mistaken, Miss Bell—but that applies only when an unexplained or a suspicious death has occurred. In this case there's no mystery at all. And there are three eye-witnessess who say that the driver of the vehicle had no chance of avoiding your brother."

"Yes—these eye-witnesses!" Eunice Bell turned abruptly towards Sergeant Lloyd and her notebook. "I thought they were suspicious, when I read about them. Three seems too many. And they were looking in exactly the same direction far too conveniently for my liking. How can you be sure that Goodrum didn't bribe them to give evidence in his favour?"

"Three old-established residents of Breckham Market?" said Hilary Lloyd reproachfully, getting up in her turn. "Two of them pensioners, all of them thoroughly respectable . . . ?"

Miss Bell hesitated for a moment, then ducked her head in acknowledgement. "Had I realised that," she said stiffly, "I would never have made such an allegation. I withdraw it, of course."

Quantrill gave a ruminative nod. "It seems to me," he said, practising kindness, "that you'd have have done better to attend the inquest, Miss Bell. You're upset by your brother's death, of course. But if you'd gone to the inquest and seen how thoroughly the matter was dealt with, I'm sure it would have set your mind at rest. As it is, you're probably imagining—"

She snapped straight back at him, proudly. "Please don't try to humour me, Mr. Quantrill. I know quite well what you think. My brother was a figure of fun in Breckham Market: poor old Clanger—yes, I know what you all called him—poor old Clanger Bell, the town drunk. None of you took him seriously in life, and you're not prepared to take his death seriously either."

The Chief Inspector started to protest. She cut him short. Her face still showed no emotion but her throat, quilted by the accumulating lines of middle age, flushed crimson with controlled indignation.

"Oh yes, there's been a police investigation. Yes, an inquest has been held. But all of you pre-judged the verdict. From the moment you heard of his death, every single one of you assumed that it was my brother's own fault—that it was the *driver* of the vehicle who didn't have a chance, rather than Cuthbert. I know, because at first I thought the same thing.

"I expected my brother to die like that, and I make no pretence of mourning for him. All I've felt, quite frankly, has been relief. But when Cub—when Cuthbert was a boy, I loved him . . . And ever since I read the report of the inquest, I've had a deep sense of injustice. I am absolutely convinced that my brother's death has not been fully investigated. Can't you *see*, Chief Inspector, how significant it is that Goodrum concealed his boyhood association with Cuthbert? Surely, now you know that the man responsible had a lifetime grudge against him, you *can't* continue to dismiss my brother's death as a mere accident!"

The woman was a tiger when she got going, thought Quantrill with respect. No wonder Molly was in awe of her— there'd be no excuses for slacking by Red Cross volunteers when Eunice Bell was anywhere about.

"I take your point, Miss Bell," he said gravely. "But there are several other factors we have to consider. For a start, Goodrum is a common enough name in Suffolk. Can you be sure you're talking about one and the same person?"

"Yes. I have local contacts, and I checked my facts. It's the same Jack Goodrum—now a self-made man, retired, with new money and a new wife."

"All the more reason, then," suggested Hilary, "for him not to go jeopardising his new lifestyle simply to settle a very old score."

"But you forget," said Eunice Bell. "Goodrum is self-made. I know about self-made men—my great-grandfather was one, and my grandfather carried on the tradition. Self-made men are ruthless. They had to be, or they wouldn't get to the top of the heap and stay there. And a ruthless man who bears a lifelong grudge against a mere town drunk is hardly likely to let either morality or sentiment stand in his way."

"You may be right," acknowledged Quantrill. "But I'm afraid, Miss Bell, that all you're offering us is speculation. You can't be sure that Mr. Goodrum ever *had* a grudge against your brother. For all you know, young Jack Goodrum came from a violent home and got regular thrashings from his own father. What you imagine to be a significant event in his life might really have meant very little to him at all."

"And even if the boy did resent the punishment, and left Breckham Market feeling that he had a score to settle with your brother," said Hilary, "it all happened such a long while ago . . . What—thirty-five years?"

That was before the detective sergeant had been born; and in her view, life was too short to be wasted by dwelling on the past. She gave the older woman a friendly, coaxing smile. "Don't you think it's more likely that Jack Goodrum will have forgotten all about it by now? People don't really harbour resentment for that length of time, Miss Bell, do they?"

But Eunice Bell, head stiff and high, throat flushed with the vivid memory of the hurts and humiliations of her own unhappy youth, knew otherwise. "Yes, Miss Lloyd," she said. "Oh yes, they do."

8

"So much," said Sergeant Lloyd, "for talking Eunice Bell out of her allegation of murder."

"She knows her own mind too well for that," agreed Quantrill. "What's more, she's obviously got a sound mind to know. We can't get away with claiming that she's off her rocker, so now we're lumbered with an investigation that hasn't a snowball's chance—oh: coffee for two, please, miss."

After they left Tower House, Quantrill had led the way in his car to the former White Hart, a Tudor inn with a Georgian brick façade that had been extended and modernised in the 1960s and renamed the Rights of Man, in honour of Thomas Paine who had ancestral connections with the town. White Hart or Rights, the hotel remained what it had always been, the best in Breckham Market.

On his own, or with a male colleague, Quantrill would have gone for refreshments to the old-established coffee tavern, just opposite the livestock market. There, in an agreeable fug behind the steamed-up windows, and in the hearty company of farmers and dealers, he could have made up for his meagre breakfast by munching a couple of pigs-in-blankets—whole sausages shawled in shortcrust pastry, succulent, steaming, fresh from the oven . . .

But he had no intention of taking Hilary Lloyd to the coffee tavern. Not that she'd have turned up her nose at its dinginess; she was too experienced a police officer to be fussy about her surroundings. He wasn't going to feed his face in front of her, though, and there was no point in tormenting his tastebuds with the smell of those home-made sausage rolls if he couldn't allow himself to eat them.

There was another reason, too. His relationship with Hilary was too delicate for him to want to expose it to the comments of the regulars either at the coffee tavern or at the Coney and Thistle, his favourite pub. After all, this was strictly a working break, a necessary pause to discuss the enquiries they were pursuing. Much better, then, to bring her somewhere where he wasn't known—and why not to the buttery of the best hotel in town while he was at it? Even if the coffee did cost—he moved the menu card surreptitiously to arm's length across the table, the better to be able to read it in the dim lighting—good grief! *Fifty pence a cup?*

The waitress brought the coffee, and left the bill. "Is this one of your eating places, when you're off duty?" Quantrill asked Hilary, trying to find out more about her than she had ever volunteered.

"Not at these prices!" she laughed, emphasising her independence by putting her share of the money on the table. "We seem to have strayed into expense-account territory. It isn't your kind of place either, I'd have thought," she added, looking round at the décor. "Surely you don't approve of fake Tudor beams?"

"No—but I don't mind 'em in a modern extension like this when the rest of the hotel's genuine. I've cracked my head on their real Tudor beams often enough to be glad not to have to duck when I come in here. Haven't been for about four years, though. They used to do a very useful all-day bacon and egg meal, but it seems that everything's changed . . ."

He held away the menu (Molly kept telling him that he ought to have his eyes tested, but he was hanged if he'd admit the necessity) and focused on the unimaginable, largely unpronounceable new-style offerings: pizzas, burgers, tacos, lasagne, enchillados . . .

"Rubbishy foreign grub," he grumbled. "This is England. Suffolk. Who wants to come here and eat *this*?"

"The briefcase brigade does," said Hilary reasonably. "They rush all over the country on business, and once they get into a hotel they don't know whether they're in Suffolk or Southampton. This is fast food, and that's what most of the customers want. If it comes to that, *I* like lasagne. You probably would, too, if only you'd give it a try."

"No *thanks*." Quantrill had never had any inclination to go abroad, and he saw no reason why he should have abroad foisted on him when he was at home. "But at least there's plenty of elbow room here, and it's not a bad cup of coffee," he conceded. "If the management has the decency to give us a free refill I might even come again."

He signalled to the waitress—the refills *were* free—then sat back and looked round the buttery. It had been completely refurbished since his last visit, but now he was here again he could recall that occasion as though it were yesterday. He was with a woman then—Jean Bloomfield, who had been head-mistress of the girls' grammar school when his daughters were pupils. Jean, a widow with whom he had fallen so blindly in love that he had publicly held her hand across the table as he tried to repudiate his marriage . . . Jean, who for a moment had returned the strength of his clasp and acknowledged that the attraction, at least, was mutual . . .

Well, that was all four years ago. The tragedy and heartbreak of that relationship had shaken him profoundly, and had taught him to keep his emotions in check. True, he'd since had some long-term eye contact with a shapely woman police con-stable—but he'd made no attempt to take it any further, and WPC Patsy Hopkins had eventually deserted him to marry his boss.

And now here he was with Hilary Lloyd, who had neither the sad beauty of Jean nor the obvious physical attractions of Patsy. What she had instead was capability, directness, a shining intelligence. Having at first resented her intrusion into the masculine world of Breckham Market CID, Quantrill had found himself increasingly glad of her presence both profes-sionally and personally. He valued her, desired her company; desired her.

He wasn't in love with her, he knew that. Having had the experience of falling in love with Jean Bloomfield, he couldn't confuse that overwhelming passion with the lesser longing he felt for Hilary. This, he supposed wryly, was probably what was known as infatuation . . . And yes, common sense told him that if he pushed his chances with her, he might not only make a fool of himself but lose her completely. One wrong move from him, and she'd almost certainly ask for a transfer.

But to hell with common sense. That was what had kept him from taking advantage of Patsy Hopkins's friendship, and look where that had got him: best man at her wedding!

Besides, time wasn't on his side. Lesser longing or not, what he wanted was an opportunity to prove to Hilary—and therefore to himself—that he was still young, still capable of ardour. He was working on the problem when he heard her say, "What about the bedroom?"

"*What?*"

"Clanger Bell's bedroom. Why did you make a point of asking Eunice Bell if you could look at it before we left Tower House?"

"Oh—sorry, I was thinking of a different person." He lit one of the appetite-quelling small cigars that he occasionally smoked. A man was entitled to *some* pleasures.

"Yes, Clanger . . . Well, when it was obvious that we couldn't shake Miss Bell's claim that her brother was murdered," he explained, "I thought we ought to let her see us starting an investigation. And having a look at poor old Clanger's bedroom was the only thing I could think of."

"His sister was completely taken aback when you asked to see it," said Hilary. "She certainly wasn't expecting that. She carried it off very well, I thought, considering that her brother can't have slept in the room she showed us for at least thirty years. It was very sad, really—all those ancient teenage adventure magazines, and the model aircraft, gathering dust in that cold room . . . I wonder where he really slept?"

"By the kitchen stove, as like as not," said Quantrill, relaxing over his cigar. "I knew an old feller—a bachelor farmer—who did that for at least the last ten years of his life. He often had to go out in the night to attend his stock, and there wouldn't have been much pleasure afterwards in returning to a cold bed. He was snug enough in his armchair, with an old greatcoat over him and his dog at his feet."

"I can't imagine Eunice Bell allowing Cuthbert to live like *that*. Though come to think of it," reflected Hilary, "she did say that she had little or no control over him—and his clothes always looked as though they'd been slept in."

"The two of them probably had separate living quarters," said Quantrill. "Tower House is plenty big enough."

"True . . . And the point isn't significant, anyway, is it? Miss Bell begged us to investigate, and it isn't in her interest to conceal anything that could be relevant to her brother's death."

"So where do you suggest we go from here?" said Quantrill with half-intended ambiguity. "You're in charge, I'm not officially on duty today."

"No you're not, are you?" Sergeant Lloyd looked unflatteringly pleased at the prospect of independent action. "Right—I suggest you go home, Chief Inspector, and make the most of what's left of your rest day. I'm going to find out whether the three eye-witnesses to the accident are the upright citizens that they led us to believe. And then I'll have a talk with Jack Goodrum, and I'll put a report on your desk first thing tomorrow morning."

"Hold you hard, Hilary!" Quantrill protested. "You're wel-

come to the eye-witnesses, but I want to see this Jack
Goodrum for myself. I'd be very interested to know how an
ordinary Suffolk boy managed to make a fortune by the time he
was fifty . . ."

"And how he might have managed to run over someone he
disliked and get away with a verdict of accidental death?"
added Hilary soberly. "Because this is what worries me—the
thought that Eunice Bell could be right."

"Yes. That's what I'm bothered about too, and why I'm
coming with you. If Miss Bell *is* right, then Jack Goodrum has
committed a near-perfect murder, because we're got a snowball's chance in hell of proving it."

9

The mid-Victorian Gothic buildings of Felicity Goodrum's son's
new school were widespread and imposing. They were
distributed over a hillside on the outskirts of the Suffolk town
from which the College took its name, and from the sloping
lawns in front of the Great Hall there was—given good
weather—an impressive view across the valley to the roofs of
Saxted and the ruins of its ancient castle.

But this was November. Fog hung over the valley and
obscured the view. Even though it wasn't raining, moisture
from the trees dripped on to the pupils as they hurried from
one part of the school to another. The new sixth-former,
dodging through the drips, found his unaccustomed rural
surroundings disenchanting.

"I say—are you Matthew Napier?"

Matthew—approaching seventeen, his eyes brown like his
mother's but his features and bearing haughtily unlike hers—
turned at the call of a stocky boy of about the same age who
came bounding up behind him. He acknowledged his identity.

"I'm Ben Clarke," said the stocky boy. "Someone said you've
come from the City of London School, and I wondered if you
knew my cousin who's there. Edward Clarke? Rugby player—
first fifteen this year!"

"Good for Edward Clarke," said Matthew in a voice that

sounded disdainful. He himself was not a games player. Then, because the disdain was a cover for newcomer's loneliness and he was not sorry to have someone to talk to, he added abruptly, "I know the name, but I don't recall having seen him. City of London's a day school, and the playing fields are miles away."

"What do you think of Saxted, then?" said Ben Clarke. The boys were making for the Technology Centre, Ben jollying through the fallen leaves, walking backwards as he talked, kicking at conkers.

"Not a lot," pronounced Matthew, turning up the collar of his blazer with a haughty flick and marching on. Although he had felt pressured and unhappy at his father's old school, he knew that it ranked a good deal higher in the public school league than Saxted. And wretched as his father had made him, he had learned from Austin Napier to be a snob.

"Oh, you'll soon get used to it," promised Ben. "Anyway, you've only got a couple of years here. What made you change schools at this stage?"

"Divorce," said Matthew shortly.

"That's tough," said Ben. "But you'll get used to that, too," he added cheerfully. "*My* parents divorced when I was eight . . . it's *really* rough at that age. But what you have to think of are the benefits! Both parents feel so guilty that they shower you with money and presents. And then when they both marry again you get two complete sets of parents and double the number of grandparents, all competing with each other to provide you with goodies. You can't lose!"

Ben Clarke hesitated, then bent to pick up a conker and fling it as far as he could across the misted grass. His bright look had changed to a momentary bleakness. "Unless of course you happen to miss your real family life, and your real father . . ."

"God, no!" Matthew Napier, preoccupied with his own problems, misinterpreted his companion's lament as a question. "I'm thankful to be free of my father. I couldn't *stand* him."

"Couldn't stand" was an understatement, but Matthew had no intention of admitting to anyone that his father had terrified him. Family life, at their home in Highgate, had been dominated by Austin Napier's moods. The atmosphere had seemed to be one of permanent tension, heightened by the fact that the barrister communicated with his wife and son almost exclusively by cross-examination.

Matthew had dreaded his father's return home each evening, because it meant the immediate exposure of his academic failings. That was why the boy had begged—in vain—to be allowed to go to boarding school, in an attempt to escape the daily torment. It was not that he had anticipated any form of punishment. His father had never punished him; he had no need to. Austin Napier was a master of sarcasm who could flay—and enjoy flaying—his son with his tongue.

"You were lucky that your parents divorced, then," said Ben Clarke. "At least you won't have to see him very often."

"Hah—you don't know my father! He's coming here today to take me out to lunch."

"On a Wednesday? We're not supposed to go out except at weekends."

"It's not *my* idea," said Matthew. "It's the last thing I want to do. Apparently my father's in court at Ipswich this week, and he rang the Headmaster this morning and fixed things."

"I expect he'll take you to The Crown," said Ben, almost wistfully. "You'll get a good nosh-up anyway . . . Make sure you go à la carte—the steak there's usually pretty good . . ."

But Matthew wasn't listening. He was dreading the meeting with his father, and angry at the way it had been engineered. Austin Napier had no right of access to him during term time. The boy's first thought, when the Headmaster's secretary had told him of today's arrangement, had been to telephone a complaint to his mother. But that would have upset her, and he would far rather endure an hour of his father's company than do that.

Matthew loved his mother. Frightened as he had always been of his father, he had grown up to realise that his mother's fear was even greater. She, Matthew had observed, trembled in her husband's presence. She flinched when he spoke harshly to her.

Even so, it had taken Matthew some time to appreciate that his mother was far more of a victim than he was. Unlike him, she had had physical symptoms: those bruises on her wrists, and on her neck; the way she sometimes used to wince when she moved. And then there had been the night of that terrible cry from his parents' bedroom, a quickly smothered, nerve-tingling shriek of pain that had hooked him, dry-mouthed and sweating, out of his sleep. *No Austin—please, please no—*

Loving her, longing to protect her, it was Matthew who had urged her on the plan of escape. They had no need to remain with his father, he had pointed out, if only she would swallow her pride and stop trying to keep up appearances.

She had a small income of her own, the boy knew; enough, he had imagined, to support them both in some interesting town a long way from London, until she could find a job. And he could go to a local school until he was old enough to leave and get a job too. They'd be *all right*, he had persuaded her, as long as they were together, and free.

And getting away would be perfectly easy. All they had to do was to leave a note, one day when Austin Napier was self-satisfiedly destroying some innocent witness in court, load their luggage into her car and take off. It would have been so brilliantly simple, so exciting, so satisfactory—if only the bloody car hadn't broken down in the pouring rain somewhere out in the wilds of Suffolk . . .

"You're on to a good thing, you know," said Ben Clarke cheerily. "Your mother'll probably marry again, and—"

"She already has."

"Quick work! What's your stepfather like?"

"He's a slob."

Ben thought it funny. "No accounting for women's tastes, is there?" he laughed. "My stepfather's a complete idiot . . . he's generous, though, I'll say that for him. Is yours?"

"Oh yes . . ." This time, Matthew's disdain was genuine. "Loaded with money, and such an oaf that he doesn't know what to do with it."

"Take him for all he's got, then," advised Ben, entirely without malice.

"I intend to."

"Good for you. Is your home far away?"

Matthew hesitated, aching with homelessness.

After they had fled from Highgate, he and his mother had settled in Colchester. It was well away from his father, and yet near enough to London for him to be able to travel by train to and from his former school, which his father had insisted he must continue to attend at least until he'd done his "O" levels.

Matthew had liked Colchester. The house had seemed cramped, after Highgate, but the atmosphere—after Highgate—was wonderfully happy. The only snag, in the boy's view, was that it had been much too close to Ipswich, and that appalling yob Jack Goodrum . . .

But the Colchester days were over. His mother had been married from there in September, two days after Matthew had left to begin his first term as a boarder at Saxted College. She and Jack Goodrum had lived in Colchester until their house in Breckham Market, The Mount, was ready, and then the only home where Matthew had ever been happy had been sold.

Presumably he was now expected to consider The Mount as his home. That was where he had been obliged to spend his October half-term holiday. The house itself, Georgian with a big garden, wasn't at all bad—if only Jack Goodrum hadn't been strutting round it, trying to ingratiate himself by making a big deal about giving his stepson a choice of rooms and furniture. What Matthew had wanted, when he had organised the escape from his father's tyranny, was to provide his mother and himself with independence. Instead, it seemed that they had become dependent on another man, and one he despised.

"My mother lives in Breckham Market now," he said distantly.

"Oh, that's almost on the way to Yarchester, where my father lives. Tell you what—my old man has access to me one weekend a month, lucky devil, and he'll be coming to fetch me for the day next Saturday. We can give you a lift as far as Breckham Market, if you like."

"No thanks."

"Why not? Good grief, don't say you'd rather stay here than be spoiled rotten by an apologetic step-parent!"

"*Much* rather," said Matthew haughtily. Bad enough to have to face the prospect of living with his mother's new husband during the Christmas holiday; but at least that was a long way ahead. "I can't abide my stepfather. My mother should never have had to marry a man like that, but she couldn't really afford to keep us both while I'm still at school. She only married him for his money."

"I expect they wanted to have sex in comfort, too," said Ben, whose parents' marriage had foundered on extra-marital affairs conducted under his childish scrutiny. "At their age, they can't make it unless they've got all night together in a double bed!"

Matthew Napier's stomach contracted. Appalled by the obscenity of the suggestion, he turned in fury on his companion. "How *dare* you say that about my mother? How bloody dare you!" He seized the shorter boy by his mist-dampened hair and shouted into his face. "Apologise, do you hear? Apologise or I'll knock your stupid teeth in!"

"S-sorry!" Ben Clarke spluttered, in pained astonishment.

"Ouch—I'm *sorry* . . . I wasn't being rude about your mother, honest. How could I be? I've never met her."

Matthew Napier pushed him away contemptuously. "And you never will. It's yobboes like you I intend to protect her from." He wiped his hands on his blazer. "Bog off, Clarke," he ordered. "I don't have to waste my time talking to you, just because your oik of a cousin went to my old school. Bog off, and keep out of my way in future."

Ben shrugged, pushed his hands into his trouser pockets and jollied in another direction, kicking at conkers and whistling nonchalantly. The taller boy, breathing hard, watched him go. Then, seeing a particularly large horse chestnut on the path in front of him, he picked it up and flung it viciously, with all his strength, against the wall of the Tech Centre.

The conker rebounded on to the path and lay there, split. Matthew Napier shattered it with his heel, ground the fragments of white nut and brown casing into the damp gravel, and stalked away.

10

Felicity Goodrum was so happy in her new marriage and her new home that as she moved lightly about the house, she sang. Her music had neither words nor recognisable tune; it was a gentle, melodious *la-la-la*, a warble of complete content.

Although she had lived for the whole of her adult life in London, she had been born and had spent her youth in the Northamptonshire countryside. Her first husband had been so much a London, Inns of Court, man that she had never anticipated returning to the country, much as she would have liked to. Coming with her new husband to settle in Suffolk was therefore a delightful bonus.

Her future life in the country would not, she realised, be the kind of life she had been brought up to know. Felicity came from an established middle-class background—her father had been chairman of the leather manufacturing company founded by his great-grandfather—and her social life before her first marriage had been active: dances, dinner parties, picnics, tennis, and frequent weekend visits to and from old school and family friends.

Her marriage to Austin Napier had soon put a stop to all that. Austin had demanded her undivided attention and had chilled off her own friends. But the network of which she had once been a part was still there, and had she been remarried to someone from her own background she would soon have fitted into the social life of whichever county they decided to live in.

Marriage to Jack Goodrum, though, had put her socially beyond the pale. Jack was, as Felicity's elderly parents had written to her in horror after they had first met him, *not one of us*. Even though, by that time, Jack's appearance and habits had considerably improved, his rustic aura made him permanently unacceptable. But Felicity, who had known this from the start of their relationship, was too happy with him to care.

Jack's money would of course have given them an entrée to a different social set. There were a good many ostentatious *nouveaux riches* living in Suffolk: land and property dealers, gravel extractors, haulage contractors, opportunists of every kind. The men were instantly recognisable by their swagger and gold jewellery, their wives (often considerably younger—their glamourous former secretaries, married after their outworn first wives had been dumped) by their structured hairstyles and Caribbean sun-tans. But Felicity was too much a product of her background to want to mix with them, and Jack was not a golfing, gambling, horse-racing man.

No; the Goodrums intended to belong to no set but their own. It was not that they were unsociable. Jack enjoyed going out on rough shoots with farming acquaintances, and playing an occasional game of snooker. And Felicity, who had been brought up to understand the importance of doing good works, had already made herself known to various Breckham Market charity organisers. She had sold poppies for the British Legion, she was on the roster for delivering Meals on Wheels to housebound old people, and she had volunteered to help man a stall at a forthcoming county bazaar in aid of the Save the Children Fund. She would have been interested, too, in doing some voluntary work for the Red Cross; but in view of the fact that the local vice president was Miss Eunice Bell, whose brother had been so tragically run over—accidentally, of course—by Jack, Felicity had thought it tactful to keep out of her orbit.

Felicity's chief interest, though, was in her new home. The Mount—early Georgian three-storeyed red brick, with a

pedimented doorway and a roof-concealing parapet—was set
in over an acre of walled garden. It was south-facing, secluded,
yet only five minutes' walk from the centre of Breckham
Market. It also had the advantage of a sloping site, and a view
across the roofs of the houses in the lower part of Mount Street
towards the wooded, undulating country on the far side of the
town.

Mount Street, a tree-lined residential road, rose steeply
from the direction of the river, passed the entrance gates of
The Mount and then forked. The right fork levelled and
continued, still residential, into the upper part of the old town
around St. Botolph's church. The narrow left fork, Hobart's
Lane, looped up and round the back of the walled garden
of The Mount. The Goodrums' property was therefore surrounded by roads on three sides; but fortunately for their
peace, the traffic in Mount Street was usually light and in
Hobart's Lane—which went nowhere in particular—almost
non-existent.

Before Jack bought it, The Mount had stood empty for some
years. It was in a state of disrepair, but because of its situation
and architectual merit the asking price was too high for the
local residential market. Only someone with Jack's resources
could have contemplated buying and restoring the house, and
he—with a secret preference for having something nice and
modern built to their own requirements—would not have
thought of doing so if his wife-to-be hadn't fallen in love with
it.

For Felicity, the house was ideal. And what had attracted
her most was the Victorian conservatory that extended from
the south-east wall. It was shaped in a hexagon, one and a half
storeys high, with a framework of slender cast-iron pillars
joined at the top by delicately curving cast-iron ribs.

When she and Jack first saw the ruined conservatory—
virtually glassless, its ironwork rusting away—it had seemed
irreparable. Jack had been all for having it demolished. But
Felicity had seen its structural beauty. And besides, there
were glossily dark-leaved camellias, so mature that they were
trees rather than shrubs, still growing there amid the broken
glass and bird droppings. From the moment she saw the
camellias, flourishing happily though it seemed that everything had fallen apart about them, Felicity had known that this
would be a good place to call her home.

And now that Jack had had the conservatory restored, at

considerable but ungrudged expense, he had become very proud of it. He would often join Felicity there so that they could do their odd jobs together in mutual contentment. That was where they were—he cleaning his shotguns, she potting up bulbs—when a large middle-aged man and a younger woman came walking round from the side of the house and tapped on the glass of the conservatory's garden door.

The man apologised for taking them by surprise. "No one answered the front door, but we saw the Range Rover in the drive and knew there'd be somebody about somewhere. County police—Detective Chief Inspector Quantrill, Detective Sergeant Lloyd."

Puzzled but hospitable, Felicity—who happened to be nearer the garden door than her husband—invited them in. She took an immediate liking to the Chief Inspector because he was very much a man in Jack's mould, solidly and unpretentiously Suffolk. The woman detective was much more stylish and sophisticated. Good bones, thought Felicity approvingly; pity about that scar on her forehead. But how strange that her eyes should move so rapidly, taking everything in . . . *his* eyes, too, despite the slowness of his voice . . .

Feeling slightly unnerved by their comprehensive scrutiny, Felicity glanced back at Jack for support. He had already moved up behind her, and now he placed his hand on her shoulder.

"And what can we do for you, Chief Inspector?" he enquired genially.

"Just a private word, if you please, Mr. Goodrum."

Jack's fingers tightened. "Has something happened?" he demanded, his voice suddenly hoarse. "You're not bringing us bad news, are you?"

"Oh *no*." Felicity sensed his alarm and her compost-soiled hands flew up towards her open mouth as if to stifle her gasp of horror. "It isn't Matthew, is it? Don't say he's—"

"It's all *right*, Mrs. Goodrum," said the sergeant quickly. She gave a reassuring smile. "We're only making routine enquiries. Matthew's your son, I imagine?"

"Yes—" Felicity relaxed. She laughed with relief as Jack gave her shoulder an affectionate pat before taking his hand away. "This is Matthew's first term at boarding school so I can't be sure what he's up to. He's nearly seventeen, and I believe he's learning to ride a motor bike. I had visions of him borrowing a machine and crashing it . . ."

"It's a worrying age," agreed the Chief Inspector. "My own boy's at day school, but I've no idea what *he* gets up to either. As Sergeant Lloyd says, though, we've come solely to ask for Mr. Goodrum's help with a routine enquiry."

Felicity dusted her hands together and gave the detective a parting smile. "I must go and see about lunch, anyway," she said. But as she began to move her husband put a detaining hand on her arm.

"I'd rather you stayed, my dear." He turned to the detectives. "There's nothing you can ask me that I wouldn't want my wife to know about," he asserted with a proud jut of his Desperate Dan chin. "*Ours* isn't the poor sort of marriage where husband and wife have secrets from each other."

The Chief Inspector looked discomfited. He opened his mouth to say something, but evidently thought better of it. Felicity, standing serenely beside her honest Jack, felt quite sorry for the man. "Do sit down," she suggested.

The conservatory was furnished, among the camellias, with bamboo chairs. Jack had—inevitably—wanted to buy brand new ones. He didn't like to provide his wife with what he called disparagingly "second-hand rubbish." But Felicity, who knew how old buildings should be furnished, had ferreted about in junk shops and saleyards and had triumphantly acquired some relics of the Imperial East: sagging, somewhat battered, but indubitably the real thing.

She had made the old chairs comfortable with chintz-covered cushions, but this had done little to muffle their tendency to creak. As the Chief Inspector's chair protested under his weight, Felicity saw him cast a glance of embarrassment at his woman colleague. Sergeant Lloyd, who wore a diamond eternity ring, gave no sign that she had noticed the creaking; not so much out of tact, Felicity guessed, as out of a studied determination to take no personal interest in her senior officer.

Oh dear, Felicity thought with gentle amusement. She was a kind woman, and certainly not a smug one, but she couldn't help rejoicing in the confidence that her newly acquired happiness had given her. She suspected that the Chief Inspector was a partner in what Jack had tactlessly dismissed as a poor sort of marriage, and that he was hankering after his unattainable sergeant. *Poor Chief Inspector Quantrill* . . .

She gave Jack a fond look, and prepared to smile kindly at their visitor. As she did so, she realised that in the last few seconds there had been a subtle change in the atmosphere.

There was now a hint of chill. The Chief Inspector was no longer a figure of pity but a massive and intrusive presence. He sat perfectly still in his chair and his eyes were still, too; they were the hard green of little apples, and they were staring straight at Jack.

"What we've come to do, Mr. Goodrum," he said in his measured Suffolk voice, "is to tie up the loose ends in the matter of Cuthbert Bell's death."

This time, Jack's was the chair that creaked. Felicity looked at her husband. His chin was jutting and he was staring back at the Chief Inspector, but his voice was completely calm as he said, "I thought that'd all been dealt with at the inquest."

"So did I. But some information has come to light that doesn't match what we thought we knew. We took you for a newcomer to Breckham Market, you see."

"That's right. So I am. We came to live here in October." Jack turned for confirmation to his wife. "What was the exact date, my dear?"

"The fifth," said Felicity mechanically. Jack seemed completely unworried, but that did nothing to lessen her unease. She had noticed that the sergeant's eyes had stilled and that they too were now focused on her husband.

"October 5th—yes, that date was mentioned in the report," agreed the Chief Inspector. "What *wasn't* mentioned, either at your interview after the incident or at the inquest, was that you were no stranger to the town when you arrived. I understand that your grandparents owned a butcher's shop just off Victoria Road, and that you often came to stay with them when you were a boy."

For a second Jack looked taken aback. Then he burst out laughing. "Why, blast, you're going back a year or two! So they did . . . So I did! There's no secret about it. I daresay a few of the old 'uns in the town can remember me delivering their meat . . . But that was all of thirty-five years ago! I haven't been near the place since I was sixteen."

"Why not?" asked Sergeant Lloyd quickly.

"Because I grew up and went out to work," said Jack, his voice civilly matter-of-fact. "I got a job near home, in Ipswich. Then m'grandad died, Grandma came to live with us, and there wasn't any reason for me to come back to Breckham. There wasn't any reason, either, for me to tell the Coroner that I used to come here in the school holidays thirty-five to forty years ago! That had nothing at all to do with the inquest."

"Except that the man you knocked over with your Range Rover was not in fact a stranger to you, Mr. Goodrum," said the Chief Inspector. "You used to know Cuthbert Bell quite well, I believe, when you were boys together?"

Jack had told Felicity all about his grandparents and their butcher's shop. She enjoyed his stories of his early life, and of the mischief he used to get up to. She knew there was no secret about his long-ago acquaintance with Breckham Market, and she agreed with his contention that the fact was irrelevant to the inquest. But she hadn't, until now, heard that he used to know the man he had accidentally killed. The revelation made her draw in her breath so sharply that both detectives immediately looked at her, hard.

"Oh Jack—and you didn't tell me!" she said reproachfully. "That must have made the accident even more distressing for you."

He took her hand. His own was big and warm and comforting. "That's exactly why I didn't tell you, my dear. You were upset enough over the accident as it was. Not that I realised who the man was at the time, o' course."

He looked straight at the detectives. "Clanger, that was what everybody called the man who walked into my Range Rover," he explained. "Just Clanger, the town drunk. I'd seen him wandering round, but I had no reason to connect him with the boy who used to follow me about all those years ago. No reason at all. As soon as I heard his real name, after the accident, I thought I recognised it. But even then, it was some time before I could call him to mind. It wasn't as though we'd ever been friends—he'd just followed me like a lost dog. Mind you, young Cuthbert always was an odd 'un. 'S not surprising, come to think of it, that he ended up as a drunk—not with the parents *he'd* got, poor little perisher . . ."

"You knew his parents, then, Mr. Goodrum?" said the sergeant.

Jack laughed. Still holding his wife's hand, to their mutual comfort, he said, "Only to deliver meat to—and then I didn't see *them*, o' course. Tradesmen went round the back in those days, and were dealt with by the servants. But I heard my grandparents talk about Mr. and Mrs. Bell, and how cold and distant they were with their children."

"So you never actually met Cuthbert's father?" asked the Chief Inspector. Though he spoke casually, Felicity couldn't fail to notice that he was watching every movement of her husband's face.

But Jack was completely relaxed. "Met him? Why yes—I got a good hiding from him, once! I can't say that actually *knew* him, but I certainly felt the weight of his leather strap . . ."

"What for?" asked Sergeant Lloyd. "What had you done?"

Jack scratched his thick hair with his free hand. "Hanged if I know, after all these years—but no doubt I deserved it! I was a young terror, always getting into trouble and having my ear clipped for it. My poor grandma used to take the sole of an old shoe to my backside when she couldn't put up with my tricks any longer. I remember the time when—"

"I'd rather you tried to remember the time when Mr. Bell thrashed you," interrupted the Chief Inspector. "My information is that he punished you severely—and that it was Cuthbert who'd told on you."

Jack make no direct reply. He went completely quiet for a moment, and then turned to his wife. "I tell you what it is, Felicity," he said in a conversational tone. "The CID has come here imagining that I recognised the town drunk, and deliberately ran him over so as to get my own back for something that happened thirty-five years ago." He looked challengingly at their visitors. "That's it, isn't it? That's what all this is about?"

Felicity was horrified. Jack was right, of course—the police *were* suspicious, that was what accounted for the unease she had felt during their questioning. But what they were imagining was preposterous, and she told them so.

The Chief Inspector's chair creaked uncomfortably. His sergeant was already on her feet and he stood too, still trying to maintain that his enquiries were merely routine. Felicity turned disdainfully away. She expected Jack to show the detectives the door, but to her surprise he seemed to have taken no offence.

"Now hold you hard, my dear," he told her. "The police have their job to do, and being suspicious is part of it. I've been glad of CID help more than once, over break-ins and thefts from my business, and I reckon an honest man's a fool if he won't co-operate with 'em. They have to act on information they receive—but what they've heard this time is just not true. What it sounds like is malicious gossip."

"We might have been misled," admitted the Chief Inspector. "Well, I'm sorry to have troubled you—and Mrs. Goodrum."

"That's all right," said Jack graciously, leading them to the garden door. "Y'know, I half expected that something like this might happen when I came to live in Breckham Market. I daresay some of the customers who knew me as a butcher's boy resent the fact that I've got on in the world, and want to take me down a peg or two."

"You've certainly set yourself up in fine style here," said the detective bluntly. "Tell me, Mr. Goodrum—as one Suffolk man to another—how did you manage to do so well?"

"Hard work, bor," Jack said promptly, and with feeling. "Twenty-five years o' bloody hard work."

"That's what I've put in, with precious little to show for it," complained the Chief Inspector. "I reckon you must have had a rare lot o' luck, too."

Jack's broad back was turned to Felicity. She couldn't see his expression but she heard his warm, confident chuckle. "That I have! I've been lucky all m' life. That's what they've always called me—Lucky Jack."

11

"You do realise, Matthew, that this new school of yours has no standing at all? *Saxted College*—" Austin Napier's elegantly penetrating voice put a sneer on the name "—is, at best, second rate. Its academic record is of no consequence, and I am not satisfied with the standard of education you're receiving here. It may be adequate for the offspring of the local minor gentry, but not for *my* son."

Matthew cast an anguished glance round the panelled dining room of the Crown. The hotel, the oldest in the small market town of Saxted, obviously served as a meeting place for the local minor gentry. A dozen of them—middle-aged, well-weathered, broad-based, tweed-clad—were tucking into soup, braised oxtail and steamed ginger pudding. They all knew each other, and had been conversing from table to table in loud, cheerful voices; but the London barrister's ringing condemnation stopped them in mid-sentence.

As they turned to stare at his father, immaculate in grey-striped trousers and black jacket, Matthew cringed. He wished—as did most people in the witness box when faced by Austin Napier QC—that he could sink into the floor and disappear. But his father, accustomed to being the centre of attention in crowded courtrooms, continued his piercing cross-examination.

"And are you seriously asking me to believe, Matthew, that despite the school's inadequacy you *want* to remain here?"

The boy pushed a piece of bread roll into his mouth. "Yes, I do," he mumbled.

"Then perhaps you will be good enough, when you have finished chewing, to tell me why?"

"I—I like it here."

Austin Napier's nostrils flared with scorn. He was a distinguished-looking man, high-browed, fine-boned, impressively bespectacled, with greying hair brushed back above his ears. His lips were well-shaped, but they turned down haughtily at each corner. Matthew watched them apprehensively, dreading what might emerge from them.

"Whether or not you *like* the school has nothing to do with the matter," his father pronounced. Matthew sat tense, anticipating the exposure of his mediocre academic progress; that, he had supposed, was the reason for this unwelcome visit. To his surprise, his father merely added, "But perhaps you've been influenced by someone from this locality? Did you—ah—"

The barrister paused, not because he was ever at a loss for words, but for effect. "The man your mother is at present cohabiting with," he continued disdainfully. "I suppose *he* was at school here?"

Matthew doubted it. Jack Goodrum was obviously totally uneducated. But much as he despised the man, Matthew wasn't going to give his father the satisfaction of knowing what a slob his mother had married.

"I s'pose so," he agreed.

Austin Napier gave a shrug. "Then he must be a local man. No one outside Suffolk has ever heard of Saxted College—as you would discover if you were foolish enough to remain here. But that," he added, lowering his voice to a hiss and leaning across the table to fix his son with pale eyes that were magnified by his spectacle lenses, "is something I refuse to allow. I insist that you and your mother return to me in Highgate."

To Matthew's relief, their meal arrived. He had asked for

steak. His father had ordered it for both of them, specifying that it must be rare. The comfortable local waitress, accustomed to serving hungry schoolboys who were out for a treat with their parents, gave Matthew a grandmotherly smile and the lion's share of the chipped potatoes.

"There you are, dear," she said. "Enjoy your lunch!"

His throat was constricted. He couldn't eat. But to continue the conversation was impossible.

Matthew knew that his father, although a brilliant criminal prosecutor, was off his rocker when it came to the subject of his own marriage. The High Court who had awarded his mother a divorce on the grounds of her husband's unreasonable behaviour had said that, as a husband, Austin Napier was unbalanced in behaviour and thought. The details of the hearing had been gleefully reported in all the newspapers, and Matthew knew them by heart.

"Did you hear what I said?" his father persisted.

Matthew rendered himself speechless by forking chips into his mouth. Head down, he began to saw at his steak. He hated it rare. The oozing redness of the meat revolted him. But he needed something to occupy himself with, something other than his father to give his attention to.

"Look at me, Matthew!"

Austin Napier had always commanded instant obedience. The boy glanced up, unwillingly, and was alarmed by what he saw. His father's forehead was gouged by a heavy vertical frown, his eyes were glittering, his lips were savagely downcurved.

"Your mother and I," the barrister said in a low, tight voice, "are still married in the eyes of God. Marriage is indissoluble, from the moment the vows are uttered until one of us draws a final breath."

Unable to swallow, Matthew tongued a mouthful of chewed potato into one cheek. "Mother's divorced from you," he mumbled. "She's remarried. We don't have to do what you say any more."

"You ignorant boy!" Austin Napier, who had just placed a forkful of blood-red meat into his mouth, sneered at his son. "Haven't you read your prayer book? Haven't you studied the Solemnisation of Matrimony? *Those whom God hath joined together let no man put asunder.* Can anything be plainer than that?"

The barrister leaned forward, his eyes seeming to bore into

his son's. "Your mother and I are *still* one flesh," he hissed.
Matthew watched, fascinated and horrified, as a dribble of
bloody juice emerged from one corner of his father's mouth
and trickled down the side of his chin. "Whatever she may say,
she knows this as well as I do. *We are still one flesh*. Do you
understand me, Matthew?"

"Yes, father . . ."

Having made his point, and subdued his son's feeble attempt at
rebellion, Austin Napier seemed to recover his composure.
Relaxing into a forced geniality he allowed Matthew to
abandon his meat course. The boy said that he had to get back
to school, but his father insisted on ordering chocolate
profiteroles for him, brandy for himself and coffee for them
both.

"When did you last see your mother?" he enquired conver-
sationally as he lit a cigar.

"At half-term," said Matthew. "She's very well," he added,
unasked. He would have liked to take a poke at his father by
saying that his mother was also very happy, but he didn't
believe it to be true.

"And the man she's living with—what did you say his name
was?"

"Jack Goodrum."

As soon as Matthew said it, he realised that he hadn't
mentioned it before. He had been careful not to do so because
he knew perfectly well that his mother didn't want her former
husband to know either her new name or her whereabouts.
Any necessary communication between her and Austin Napier
was carried out through her solicitor.

Well, he'd said it now. And surely it couldn't really hurt his
mother if his father knew his stepfather's name? There seemed
to be a lot of Goodrums in Suffolk, and she and her new
husband had made a point of keeping themselves out of the
telephone directory.

"*Goodrum?*" said his father, voicing the name with distaste.
"How could your mother descend to a peasant surname like
that, after Napier? What does she see in the man?"

Matthew shrugged. "He's loaded with money," he said.

"And yet this is the best school he's prepared to afford for
you?"

The boy tussled with his conscience. Much as he'd resented
his mother's new husband, he had always been willing—until

this morning—to acknowledge Jack Goodrum's generosity. But his conversation at school with Ben Clarke had turned him against the man completely. The thought that Goodrum, old and hairy as he was, might be forcing sex on his mother was more than Matthew could bear.

There was, though, the other thought that Ben Clarke had implanted in his mind: that divorced parents compensated for their feelings of guilt by competing to load their children with gifts.

Take him for all he's worth, Ben had advised him, of his stepfather. And that, it occurred to Matthew, might as well apply to his father as to Jack Goodrum.

"Jack's not tight-fisted," he said, thinking himself cool and calculating. "Guess what he bought me at half-term—an Amstrad computer, with a colour monitor and a printer!"

"Bribery . . ." said his father disdainfully. "The man's trying to buy your affection, surely you can see that?" But after another sip of brandy, Austin Napier began to question his son about his other interests.

Matthew mentioned that he was taking a course, sponsored by the school and with a qualified instructor, on motor bike riding. He had already acquired a provisional licence, he said, and his own crash helmet. But the boys who didn't have bikes of their own had to take it in turns to practise on a battered old scooter.

"I had a motor scooter, when I was an undergraduate," said Austin Napier unexpectedly. "A Vespa . . . One taught one-self to ride, in those days, but I'm glad to hear that you're taking a proper course. Would you be allowed to keep a machine at school, if you had one?"

"Oh yes!" Matthew was overjoyed that his father had taken the bait. "We're not allowed to go outside the school grounds during the week," he added, anxious to make it clear that he was thoroughly responsible. "But we can go out on either Saturdays or Sundays, as long as we don't just zap about the town."

"I see . . . And is there a motor cycle retailer in Saxted?"

"*Yes*. I went past the shop last weekend, and there was a nearly new Suzuki CS50, already licenced, in the window! All I'd need would be insurance, and the dealer would fix that for me. I could be riding it by Saturday. That is, of course, if . . . ?"

Austin Napier slid back his stiff white cuff and looked at his

watch. "Yes, I think I can spare the time." He beckoned the
waitress for the bill, and then gave his son a restrained smile.
"Very well. We'll go out now and I'll see what I can do for you."

"Thank you—very much," said Matthew in a happy daze.

"Not at all. You're *my* son, and when you need anything *I* am
the person you are to turn to. Remember that."

"Yes, I will."

"No doubt you'll want to show the machine to your mother.
Do you think you'll be able to travel there and back in a day?"

"No problem! Breckham Market isn't more than twenty
miles."

"Is it not?"

The barrister paid the bill, adding a generous tip. "But you'll
find it a long journey on a low-powered motor cycle," he
advised, "particularly at this time of year. I don't think you
should consider it until you've gained some experience. These
are potentially dangerous machines, and I am buying you one
on the strict understanding that you will ride it sensibly and
carefully. You realise that, don't you?"

"Yes, I do. And thank you, father!"

Austin Napier gave his son a strange reply. "Thank *you*,
Matthew," he said.

His mouth was curved in an unpractised genial smile, but
his tone was ironic, and it took Matthew a long time to work
out why.

12

The following morning, when Detective Chief Inspector
Quantrill returned officially to work after his nominal day off,
he found a report from Sergeant Lloyd among the other papers
piled in his In tray. He read it first, and sent for her
immediately. Not that her report contained anything urgent;
he was, quite simply, feeling disgruntled because Molly had
spent the whole of the previous evening knitting a very small
garment and chattering about their future grandchild, and he
hoped for some kind of reassurance from Hilary that he was
still in his prime.

"You weren't able to shake the eye-witnesses to Clanger

Bell's encounter with Goodrum's Range Rover, then," he said, summarising her report.

"No, they were quite certain of what they'd seen. It does seem a heavy coincidence, as Miss Bell pointed out, that three people standing in different parts of the street should have been so conveniently looking in exactly the same direction at the same time, but I'm satisfied with their explanations. All three witnesses had known Clanger—at least by sight—for years, and they knew his habits. They told me, individually, that whenever they happened to see him emerge from a pub they always made a point of watching him, to see whether he was finally going to get himself run over."

Quantrill rubbed his jaw. "Hmmm—yes, I've done the same thing myself. And seen other people do it, too. Poor old Clanger provided Breckham Market with free entertainment for years . . . Well, there it is. His sister won't be pleased that we've found no evidence to support her theory that his death wasn't an accident, but she'll have to accept it. Good thing she approached the Super in the first place—*he* can have the job of soothing away her suspicions."

"I doubt he'll succeed," said Hilary.

"Probably not. And she could be right. Chances are that Lucky Jack Goodrum's been in luck again."

"I know that's what you think," Hilary acknowledged. "You didn't like him, did you? I was surprised about that, because you seem to have a lot in common."

Quantrill snorted. "Because we both sound Suffolk?"

"That, yes. But I was thinking more in terms of directness and honesty."

Dazed by her compliment, Quantrill bent his head and rummaged about among the dog-eared forms, match boxes, spare torch batteries, empty cigar tins, useless ball-point pens and gritty fluff that occupied the bottom drawer of his desk. He would have preferred to hear something more vigourously masculine about himself, but any comment from Hilary—any indication that she took a personal interest in him—gave him cause for hope. The compliment was, though, on rapid reflection and in view of his own opinion of Jack Goodrum, a bit of a back-hander.

"Well, *I* don't trust the feller," he said, surfacing abruptly. "Miss Bell suggested, and I agree with her, that anybody who starts from nothing and makes a fortune is bound to have a ruthless streak."

"That," Hilary pointed out, "sounds remarkably like envy. Or like the resentment Jack Goodrum told us he expected to meet from local people."

"Pah! You've let him con you, Hilary. Just as his wife has. All that touching, and holding her hand, and the 'my dear' stuff, and claiming they've got no secrets from each other."

"I happened to believe him. I think his affection for his wife is absolutely genuine. We see so many problem relationships in this job that it's a real pleasure to come across a couple who are so obviously happily married."

"*Any* husband and wife," said Quantrill sourly, "can give that impression for the first few months . . ."

"It's a good deal more than an impression," Hilary retorted. "The Goodrums obviously *care* for each other. Surely you saw that, just as well as I did? He's very kind to her, very gentle and considerate. And she trusts him completely—not with newly-wed bedazzlement, but with mature calm. That's why I liked him. I think it means that he's a nice man, and genuinely trustworthy."

Quantrill muttered disagreement. He saw no reason why he should acknowledge that his sergeant might well be right about Jack Goodrum as a husband, because it still didn't invalidate his own opinion of Jack Goodrum as a man. But to discuss it further—Hilary liked arguing, and argument became her, adding sparkle to her eyes and colour to her cheeks— would be sheer self-indulgence on a busy morning.

"Anyway," he said, "whatever we think of Jack Goodrum, the enquiry's now closed. We've got enough to do without wasting any more of our time. Just give me a quarter of an hour to sift through these new reports, and then you can bring back this file on the post office raids and tell me what action you suggest."

He gave his sergeant the file, and what he intended to be an impersonal, dismissive nod. It was a matter of surprise and confusion to him that the movement of his head beckoned rather than dismissed her. At the same time he heard himself saying, without premeditation or truth and in a sickeningly ingratiating tone, "Er—as it happens, I've got to go and see somebody over at Ashthorpe this evening. I hear that the old bakery in the village has been turned into a very good restaurant. Would you like to meet me there and have a bit of supper? It'll give me a chance to tell you all about the computer course."

Hilary was already half-way out of the door, the bulging post office robbery file cradled in her arm. She paused, then turned back, her face lively with interest. "Oh, the computer familiarisation course at Yarchester? Yes, I do want to hear about it. Did you enjoy it?"

"Fascinating," he said, and this time the lie was pre-meditated. No point in giving her the impression that he was too thick to master the new technology.

She smiled at him, and he realised how much he liked her new short hairstyle. "Good," she said. "I'll look forward to hearing the details—the computer'll be a great help when we're dealing with major enquiries. But I can't join you tonight, I'm afraid. I've arranged to play squash."

"Tomorrow night?"

"Squash again. A club tournament. But thank you for the invitation."

"Some other time, then," he muttered, crestfallen. But Hilary was already walking away, and failed to hear.

13

It wasn't as though he would have been deserting Molly, Quantrill argued to himself as he drove home through the damp darkness of the early November evening. She was used to being left on her own, anyway, because he was very often called out on a case. But tonight Molly was going out herself, to a rehearsal for some nonsense that the Amateur Operatic Society was shortly putting on at the Town Hall, so she wouldn't even have noticed his absence.

And quite apart from the enjoyment of Hilary's company, he would have been glad of the chance to eat a second supper. He looked gloomily at the pale piece of skinless grilled chicken, the spoonful of peas and the small, butter-free jacket potato that his wife put in front of him as soon as he arrived home, just after six o'clock. Peter, he noticed, qualified for juicy brown skin on his chicken and butter on his large potato as well.

"It's all right for growing boys . . ." Quantrill said, attempting fatherly joviality; but Peter was in one of his withdrawn moods, and ignored him.

"You'll never guess who spoke to me at the health centre today, Douggie," said Molly brightly. Eager as she was to get the meal over early and go off to rehearsal—she was a backstage helper rather than a performer, but she liked to lend her support in the choruses and she was particularly fond of the music of *My Fair Lady*—she felt that supper was an occasion for family togetherness. "You'll *never* guess!"

"No, I shan't," said her husband.

"Well—it was Miss Bell. Eunice Bell from Tower House, one of the county Red Cross vice presidents! There, I knew you'd be surprised. She's a patient of Dr. Fieldhouse, but we hardly see her from one year to the next. I can't reveal why she came in, of course—patient confidentiality! Well, actually she was only having her annual flu injection. But she came over to me on her way out, and she said, 'It's Mrs. Quantrill, isn't it? You're one of our invaluable Red Cross workers.' And then she asked me all about the way I run the medical loan service. She was so pleasant and friendly!"

"No reason why she shouldn't be, was there?" said her husband, irritated by her deference.

"Oh, but I had no idea she knew my name. She's certainly never spoken to me before. But I think perhaps, now her poor drunken brother's dead, she feels she can hold her head up in the town and she wants to be more sociable. Anyway, she made a point of chatting to several people, and then she saw the poster, just by my desk in the waiting room, for *My Fair Lady*. And she's coming to see it, Douggie—she bought a ticket from me for the final performance on Saturday week!"

Bored, disappointed, inadequately fed and thoroughly ill-humoured, Quantrill muttered unkindly, "Rather her than me."

"If you want a cup of tea you must make it yourself," snapped Molly; but her hurt, flushed face showed him that she hadn't really misheard his remark.

"That was very nice—my dear," he said quickly, trying to retrieve the situation and at the same time set a better example to his son. He passed her his plate, empty of everything but the pattern. "Is there any pud?" he asked, hoping that in some moment of dietary aberration she might have baked him an apple pie.

Still flushed with indignation, but now tight-lipped, Molly slapped down in front of him a baked apple. It looked well cooked, with the pale fruit fluffing out of the burst skin and a few sultanas steaming plumply on top, but it cried out for an accompaniment of crunchy brown sugar and custard. Either custard or cream . . .

"Anything—er—with it?" he ventured.

"Certainly not," said Molly. "Except for Peter, of course. There's sugar on yours already, dear," she told her son indulgently. "Would you like some cream?"

A silence fell over the supper table, broken only by the sound of Peter blowing on the hot sultanas as he picked them one by one off his apple and ate them idly with his fingers.

"*Answer* your mother when she speaks to you!" roared Quantrill. "And for heaven's sake sit up and eat your food properly, boy."

"What?" said Peter, with a dazed look. But he accepted the cream that his mother poured over his apple, took his elbows off the table and picked up his spoon and fork. "I say, Mum—"

"Yes, dear?"

"Darren Catchpole's seventeen tomorrow. He's going to have a Yamaha 125 for his birthday."

"Is he really?" said Molly, in a comfortable tone that conveyed her complete ignorance of what her son was talking about.

"No!" said Quantrill forcefully.

Molly frowned at her husband. "What do you mean, *no*? Is he or isn't he?"

"What I mean," said Quantrill, abandoning his hot, sour apple, "is that it's no use Peter trying to wheedle round you. Because there's no chance at all of *him* having a motor bike for his birthday."

"Oh . . . well I'm sure he was thinking of no such thing," said Molly.

"Of course he was. But he needn't bother. He is not going to have a motor bike, not at *any* age, and the sooner he gets that into his head the better."

"But Dad! Darren Catchpole—"

"Darren Catchpole's parents must have more money than sense. Motor bikes are too dangerous."

"Your father's quite right, dear," said Molly, horrified. "We wouldn't *dream* of letting you have one. Just think what happened to poor Stephen Carter—only twenty, and paralysed from the waist down after his accident! We couldn't possibly let you take that risk."

"But Steve was on a Kawasaki 750 Turbo! I don't want a big bike—even a Honda 50 would do. I just need something to get about on."

"You've got exactly what I had when I was your age," said his father ponderously. "A perfectly good bicycle. And buying you that cost me more than enough . . . Of *course* I'm not going to buy you a motor bike. Do you think I'm made of money?"

"But I'm not asking you to buy it! I can use my own money— the money in my savings bank."

"You can't use that," said his mother in a scandalised voice. "That's put aside for your future."

"*What* future?" Peter demanded dramatically. "I probably shan't *have* a future—not unless this country changes its defence policy! Don't you realise that Suffolk is full of American military bases? Don't you realise that all it needs is for some hawk in the Pentagon or the Kremlin to start even a limited exchange of nuclear weapons, and Suffolk will be the first place to be flattened? And if any of us survive that, we'll be plunged into a nuclear winter. We'll be covered by such dark clouds of smoke and dust that the sun will be completely excluded. The temperature will drop so far that crops and animals won't survive, and we'll all starve to death in a few weeks. And what good *then* will my savings bank account do me?"

It was the most that Peter had said to them, at any one time, for as long as his parents could remember. They stared at the pale-faced, impassioned, man-sized stranger on the other side of the supper table with amazement and unease.

Then Quantrill said, "Well I'm not having you killing yourself on a motor bike, anyway. You're not going to buy one, and that's that."

And Molly said, "Would you like some more cream, dear? Do finish up your apple, before it gets cold."

Peter jumped to his feet, sending his cutlery clattering to the floor in his fury. "For God's sake stop treating me like some stupid kid!" he shouted. "I'm a *person*. I've got ideas, and feelings, and needs, and I've got the right to live my life the way I want to. All you ever do, both of you, is patronise me and put me down, and I've had as much of it as I can take. If I want to use my *own* money to buy my *own* bike, I shall. And there's nothing you can do or say to stop me!"

He slammed out of the door and bounded up the stairs to his room. Molly turned to her husband, aghast.

"Oh Douggie—you *must* stop him! If he buys a motor bike I shall never have a minute's peace of mind, never."

"It's all right," said her husband, his confidence returning with the recollection that he was still master in his own home. "He can't get hold of his savings bank book, because it's locked away with ours and I'm the only one with the key. So there's nothing for you to worry about, is there?"

Later, after he had shooed Molly off to her rehearsal with a promise that he would do the washing up, he went upstairs and knocked on Peter's door. There was no reply.

Remembering that they had bought the boy a Sony Walkman the previous Christmas, principally in self-defence against the peace-shattering noises that had been issuing from his room, Quantrill decided that he was justified in opening the door without invitation. The poster-pasted room was dimly lit by one small lamp. Peter, earphones on, eyes closed, was stretched out on his bed. As it was obvious that neither word nor shout would get through to him, Quantrill switched on the main light.

Peter jerked up into a sitting position, his expression dazed, his eyes heavy. "Wass 'at?" he demanded hoarsely. "What d'y want?"

His father gestured to him to remove his earphones. Peter did so with reluctance, and turned down the volume of the cassette player. "What d'y want?" he repeated aggressively.

Quantrill had decided to be mild and conciliatory; friendly, if possible. He switched off the bright light. "Don't know about you," he said, "but I'm damn hungry. What say we have some cheese and biscuits?"

"Oh, for heaven's *sake*," said Peter contemptuously. He flopped back on to his pillow and closed his eyes again.

"All right, forget the food. We can have a chat, though, can't we? Don't often get the chance."

Quantrill looked round for somewhere to sit, and found that the one armchair, beneath a Mediterranean poster of a well-built girl wearing nothing but a sun-tan, was already occupied. The grubby toy animals that had been Peter's childhood joy and comfort were still accorded a place of honour in his room. Quantrill picked them up and, as there seemed to be nowhere else to put them without risk of offending their owner, sat down with Teddy, Peter Rabbit and Eeyore on his knee.

"I didn't realise you were in favour of nuclear disarmament,"
he began tentatively. "D'you belong to the CND?"

"No," said Peter. He opened his eyes. "Not yet. But I *think*
about the issue, because it's *our* future that your generation
has screwed up. And if I decide to join CND, I shall, whether
you like it or not."

"Fair enough," said his father quickly. "As you suspect, I
don't agree with you. In my opinion, it's only because of our
defence policy that you've never had to live through a war. But
even so, if you want to support the campaign I shan't object.
All I ask is that you don't go making a public nuisance of
yourself by blocking the highway outside the Cruise missile
bases. The police there have got quite enough to—"

"There you go again! Don't do this, don't do that—you're
dictating to me all the time. And as for the Cruise missile
bases," Peter went on bitterly, "some chance I'd have of
getting *there* without any transport of my own . . ."

It was this subject that Quantrill had come prepared to
discuss. He was, he considered, not an unreasonable father.
On reflection, he was willing to concede that times had
changed since he was Peter's age. Young men expected, now,
to learn to ride or drive as soon as they were old enough to
hold a licence, and it was something to be thankful for that
Peter hadn't wanted to take to the roads on a moped, with a
provisional licence and L plates, just as soon as he turned
sixteen.

And now that the boy was nearly seventeen it was no use,
Quantrill realised, simply saying "No" to him. Much better to
give him something to hope—and, hopefully to work—for.

"*Not* a motor bike," Quantrill insisted. "I'll never agree to
that because I know of too many youngsters who've come to
grief on the wretched things. What you really need to aim for
is a car."

Peter sat up, open-mouthed with astonished hope. "A car!
D'you mean—?"

"No promises," his father warned him. "What I mean is that
if you buckle down to your school work and pass your exams
next summer, I'll be willing to pay for you to have driving
lessons. Then, when you get yourself a job, and after you've
settled in it and proved that you can afford to run a car, I'll
consider helping you to buy one."

"You're telling me that I can't have any transport until after
I'm settled in a job?" Almost crying with disappointment,

Peter snatched his toy animals away from his father and bundled them on to his bed. "What kind of an offer is that? Bribery, that's all! You *know* how hard it is for school-leavers to get jobs round here. Even if I do pass the rotten exams, I'll probably still be unemployed by the time I'm ninety."

"Now you're being childish." His father got up to go. "I've made you a very fair offer, and if you're not prepared to—"

Quantrill paused, one hand on the door handle, and sniffed the air. Peter's school blazer was hanging behind the door. His father seized it and pressed the cloth to his nose. Then he turned on his son, his face dark with fury.

"Glue . . ." he said. "My God, you young fool! After all I've told you, you've been sniffing glue—"

Peter denied it. He'd been doing woodwork at school, he said. They used glue in the craft workshops, that was all.

"Don't lie to me!" stormed Quantrill. He switched on the main light, made a grab for his son, caught a fistful of pullover and shirt front, and pulled him close. Peter, not far off the same height, jerked his head backwards to avoid his father's thrusting jaw and turned his own face away.

"Let me look at you!" Quantrill commanded, shaking him. "And *breathe*! Breathe on me, blast you—"

Slowly, with a look of dislike and anger, Peter straightened his head. Holding his breath, he stared his father unwavering-ly in the eye. Then, as deliberately as though he were about to spit, he exhaled.

The boy was a smoker, there was no doubt about that. But the trace of stale smoke on his breath smelled unarguably of tobacco. There was no herbal smell of cannabis, and none of the chemical smell of solvent abuse.

It was true that Peter looked out of sorts. But now, at closer quarters than he had been for months, Quantrill could see that the pupils of his son's eyes were not drug-dilated. There was no glue-burn round his mouth, no rash round his nose. He had no sniffer's catarrh, and the odd fiery spot of his skin was almost certainly nothing more than adolescent acne. As for the boy's heavy-eyed pallor, it would probably be cured if he spent more of his time on healthy outdoor activity, and less of it lying about on his bed listening to his favourite tapes and indulging in heated fantasies.

But it was breath that was the decider. And Peter's breath smelled predominantly of his recent supper, of apple and sugar and cream . . .

Quantrill released his grip on the boy's clothing. "Sorry," he said lamely, trying to make amends by straightening his son's shirt collar.

Peter pushed him away, sneering at him. "Thanks for your trust in me, Dad," he said with contempt.

"I'm *sorry*. It's just that . . . well, I know my job makes me over-suspicious. But, really, it's only because your mother and I care so much about your welfare. We're anxious that you shouldn't come to any harm . . ."

Peter turned his back and picked up his earphones.

"No, just listen a minute—" Quantrill cast about desperately for some way of changing the subject and at the same time appeasing his son. "It's your mother's birthday next Wednesday. You know how much store she sets on our remembering it. Look—" he pulled out his wallet, plucked from it a five pound note, and then hastily exchanged it for a tenner. "Buy her a nice present, and keep the—"

"Her birthday's *Tuesday*, not Wednesday," said Peter with scorn. "And I've *made* her a present. I've been making it all term—in *woodwork* classes."

He strode to his cupboard and fetched from it a stool—or possibly a coffee table—in attractively grained elm. Turning it upside down, he demonstrated its construction loudly and crossly, as though to a wilfully obtuse child. "T-joints," he pointed out. "They're held in place with *Duroglue*. *Glue* . . . OK?"

Quantrill, still holding his ten pound note, nodded shame-faced approval. "Very nice," he said. "You've done well—your mother'll be really pleased with that." Then he proffered the money again. "Don't forget to buy her a card as well."

"I've *bought* her a card," said Peter, tight-lipped with anger. He banged down the stool and pulled from his cupboard a flat white cardboard box that measured all of two feet by eighteen inches. Yanking off the lid, he revealed a huge birthday card depicting a curious hybrid animal, with Minnie Mouse ears, big blue eyes, pink fur and a kitten's nose and paws. The fluffy, cuddlesome creature was wearing a mob cap and a long flower-sprigged dress. It held a banner that proclaimed, in letters of gold, HAPPY BIRTHDAY TO THE BEST MUM IN THE WORLD.

"Very nice," mumbled Quantrill. "Very nice indeed . . . She'll like that." Then he added, haltingly, "You're a good lad. Look, take the money anyway. Buy something for yourself—"

But Peter, clenching his fists in an attempt to contain his
rage, spurned his father's offer. "*Stuff* your tenner," he said.
"You keep your rotten money, Dad. And much good it'll do you
when the nuclear winter comes."

14

Two days later, on Saturday November 15th, the Goodrums'
house was burgled.

It was the day of the county bazaar, held annually in the
Assembly Rooms at Yarchester in aid of the Save the Children
Fund. Felicity Goodrum's offer to help with one of the stalls
had been gladly accepted by the organising committee, who
promptly earmarked her, as she had hoped they would, as the
right kind of person to become a future committee member.

As it was going to be such a long day for his wife—she
needed to leave home soon after 10 a.m., and didn't expect to
return much before six—Jack Goodrum had insisted on
driving her to Yarchester. Besides, his Range Rover had more
carrying capacity than her Renault for all the bits and pieces
she was taking to sell.

After unloading, and helping her to set up her stall, Jack had
made himself scarce. He strolled about the misty city and
spent some time in Bignold's, the gunsmith's, where he
ordered a heavy metal security cabinet to keep his shotguns in.
The detective chief inspector who had come nosing round The
Mount earlier in the week had seen him cleaning his guns,
asked where he kept them, and told him that an ordinary
locked cupboard wasn't good enough. The old Jack would have
seen the detective damned before going to the trouble and
expense of getting a security cabinet; but now he was a
reformed character and a responsible citizen. And besides, he
didn't intend to give the police any cause for aggravation if, as
he suspected they might, they came back to do any checking.

He ate a pub lunch, toured the fruit and vegetable market,
bought a large pineapple and a fine crimson potted cyclamen
as surprises for his wife, and finally returned through the
November afternoon dusk to the Assembly Rooms. The bazaar
was almost over, and there was little of interest left on the

stalls. Jack had intended to do his bit by buying something, but he saw no point in acquiring useless pieces of handicraft, or someone's unwanted last year's Christmas presents, or someone else's mountain of green tomato chutney. But then Felicity whispered to him that the purpose of attending a charity bazaar was to support the cause by buying things *whether you wanted them or not* and Jack, ever anxious to please her, immediately went over the top and spent money by the handful.

Eventually, having collected nonsenses enough to stock an entire stall for his wife at her next charity event, he had loaded up the Range Rover and driven her home to Breckham Market. Felicity, sitting beside him nursing her cyclamen, felt satisfactorily tired. She had done some useful fund-raising, and had also become re-acquainted with the kind of social circle she had been brought up in. Other stallholders had welcomed her, and she had received several unspecific invitations ("You must come for coffee, or a drink, whenever you're in our vicinity. *Do* telephone") to houses in distant parts of the county.

The invitations pleased Felicity, but it pleased her more that she felt no great eagerness to take them up. Against all the expectations of her family and friends, she really was content to be with Jack. And not merely content; she felt so happy that, as they drove, she began to sing. Her new husband hadn't attempted to sing since he was in short trousers, and he knew hardly any of the words of her carols, but he shared her mood so completely that he growled an unmusical accompaniment.

By the time they reached The Mount, the light mist had turned to rain. To save Felicity the trouble of cooking after her busy day, Jack had booked a table for dinner at the Old Bakery restaurant at Ashthorpe, and so he left the Range Rover at the front door while they went in to change.

Hurrying in out of the wet, and laughing because he was holding the pineapple like an exotic umbrella over her head, they were not at first aware that anything was wrong. Pausing to exchange a kiss in the hall, they failed to notice that all the doors were ajar. But then Felicity entered the kitchen and saw the wanton damage that had been done. In a state of shock, she dropped her pot of cyclamen and added its compost and crimson flowers to the foul-smelling mess on the floor.

And when she saw what had been done to defile the other

rooms of her lovingly decorated and furnished house, and especially the bedrooms, she sat down on the stairs and wept.

The burglary at The Mount was investigated by Detective Sergeant Lloyd. It was a long job which she and the scenes of crime team took particularly seriously, because among the stolen items was an AYA side-by-side 12-bore shotgun.

Chief Inspector Quantrill was angry when he read the sergeant's report.

"That bloody man Goodrum! I *told* him to get a proper security cabinet for his guns."

"To be fair," said Sergeant Lloyd, "he'd ordered one from Bignold's only that morning. And his other three guns were locked in a cupboard which the burglars didn't force."

"They didn't need to, did they? Not when he'd left one gun lying about for them! Of all the irresponsible—"

"Goodrum denies that he left it 'lying about,'" said Hilary. "He says it was propped in a corner of the downstairs cloakroom, in a leather and canvas gun bag. He'd overlooked the fact that it was there because it was hidden by some coats."

"That's no excuse for not locking it up. But I might have known you'd sympathise with the man . . ."

"I sympathise with both of them. And you would, too, if you'd seen the damage. I can't recall ever having come across such a viciously destructive burglary."

"Hmm." Quantrill mellowed a little towards the Goodrums. He flipped through the report again, and rubbed his jaw. "What d'you make of it, Hilary?"

"I'm not sure," she admitted, frowning. "Seven or eight years ago, I'd have said that a disgusting mess like that would only be made by someone who had a personal grudge against his victims. But times have changed—and so has the population of Breckham Market. There's so much disaffection in the new part of the town, now that a lot of the jobs that people moved here for have folded . . . And with drug-taking on the increase, and horror videos being regarded as a form of entertainment, it's quite possible that this particular burglar didn't need any reason for making a beast of himself."

"We can't rule out mindless vandalism, I agree. But in this case," said Quantrill bluntly, "I think it's a lot more likely that someone who has good reason to hate Jack Goodrum has deliberately fouled his nest for him. What does he say about it, anyway?"

"He insists that it was mindless vandalism."

Quantrill snorted. "If you believe that, Hilary, you've let the man con you again!"

"Ah, but I don't necessarily believe it. I'm prepared to consider it as a possibility, that's all. The point is that I knew *why* he was denying that the burglary was a personal attack. His wife—understandably, poor woman—is extremely shocked. Jack Goodrum is a loving husband, and he doesn't want to cause her any more worry or distress."

"Hah!" said Quantrill, who was determined to disagree with her opinion of the Goodrums' marital harmony.

"But although I like him," Hilary went on, ignoring the Chief Inspector's interjection, "I don't trust him. So I made a point of getting him alone, and telling him to come off it."

"That's better! Goodrum told us himself that there're people in the town who resent his rise from butcher's boy to wealthy man. He said he'd half expected them to have a go at him, so it's pointless for him to pretend that he's got no enemies."

"That was what I told him. I hoped, when he was alone, that he'd start naming names. But he simply shrugged, and said that anybody he delivered meat to thirty-odd years ago is too old and too respectable to take up burglary. I pointed out that he or she could have bribed a disaffected youngster to do the job, but Goodrum shrugged that off too. And *that* suggests that he has a pretty good idea of who might have done it, and it's someone from outside Breckham Market. But he's not telling."

The scenes of crime officer had concluded that the burglary at The Mount was a one-man job. The burglar had protected his identity by wearing gloves, but he had left his damp footprints on the tiled floor of the downstairs cloakroom and on the polished floorboards in the upstairs corridors. His shoes were size nine, with a ridged composition sole common to several popular makes of leisure and training shoe.

The burglar had entered the house by forcing the downstairs cloakroom window. He had stolen between two and three thousand pounds' worth of property, including the shotgun, five hundred pounds in notes, a Pentax camera, a Rolex watch, an antique ruby and diamond cluster ring, several lesser items of jewellery, and some domestic silver. Although the house contained a number of other valuable items of the kind normally attractive to burglars—a video recorder, two portable colour television sets, a stereo record player, an Amstrad computer—none of these larger items had been taken; most of them, though, were included in the long list of things that had been wantonly damaged or destroyed.

Because the house was comparatively secluded, it would have been possible for the burglar to enter the gates—even to drive in, and park—without being seen. If any significant tyre marks had been made, though, they had since been obliterated by the rain and the passage of the Goodrums' Range Rover. But the fact that no large items were taken suggested either that the burglar had not used a vehicle, or that he had parked it elsewhere. The other residents of Mount Street had been questioned, but they had noticed no suspicious movements during the course of that day.

Apart from his footprints, the burglar had left behind some smears of blood and a few dark brown woollen fibres. The fibres were caught on the jagged edges of glass left in the frame of the cloakroom window, where there were also traces of blood. There was nothing about the m.o., or the size of the feet, or the footwear, that suggested the work of any particular villain known to Breckham Market police. But although it was the worst—in the sense of the most gratuitously nasty—burglary in the well-heeled Mount Street area of the town, it was by no means the first. The CID knew where to look for those of its regular villains who were not currently in gaol, and Sergeant Lloyd had had them sought out immediately after the burglary; so far, without result.

Quantrill got up from his desk and walked to the window. Looking out from his first-floor vantage point, across the busy Yarchester road to the gabled roofs of the old town, he speculated on the lengths to which a resentful resident might go. Would anyone in Breckham Market have felt so strongly anti-Goodrum as to seek out some yob who wasn't known to the police, and persuade him to break into and dirty the man's home? It seemed unlikely, if only because it would leave the resident wide open to blackmail. But it wasn't impossible.

"You don't suppose it was Eunice Bell who put somebody up to this burglary, do you?" he asked, turning to his sergeant. "After all, she did allege that Goodrum murdered her brother, and she must be feeling frustrated because we found nothing to substantiate her claim. D'you think this might have been her way of getting even?"

Hilary thought about it. "Miss Bell hadn't occurred to me in this connection, I must say. But it really isn't in character, is it? After all, it wasn't as though she showed any personal animosity against Goodrum—she didn't actually know the man, it was just that she wanted justice to be done."

"There're probably a few others who've been wanting that," Quantrill pointed out as he returned to his desk. "Lucky Jack Goodrum has done very well for himself over the years, almost certainly at other people's expense, and I reckon somebody's finally got tired of waiting for justice to be done. If you ask me, he had this burglary coming to him."

"Tough on his wife," protested Hilary.

"Yes—but that's what comes of marrying that kind of man. Anyway, no doubt he's well insured. He can easily put things to rights and replace what was stolen, so you needn't waste your sympathy. If Goodrum's not prepared to co-operate by telling us who he thinks might have done the job, I don't feel inclined to waste much more of our time on it."

"Except that a shotgun was stolen," Hilary reminded him.

"I know . . ." Quantrill scowled, then burst out irritably, "*Blast* the wretched man! I hate a stolen shotgun—it's almost certain to be used in furtherance of another crime. And here we are in the middle of a spate of raids on post offices . . . So far the villains have threatened the subpostmasters with concealed handguns, real or false, and that's bad enough, God knows. But if they've now got hold of this shotgun that Jack Goodrum had the criminal folly to leave lying about, some innocent person's liable to end up dead."

15

The following week was a busy one for all the members of Breckham Market and District Amateur Operatic Society. Although she only helped backstage, Molly Quantrill was needed at the costume run-through on Monday and at the dress rehearsal on Wednesday, as well as at the Thursday, Friday and Saturday performances. Ordinarily she would have felt guilty about spending so many evenings away from home; but this week she was glad to have somewhere else to go.

After Douglas's confrontation with Peter, the atmosphere at

number 5 Benidorm Avenue had deteriorated. No longer content merely to ignore his father, the boy had worked at developing dumb insolence into an art form. Molly regretted her son's attitude, but although she didn't know exactly what had passed between him and Douglas she was aware that Peter had been treated unjustly, and naturally she took his part.

Quantrill himself had hoped that her birthday—on the Tuesday, not the Wednesday, as Peter had had to remind him—would provide an opportunity for family reconciliation. He had offered to take them both out for supper, even going so far as to suppress his prejudice against foreign food and suggest, entirely for Peter's benefit, the town's only Chinese restaurant. But his son had sneered a refusal, without even bothering to make an excuse. And although Molly had been glad enough to accept—as long as they went somewhere *clean*, like the Rights of Man Hotel, and confined their gastronomic adventures to avocado vinaigrette and scampi—Quantrill was called out at the last moment to yet another post office break-in and the opportunity had been lost.

Even his birthday present to his wife had misfired. In the days when his favourite uniformed policewoman, Patsy Hopkins, had been willing to undertake his shopping and wrapping, Quantrill had been confident of providing Molly with suitable surprises. Since Patsy's defection, however, he had played safe by presenting his wife with birthday and Christmas cheques. Acceptable, surely? But perhaps a bit routine—and liable to seem uninteresting beside Peter's handicraft and his extravagant card.

And so this year, guilty because he'd offended Molly by denigrating her amateur operatic society, and guilty because he'd offended her further by offending her beloved son, Quantrill had decided to give her a surprise of his own. His cheques had always been for twenty-five pounds. This time, he made one out for fifty.

"Oh, Douglas—" she'd said when she unfolded it. (He'd included a card, too, of course—an ordinary small one, chosen by himself, with a picture of a proper cat not unlike their own family moggy, and a straightforward, unsentimental message.) For a moment, staring at the cheque, Molly had gone quite pale with astonishment. Then she'd turned pink, and had given him an embarrassed, quizzical, *hurt* look. Not a look of pleasure at all, but of insight: a recognition that her husband felt guilty and that rather than admit it he had tried to obtain domestic harmony by purchase.

She'd thanked him, certainly. But his gesture of generosity had fallen flat. And it was in a last-resort attempt to redeem himself that he volunteered to accompany her to the final performance of *My Fair Lady*, on Saturday evening. Molly had said that she felt bad about always having to cadge lifts from friends, and so he offered for once to put himself out on her behalf: to drive her to the Town Hall, support the performance, be nice to her friends afterwards, and drive her home when the backstage party ended.

Always providing, of course, that he wasn't needed on a case . . .

In the event, no criminal activity came to his rescue. And neither did Hilary Lloyd, when he offered to get her a ticket on a see-you-there basis. Sitting beside Hilary, and buying her a cup of coffee in the interval, would have given him pleasure whatever was happening on-stage; but she had thanked him nicely and declined.

Quantrill sighed. Then, at Molly's behest, he put on his best suit—the Op, as the amateur operatic society was known, was an old-established institution in Breckham Market, and the last night of the annual production was always one of the town's dressiest occasions—and prepared to endure a long and tedious evening.

Fog had been forecast, and Molly had worried that this might keep some potential members of the audience away. But all it amounted to, as the Quantrills drove into the town, was an occasional swirl of thin mist. They parked in the market place, which was already filling up with the other Op members' cars, and stepped out into the evening dank.

There were numerous things to be carried from the car—a plumed Edwardian cartwheel of a hat that had needed emergency repair, some small but vital props that were Molly's personal responsibility, and a cling-wrapped dish of mince pies that she was contributing to the party. Her husband, who had already been refused a mince pie, tried to lighten the atmosphere by offering, in a boyishly mischievous tone, to carry them. But Molly was now worried about all the things she had to remember to do or to have ready during the coming performance, and she couldn't be bothered with any of Douglas's nonsense. She plonked the hat on her head, snatched the mince pies crossly away from him, and swept off like a domesticated duchess, leaving her husband to follow in her wake with the box of props.

Quantrill was well acquainted with the magistrates' court which occupied the rear of the Town Hall, but he was less accustomed to going up the front steps of the imposingly Italianate building. Molly, however, knew her way across the pillared antechamber and through the warren of corridors that led to the area behind the stage. Douglas followed her closely, making himself agreeable to the other newly arrived members as he went; having set out to mollify his wife by doing his husbandly duty, he intended to make sure that he was both seen and heard to do it.

His original plan had been to deposit Molly and then nip round to the Coney and Thistle for a quick anaesthetic before the performance. But now he had a better idea. Having found his way back to the antechamber, he discovered that the audience had already begun to arrive. It was the custom for them to gather and socialise in the antechamber before taking their seats in the main hall, and Quantrill saw this as an ideal opportunity to establish his support for his wife.

Happily, there was no system of numbering for the seats. Once he'd let it be known that he was there, and the performance had started, he could sneak off to the pub for most of the evening without anyone (except possibly the Town Hall doorman, who wasn't likely to stop him) being any the wiser. As long as he returned for the last half hour of *My Fair Lady*, so that he could make appropriate comments as they drove away—whistle a tune or two, even—Molly would never know that he hadn't sat through the lot. And with a little bit of luck he might be able to prise her away early from her backstage party and get home in time to watch Match of the Day on television.

Cheered by this prospect, he began to loiter as conspicuously as possible. He knew no one among the earliest arrivals, so he passed the time by taking a good look round the antechamber. It was a chill, echoing marble vault dominated by the statue of Alderman Redvers Fullerton Bell, Mayor of This Borough 1867–68, 1875–76 and 1881–82 and Benefactor of Breckham Market.

Yes, of course . . . poor old Clanger Bell's forefather. The fellow who'd built Tower House in much the same style as the Town Hall. No doubt he'd impressed his contemporaries, but at the same time he'd condemned his family and his descendants to live in permanent cold gloom. It wasn't surprising that Clanger had taken to drink.

But had Lucky Jack Goodrum really *intended* to kill him . . . ?

The antechamber was beginning to fill. Quantrill was soon among people he knew, or people he knew Molly knew. The current Mayor and Mayoress were there, in their chains of office, and so was anyone else who was anyone in Breckham Market and district. Whether or not they came out of a sense of duty, they were all buzzing with cheerful anticipation.

Quantrill reluctantly dismissed his own concerns and set about playing the unaccustomed role of his wife's husband. Yes, he agreed, nodding and smiling to as many people as possible: Molly was busy behind the scenes, as usual! And where indeed *would* the cast be without all the members who worked so hard backstage?

Yes, *My Fair Lady* was a very good choice for this year's production, wasn't it? Very lively and tuneful. Yes, there was certainly a good turn-out for it—nearly every seat had been sold, so his wife told him! Yes, it was obviously going to be a very good evening . . .

With ten minutes to go before the performance started, newcomers came crowding in. Most were in couples, or parties; but among them, stiff in navy blue and fastidiously solitary, was Clanger Bell's sister, Eunice.

Quantrill was surprised to see her. He remembered that Molly had said that Miss Bell had bought a ticket for this performance, but—though he hadn't said so, knowing that the suggestion would only offend his wife—he had assumed that Eunice Bell was merely offering token support. He couldn't imagine her wanting to go to a musical, at the best of times. And it was only at the beginning of the week that her brother had been buried.

But then, as Miss Bell had said when he and Hilary interviewed her, she was making no pretence of mourning Cuthbert. Perhaps Molly had been right: with her drunken brother dead, Eunice could now hold up her head in the town. And as the sole remaining descendant of the man who'd developed Breckham Market into the civic centre of the district, she might feel an obligation to put in an appearance on a major social occasion such as this.

If she did happen to be attending as a duty, it was something that he and Eunice Bell had in common. But Quantrill avoided her eye. She was probably annoyed by his failure to come up with any proof that her brother had been murdered. Worse, she might want to take the opportunity to tell him so . . .

"Good evening, Chief Inspector."

There was no mistaking that strong, spiny, authoritative voice. Quantrill's spirits sank, but he turned to her with a smile and what he hoped was a disarming greeting.

"Good evening, Miss Bell! My wife told me that you'd bought a ticket. She's backstage, of course, helping with props and costumes and things—"

"So I imagine." Eunice Bell ducked her head in brusque acknowledgement. Then she added, unexpectedly: "I understand that Mrs. Quantrill is one of those modestly invaluable ladies who receives scant recognition for all the work she does. After I'd bought my ticket from her, it occurred to me that she might think I had no real intention of coming to see the performance. That would have been patronising of me, and I should be sorry if she made that assumption."

Quantrill assured her, with truth, that Molly hadn't done so. "But I don't suppose," he added bluntly, "that this sort of caper is your cup of tea, any more than it's mine."

"On the contrary," said Eunice Bell. Her features cracked into a small, stiff smile. "I have happy memories of a summer spent with my cousins at Southwold, many years ago, when *My Fair Lady* was new. They had a recording, and we played it most of the time . . . I don't expect amateur singers to reach that standard, but I've come here tonight with every intention of enjoying the production. And I recommend, Mr. Quantrill," she added severely, "that you do the same."

He stood rebuked. But that was better than getting an earful of complaint about the way he did his job.

Miss Bell took an audible breath, obviously in preparation for saying something far more serious. But the orchestra had begun to tune up in the main hall, drawing the latecomers out of the antechamber.

"On the subject we discussed at Tower House—" she said, fixing Quantrill with her stern dark eyes. "I want you to know that my opinion remains unchanged. But this is not the place to discuss it."

"No," he agreed with relief, gesturing her towards the hall. "Besides, it's time we went in."

As she offered up her ticket at the door, Miss Bell glanced back. "Some friends are keeping a seat for me," she said, distancing herself from him.

"I was just about to say the same thing."

Honours even, they gave each other a cool parting nod. Even so, Quantrill lingered to let her go in well ahead of him. Two of Molly's Op friends, who knew him by sight, were on the door and he made his number with them by giving his ticket to one and buying a programme from the other.

When he finally entered the auditorium the house lights had already been switched off and the orchestra was going full blast. He lurked at the back until the ticket collectors closed the door and took their own seats; then he slipped out into the antechamber. He gave a wink to the indifferent doorkeeper, a man he didn't know who sat in a glassed booth keeping an eye on the main doors to stop undesirables coming in, and at last made his escape to the companionable comfort of the Coney and Thistle.

What Quantrill had intended to do, as soon as he got there, was to ring the CID office and let them know where he was. If they happened to need him, he didn't want them to blow his alibi by trying to find him at the Town Hall. But his intention was forgotten when, on his way into the pub, he met PC Ronald Timms hurrying out. The off-duty constable, also in his best suit, with beer-froth on his Kitchener moustache, a worried look on his face and a ticket for *My Fair Lady* in his fist, was attempting to make the Town Hall in time for curtain-up.

Ron Timms's wife had recently been promoted assistant wardrobe mistress of the Op. He hated musicals, and everything to do with them. Only the previous day, in the canteen at Breckham Market police HQ, he had been heard to say that for the past three months his home life had been completely disrupted by the preparations for the show. He was sick of the sight of the costumes. And now that they'd finally been taken away, he was damned if he was going to waste a precious free Saturday evening by *paying* to see the things on stage.

"What's all this then, Ron?" demanded Douglas Quantrill jovially.

"Well . . . You know how it is. Thought you were supposed to be at the show yourself?"

Quantrill, who knew only too well how it was, pointed out that there were no good conduct marks to be won for actually watching the performance. He bought Ron Timms a beer and outlined his own tactics. His colleague congratulated him on his policemanly aptitude for low cunning, and bought him the other half.

And that was where they were, drinking companionably, when an urgent message for Detective Chief Inspector Quantrill was received at the Town Hall. When it eventually reached him—but not before the performance had been interrupted, to Molly's chagrin, twice—he pushed aside his mug and hurried out into the November night.

Somebody in Breckham Market had been blasted with a shotgun.

16

Felicity Goodrum was another middle-aged resident of Breckham Market who had happy memories of the music of *My Fair Lady*. Years ago, before her marriage to Austin Napier, she could have danced to it all night.

And so when she first heard that the musical was going to be performed in Breckham Market, she had wanted to see it. She had almost said to Jack, impulsively, "Oh, do let's go!"

Had she done so he would have bought tickets straightaway, of course. Dear Jack—he was practically tone deaf, and he'd never been to a theatre in his life, and the performance would almost certainly have mystified and bored him; but he would have gone with her and pretended pleasure simply for the sake of pleasing her. And that was why Felicity had eventually decided not to mention it.

She knew, without consulting him, that at this stage in their marriage he wouldn't dream of letting her go out for an evening unescorted. Nor would he consider leaving her at home alone. Though he had been gallant throughout their courtship, she had assumed that once they were married he would want to revert to some of his old habits; but when she had told him that he must feel free to spend an evening on his own occasionally—to go off to a pub, if that was what he wanted—he had declared that he preferred to stay with her. Pubs, Jack had said pityingly, stretching out his legs at his fireside like a contented dog, were for men who had nothing to go home for . . .

And now, of course, after the burglary that had occurred
while they were out the previous Saturday, the Goodrums had
an additional reason for staying at home.

What had been stolen was not significant: it was the
disgusting mess that had appalled them both. Felicity had
been badly shocked by it. Jack had at first been furiously angry,
but then he had simmered down and tried—obviously for his
wife's sake—to brush it off. The damage hadn't been directed at
them *personally*, he insisted. He'd heard that was the way
some wild young amateur burglars carried on, fouling their
victims' property just for the hell of it. It didn't *mean* anything.
Of course Felicity was upset—but she had no need to worry
about it. Lightning never struck the same place twice!

Felicity was not reassured. She remembered all too well
what Jack had told the police about the resentment some
Breckham Market people might feel because of his new
wealth. But if her husband was trying to prevent her from
worrying, the least she could do was to keep her fears to
herself.

She had spent a busy week replacing soft furnishings and
bedding, and obsessively cleaning the house. Jack had tried to
take the burden from her and her two-mornings-a-week
domestic help by bringing in a team of professional cleaners,
but even so Felicity could not convince herself that all traces of
defilement had been removed. She felt that the house was still
smeared. She felt that their privacy had been invaded, that an
attempt had been made to violate their marriage.

She also felt closer to and fonder of Jack than ever. As long as
she was in his company, she knew she was safe. And she was as
glad as he was to spend their evenings at home—after all, it
was still a wondrous novelty to be in a domestic atmosphere
where there was none of the stress of her first marriage. With
her second husband there was no tension, no fear of violence;
nothing but trust and contentment.

Jack got up from his armchair, put another log on the fire, and
sat down again without taking his eyes from the television
screen for more than a few seconds. "Shot!" he crowed, as his
favourite snooker player potted a difficult red and brought the
cue-ball back for the black. Then he turned to his wife. "You're
sure you wouldn't rather be watching something else, dear?"
he asked considerately.

"Quite sure." Felicity, her neat gold-rimmed reading glasses
half-way down her nose, was embroidering a cushion cover in

petit point while glancing every now and then at the screen. "I'm really beginning to enjoy snooker now you've explained it to me. Bet he tries to put that second red on the left into the middle pocket . . ."

The player did, and Felicity felt as pleased as though she'd made the pot herself. "I think you should buy that snooker table you were talking about," she added. "We've got plenty of room for it, goodness knows, and it'll give you a lot of interest. Besides, I'd rather like to have a go, too."

"Good girl! I'll order it, then. If we can get the table set up in time for the Christmas holidays, it'll be fun for young Matthew as well. Oh, *shot!* Did you see that, sweetheart—?"

Felicity hadn't seen it. What had made her look up from her embroidery was a sound she thought she heard from outside the house. And ever since the burglary, strange sounds had worried her.

"Did you hear anything, Jack?"

He turned down the volume of sound by remote-control and cocked his head, listening. "Where from?"

"The conservatory, I thought—"

Both listening, they heard the crash of breaking glass.

"Bloody hell!" Jack leapt to his feet, shouting. He made for the glassed door that led directly to the conservatory, unlocked it and wrenched it open. Switching on the soft lighting, he illuminated the cast-iron columns, the budding camellia trees, the bamboo furniture and the chintz "Indian Tree" cushions with their stylised birds perched on stylised branches.

There were shadows in the conservatory, but none of them was dense enough to conceal an intruder. Nothing moved except a wraith of November mist that insinuated itself through a broken pane of glass and wavered across a spotlight's beam. On the tiled floor, surrounded by shattered glass, lay a sizeable chunk of rockery stone.

"Bloody hell—" Jack repeated.

Felicity had followed him. "What's happening? What is it?" she said anxiously.

"I dunno. Somebody fooling about, probably—you get back inside, my dear, I'll handle this."

Jack strode masterfully through the conservatory. Felicity, too anxious to think of obeying him, stood hovering. He

unbolted and flung open the garden door. Standing with his
back to the light, he bellowed into the gathering mist.

"Who's there? What the hell do you think you're doing?"

Felicity Goodrum watched as the reply came roaring at her
husband out of the darkness, and blew away his head.

17

From the extent of the wounds in the dead man's head and the
diameter of spread of the pellets in his neck and shoulders, a
forensic expert estimated that the shotgun had been fired at a
range of not more than eight yards.

The incidental damage caused by the shot was extensive.
Some pellets had bypassed their target and cut a swathe
through the camellias. Some had shredded the bamboo
furniture. Some, having ricocheted off the cast-iron pillars of
the conservatory, had smashed glass. Mrs. Goodrum, who had
been standing in the doorway that led into the house, had
sustained cuts from flying glass and flesh wounds from stray
pellets.

She had also been hit by debris from her husband's skull.
Fragments of scalp and flesh and bone and brain had been
blown all over the conservatory. The budding camellia trees
that had escaped destruction appeared to have burst into
unusually early crimson blossom.

Splattered with blood, not all of it her own, Felicity
Goodrum had turned and ran. Too shocked to use the
telephone, or to close the front door of The Mount behind her,
she had staggered down the drive moaning, her arms out-
stretched in a plea for help.

She was incapable of thought. The fact that there was a
gunman out there in the dark garden, and that he might be
waiting to kill her, never entered her mind. What she feared—
what she was running from—was the scene in the conservatory . . . Her husband lying on his back on the tiled floor,
with blood gurgling out of what remained of his head. The
horror that dripped from the camellias.

* * *

In the dank grey first light of Sunday November 23rd, a team of policemen began searching the walled garden of the Goodrums' Georgian house.

Chief Inspector Quantrill, on the advice of the forensic expert, established the approximate spot where the gunman must have been standing. It was on a slope, slightly above and directly overlooking the garden door of the conservatory. The slope had been made into a rockery, brightened at this time of the year by winter-flowering ericas, and the gunman had stood on a partly paved, partly gravelled path that traversed the rockery. His probable firing position was marked by some scuffed gravel, but the daylight failed to reveal any identifiable footprints, either there or elsewhere.

"He must have known the layout of the garden," said Quantrill, pausing on his way back to the house to survey the rockery from the paved terrace outside the conservatory. "He'd picked his spot in advance, there's no doubt about that. If he hadn't, he couldn't have made his way there in the dark without first treading on a flowerbed and providing us with a footprint. So we're after somebody who's been here before— though not necessarily by invitation."

"I suppose you mean last week's burglar," accepted Sergeant Lloyd. She turned away from the garden and went back— though not by way of the conservatory—to the room they were temporarily using as an office. She felt unusually despondent: it was vexing enough that she had failed as yet to catch the burglar, without having on her conscience the possibility that he had used the stolen gun to commit murder. And whatever Jack Goodrum's past crimes—himself a murderer, even?— Hilary was saddened that his death had put an end to what had so evidently been a happy middle-aged marriage.

"No need to jump to the conclusion that Goodrum was killed with his own gun," Quantrill protested as he followed her. "Good grief, there're enough shotguns in Suffolk to provide one for every third household in the county—and that's only the legally owned ones! If the fellow who stole the gun last week had wanted to kill Jack Goodrum with it, he could have hung about and done it later that evening. Couldn't he?"

"Not if he was doing the burglary—getting hold of the gun— on behalf of somebody else . . ."

Quantrill had never before seen Hilary so downcast. She was tired, of course; they'd both been working at the murder scene until the early hours, and had returned after only a brief snatch of sleep. And then, too, she must have been distressed—though she'd been too professional to do more than close her eyes tightly for a few moments and gulp—by the sights and smells in the conservatory. Longing but knowing better than to offer her a shoulder to lean on, he wondered for a moment whether he could get away with some minor physical contact, like putting a sympathetic hand on hers. But he decided not to risk it.

"Look," he said vigorously, instead: "Jack Goodrum's stolen gun was a 12-bore, we know that. But there's a wide variation in shotgun calibre: four-ten, 28, 20, 16—even 10 and 8, as well as 12. So the chances are that he was shot with a gun of a different bore, anyway. And if the searchers can find the spent cartridge case, that'll prove it."

Some minutes later, a message came from the garden that the cartridge case had indeed been found. It was an Eley GP 12-bore.

"Proves nothing!" asserted Quantrill briskly. They had just been informed that the mobile police canteen had arrived at The Mount, and he was looking forward to biting into a bacon roll. "Unless we can recover Goodrum's stolen shotgun and send it to the forensic lab for a test firing, a cartridge case proves nothing either way."

"It begins to look significant, though, doesn't it?" Hilary had been making use of the Goodrums' downstairs cloakroom to rinse the persistent abattoir-taste of the conservatory out of her mouth, and now she was beginning to feel more detached and positive. A mug of coffee—even canteen coffee—and a couple of Anadin, and she'd be back to normal.

"The shotgun was stolen on Saturday 15th," she went on. "And we know now that the burglary took place just after enquiries had been made in the town about where Jack Goodrum lived."

Information had started to come in as soon as the news of the murder had percolated through Breckham Market the previous evening. Jack Goodrum had not been a customer of any of the town's pubs, but as a rich newcomer he was known by name and sight by many more people than he knew. When one of the barmaids at the Coney and Thistle heard about the murder, she had told the landlord—who had immediately telephoned the police—that a stranger who had called in for a drink during the previous week had asked where he could find Mr. Goodrum.

A second report had just come in. A detective making enquiries in Mount Street had called at the home of the owner of the principal newsagent's shop. The newsagent had seen and heard nothing suspicious in Mount Street on the evening of the murder; but he remembered that a stranger who had made a token purchase in his shop the previous week had asked if he delivered newspapers to Jack Goodrum, and at what address.

According to the descriptions, the stranger in the pub had been a bit of a punk, with one gold ear-stud, and the stranger in the shop had been middle-aged, bespectacled and well-spoken. The middle-aged man had made his enquiry during the afternoon of Wednesday 12th, the punk at lunch time on Saturday 15th.

"The fact that two men wanted to find Jack Goodrum doesn't mean that either of them intended to rob him, let alone murder him," said Quantrill. "There could be a perfectly legitimate reason for their enquiries. The older man might well be an inspector from the Inland Revenue, or the VAT-man, chasing Goodrum for unpaid taxes and catching up with him at last. If either one of them had come here intending villainy, he'd hardly have taken the risk of advertising his presence by asking where to find his victim."

He paused, rubbing his chin. "All the same," he added, "bearing in mind that the shotgun was stolen that same Saturday evening,—"

"—we've got a useful lead on the burglary, at least," concurred Hilary. "And since it's possible that Jack was murdered by his own gun, we need to set up a search for the partial punk with the ear-stud."

18

The detectives' more immediate concern was to interview the dead man's wife.

Felicity Goodrum had been found, staggering distraught and bleeding out of the gates of The Mount, at approximately 8:25 the previous evening. Mount Street was usually very quiet at that time in the winter, but fortunately for her some near neighbours were returning home after a visit to Ipswich, and had picked her up in the headlights of their car.

They had immediately helped her into their house and called the police. Too shocked to give any coherent information, Felicity had been taken by ambulance to Yarchester Hospital. There, a number of shotgun pellets were removed from her arms and upper body, and fragments of glass from her face; her wounds were dressed, and she had fallen into a merciful, sedated sleep.

Detective Chief Inspector Quantrill and Sergeant Lloyd arrived at the hospital shortly before ten on Sunday morning. Hilary, who had begun her working life by qualifying as a nurse, went in search of the ward sister.

The sister, busy and warm, clearly regretted the detectives' intrusion. "Mrs. Goodrum? Physically, her condition's satisfactory. She'll be fit for discharge in a couple of days. But she's had a shattering ordeal, you know. I suppose you couldn't leave her in peace for a bit longer?"

"I only wish we could," said Sergeant Lloyd.

Mrs. Goodrum had been put into a private room. As the sister led the way there, she said, "You'll find her son with her. A nice boy, and obviously fond of his mother, but the situation's more than he can handle." She paused. "It wasn't his *own* father who was killed, I take it?"

"No—his new stepfather."

"Ah, that accounts for his lack of emotion. Pity, in a way, that he wasn't fond of his stepfather. Better for him, of course. But it'd help his mother if they could grieve together, and it'd give her an incentive to keep going for the boy's sake . . . Well, there you are, m'dear—second door on the right, please don't stay too long, and I hope you soon catch the bastard who fired the gun."

PC Barry Brown, a porky young constable from the Yarchester division who was officially on duty outside Mrs. Goodrum's room but in fact loitering by the nurses' station and doing his best to waste their time, got a whiff of CID as soon as he saw the plain-clothes couple and hurried to intercept them.

"Mrs. Goodrum's son arrived about half an hour ago, sir," he reported to the Chief Inspector. "One of the masters drove him over from his school. The hospital notified the headmaster last night, but they agreed there was no point in telling the boy and bringing him here until this morning."

"Fair enough," said Quantrill. "Has anyone else wanted to see Mrs. Goodrum?"

"No, sir. But her parents are expected from Northamptonshire later today."

"Thank goodness for that," said Hilary. She knocked and went in, followed at a discreet distance by the Chief Inspector.

A tall adolescent sat beside the bed, with his back to the door. He stood up and moved to the window as the sergeant went in, but she gave the whole of her attention to Mrs. Goodrum. Felicity, huddled in a hospital dressing gown, was sitting up on the bed, propped against a pillow. With her prematurely grey hair and grief-ravaged face, she could have been mistaken for the boy's grandmother.

Her forehead was marked by cuts and abrasions, livid against her pale skin. Hours of crying had swollen the rest of her features, and they had now stiffened into immobility. She made no attempt to raise her heavy eyelids as her visitors approached.

"Hallo, Mrs. Goodrum," said the sergeant gently. "D'you remember us—Hilary Lloyd and Chief Inspector Quantrill?"

The bereaved woman's hands, lying limply on her lap, opened and closed in a gesture of indifference. Hilary sat on the bed and took one hand in her own. It was cold and unresponsive. She pressed some warmth into it, and as she did so a remnant of moisture seeped out from under Felicity's lowered lids and, too weak to form tears and fall, dampened the puffy skin immediately below her eyes.

"I'm glad your son's with you," Hilary went on. "Matthew, I think you said." She looked up and gave the boy a friendly grin: "Hallo, Matthew."

His brown eyes were, she recollected from her visit to The Mount, those of his mother; but his high-browed, fine-boned features and the downward curve of his mouth gave him a haughty look quite unlike hers. By way of reply to the sergeant, he mumbled with embarrassment. He was patently relieved when the Chief Inspector suggested that, while they talked to his mother, he might like to go out and chat to the duty constable.

"And I believe you're expecting your parents. Do they have far to come?" Hilary continued, trying to coax Mrs. Goodrum into speech. Quantrill stood well back, content to watch and listen. This was one of the occasions when he was operationally thankful that his CID sergeant was a woman.

Mrs. Goodrum's voice, when it emerged, was a bleak whisper. Hilary encouraged her halting words about her parents, at the same time disengaging her own hand so that she could take her notebook from her bag. But as soon as the notebook appeared, Felicity's voice faltered to a stop.

"I'm sorry," said Hilary. "I hate to do this but I'm afraid we

have to take a statement from you about what happened last
night. I really am so very sorry . . ."

She hesitated, momentarily speechless herself. Grief was an
old acquaintance of hers; ten years ago, she had watched the
man she loved waste and die.

That had been terrible enough. Even having known for
months that Stephen's disease was terminal—having accepted
that he would die, having prayed for an end to his pain, having
rationally contemplated, and planned for a future without
him—she had found herself totally unprepared for the finality
of his death and for the emotionally disabling effect of
bereavement.

And so how much worse it must be for Felicity Goodrum!
Bad enough for her to have had her happy marriage brought to
such a shatteringly sudden end; bad enough for her to have
seen her husband die. But to have seen him murdered . . .
to have been splattered with the contents of his skull . . .
that was beyond Hilary's imagining. Suppressing a shudder,
she clasped Felicity's hand in sympathy and was glad to feel a
tentative response.

But there was work to be done. Considerate but firm, she
took her witness through the events of the previous evening.
Mrs. Goodrum's voice, though toneless and barely audible,
was reasonably steady, but her eyes remained downcast. Then
Hilary came to the critical period.

"And so your husband stood in the open doorway of the
lighted conservatory and shouted, 'Who's there?' or words to
that effect. What happened then?" she asked.

Felicity's face remained stiff, mask-like. Her swollen eyelids
were lowered so far that they might have been closed. She
made two attempts to speak, sipped some water from the glass
that Hilary offered her and then, hardly moving her lips,
whispered "There was a flash . . . and a roar . . . and
everything blew apart . . ."

"And you saw no one? Before the flash, I mean."

"No one."

"But why do you think it happened? Why do you think
anyone would want to kill your husband?"

Painfully, as though her eyelids were fastened together with
lashes made of velcro, Felicity forced herself to open them.
Her eyes, brown as her son's but dulled and bloodshot, stared
at nothing but horror and desolation.

"I have no idea . . ."

* * *

Nothing could persuade Felicity Goodrum that her husband might have had enemies. He had never claimed to her that he was a saint, but she knew for a fact that he was honest, reliable and considerate. She believed him to have been a good (though no doubt mischievous) youngster, a good (though no doubt exacting) employer, and a good (though strangely unappreciated) first husband. And she knew that he was kind: the kindest man she had ever met.

No, she had seen none of Jack's former business associates. All his affairs, whether in connection with business or with his first marriage, were dealt with through his solicitor and his accountant. Jack had wanted to keep their life at The Mount private. As far as Felicity knew, no one had ever called there to see him, and no one had telephoned asking to speak to him personally. He had not seemed worried by anything, not even by the burglary; annoyed, but not worried.

"How did his first wife take their divorce?" asked Hilary.

"Badly, I believe." Felicity was talking more easily now. "I can't blame her for that . . . But Jack was very good to them financially, of course. He settled their house and its contents on her, as well as making provision for all of them." A peripheral anxiety deepened the lines on her face: "He has two grown-up daughters. They've never bothered to keep in touch with their father, but they must be told . . ."

The Chief Inspector assured her that it would be done. "And that's a fine young son you have," he said, hearty now that the emotionally charged interview was over. "About the same age as my own boy."

And if Matthew was anywhere near as difficult, surly and uncooperative as Peter, Quantrill reflected, a fat lot of comfort he'd be. But it would hardly do to imply that. "He'll be a great comfort to you, I'm sure," he asserted, and escaped into the corridor, leaving Hilary to do and say all the appropriate, policewomanly things in farewell.

Quantrill had intended, anyway, to have a word with the boy, but it was Matthew who interrupted PC Brown's eleventh jolly anecdote and made the approach.

"Excuse me, sir," he said, diffident and anxious. "I'm Matthew *Napier*, not Goodrum. It wasn't *my* father who was killed."

"So I understand," said Quantrill. He looked the boy over

approvingly, glad that his haughty appearance was countered by good manners.

"I thought I'd better tell you," went on Matthew. "I didn't want you to think there was anything . . . well, suspicious about my being dry-eyed. I mean, I'm sorry for my mother, of course, but—"

"You've no need to explain. I don't suppose you had time to get to know your stepfather very well?"

"No, I'd already started boarding school when they were married. I stayed with them at The Mount for the half-term holiday, last month, and that's the most I ever saw of him." Matthew frowned, obviously wanting to say more, but intent on choosing his words carefully. "Jack was very . . . generous."

"So I understand from your mother. She either can't or won't believe that he had any enemies, but the fact that he was murdered disproves that. And what I'd like to ask you, Matthew—" the Chief Inspector gave the boy an avuncular smile "—since you're a dispassionate observer, is whether you think Jack Goodrum *knew* that somebody was after him? Did he give you the impression, when you were there at half-term, of being worried, or wary? Did he seem uneasy when the doorbell or the telephone rang?"

Matthew shook his head. "I don't think anyone came to the door while I was there. I don't remember hearing the telephone, either—but I do know that Jack had asked for their number to be kept ex-directory."

"Why was that, d'you think?"

"My mother said it was because they wanted to make a fresh start." Matthew paused, his eyelids lowered as hers had been. Choosing his words again, he stood scraping the toe of his shoe on the polished floor of the hospital corridor. "I suppose he might have been trying to shake someone off . . ."

"And you know who that was?"

"I can guess."

The boy looked up, his brown eyes hot and unhappy. Then he said, plunging into the narrative: "My father came to see me at school last Wednesday week—the 12th. He's Austin Napier QC. He took me out to lunch and told me he was still married in God's eyes to my mother, and that we had to go back and live with him in Highgate. I told him that we didn't have to do as he said any more, and then he started to <u>smarm</u> me up. I knew I wasn't supposed to tell him my mother's new name, or where she was living, but he tricked it out of me. He's brilliant at that kind of thing . . ."

PC Brown, who had been listening, fascinated, couldn't contain his incredulity. "Your father's a *barrister*? And you're suggesting that he went after your stepfather with a shotgun—?"

Matthew dismissed the constable haughtily. "Not in person, no. I don't suppose my father knows how to handle a shotgun," he told Quantrill. "He certainly doesn't possess one. But—look, sir, if he wanted murder done, he'd know how to find someone to do it."

"Oh yes?" said the Chief Inspector drily. He was interested, but not sure how far Matthew Napier was telling the truth. If the boy disliked his father—held him responsible for the break-up of the family, perhaps—the accusation could be nothing more than an act of vindictiveness.

Matthew reddened with vexation. "*Yes*," he insisted, almost tearfully. "I'm not making this up, you know—my father's capable of anything! He's mad—I mean *seriously* mad. If you don't believe me, read these!"

He pulled from his pocket a bulky manilla envelope and thrust it at the Chief Inspector. Mystified, Quantrill discovered that it contained cuttings, six months old, from most of the national newspapers. They turned out to be reports, in gleeful detail, of the unsuccessful appeal of a London barrister against a divorce that had previously been granted to his wife on the grounds of his unreasonable behaviour.

The reports were headed by separate photographs of the couple. The woman was Matthew's mother, looking a good deal older and more strained than the happy woman Quantrill had first met as Jack Goodrum's wife. The barrister was unfamiliar. But he answered to the description of the stranger who, on the afternoon of Wednesday November 12th, had asked a Breckham Market newsagent for the address of the man whose murder Quantrill was now investigating.

19

Shortly after midday, Chief Inspector Quantrill and Sergeant Lloyd set out for London to interview Felicity Goodrum's first husband.

Quantrill decreed that they would go by train rather than by car. He saw no shame in admitting that he didn't know his way round the capital, but when Hilary said she had a street map and offered to navigate he was quick to assert that the journey would be faster by train. What worried him about driving in London was the possibility that he might make a fool of himself in front of her by getting stuck in the wrong traffic lane; much better for his image to use trains and taxis—and if the Super wouldn't wear his subsequent claim for expenses, he'd gladly bear the cost himself.

It was a very long time since Quantrill had been to London. The capital was less than two hours by direct train from Breckham Market, but he saw no reason to go there if he could help it. A dirty, noisy, overcrowded place, in his opinion, and populated almost exclusively by foreigners. Even some of the graffiti were in Arabic . . .

It was even longer since he'd been on a train. When he heard the cost of the tickets, he blenched. But he had been impressed by British Rail's advertising campaigns for their high-speed inter-city service, and he looked forward to travelling in executive comfort with Hilary by his side, and to buying her a really good Sunday lunch in the restaurant car.

What had not occurred to him was that the high-speed inter-city service didn't extend to the Eastern region. The rolling stock on the Yarchester–Breckham Market–London line was some high-speed region's cast-off, shabby and unreliable; and although a restaurant car service was advertised on the Sunday lunch-time train, it was not available on that particular day.

"It's not your fault," Hilary pointed out as he apologised for the second time. "And at least," she said philosophically as they joined the queue for light refreshments in the buffet car, "we can get a drink."

"I've never heard you say that before," Quantrill said, surprised. "I thought you didn't drink anything but wine . . ."

Hilary looked at him gravely. "On days when I've had to help account for the scattered pieces of someone's head—especially someone I'd met and rather liked, even though he might have been a villain—I go for the hard stuff."

The sergeant lunched on brandy with a splash of dry ginger, and a quarter of a small packet of cheese-flavoured biscuits. The Chief Inspector—reluctant to be seen making a pig of himself, but he couldn't help the fact that he was both hungry and thirsty—consumed two cans of beer and a pork pie.

It was while he was enjoying the pie, which his wife would never allow him to eat, that he realised he'd forgotten to tell Molly his whereabouts. She knew that when he was on a murder enquiry she could expect him home when she saw him, but he wouldn't ordinarily take off for London without letting her know.

Today wasn't ordinary, though. Today he was going to spend four uninterrupted hours on trains with Hilary, and it was a perfect opportunity to establish a more personal relationship. He pushed aside his cardboard plate, with a remnant of pastry to indicate that he wasn't really greedy, leaned forward with his elbows on the table and gave her his warmest smile.

"Feeling better?"

Her own smile was a good deal more circumspect. "Yes thanks. Did you remember to ring your wife before we left, by the way?"

He could have done without the reference to his marital status. "She wouldn't expect me to," he said untruthfully. "We're . . . well, we're not that close any more . . ."

Hilary's mouth twitched. "Would that be anything to do with last night, when you couldn't be found at the Town Hall because you'd sneaked off to the pub instead of watching *My Fair Lady* . . . ? If that put you in the dog-house, I'm not surprised."

"Ron Timms as well, I shouldn't wonder," Quantrill said. "We could have got away with it if the performance had been interrupted just once, but twice was bound to mean trouble." He sighed, for effect. "Are you thinking of getting married, Hilary?" he asked, with a casual don't-do-it air that he hoped would conceal the importance, to himself, of the question.

"Oh yes—I quite often think about it," she said lightly. "In general terms, that is."

"You're not actually engaged then?" he persisted, indicating the ring on the third finger of her left hand. Its significance had always puzzled him.

Hilary looked at her diamond eternity ring with something like surprise. Obviously it was so familiar to her that she no longer noticed she was wearing it.

"That's . . . different," she said. "More of a grand romantic gesture, made when I was very young."

Quantrill knew then that he'd already overstepped the bounds of politeness. Hilary's private life ought to be none of his business. But having trespassed as far as this, he couldn't stop himself from asking a final question.

"So there isn't anyone . . . special, at the moment?"

"When would I find the time?" She laughed as she said it, but he detected a warning of frost.

"Another brandy?" he said hastily.

"No thanks. Coffee would be a good thing, though. I'd better keep a clear head for our interview with Felicity Goodrum's ex."

When Quantrill returned from the buffet car balancing waxed-paper cups of coffee for them both, he found Hilary re-reading the newspaper cuttings about the Napiers' divorce.

"It was an impossible marriage, wasn't it?" she said. "Austin Napier's obviously a very difficult man. And I don't suppose he'll take kindly to being interviewed."

"What seems so odd," said Quantrill, "is that if he did sus out for himself where Goodrum lived, and then sent a yob a few days later to burgle and foul the house, the yob should have had to go to a pub and ask where he could find Mr. Goodrum. That doesn't make sense. And of course it doesn't make Napier a murderer either. He'll certainly deny that."

"I suppose he may not be prepared to talk to us at all," said Hilary.

"Or he may insist on doing so only in the presence of his solicitor." Quantrill looked at his watch. "That could keep us hanging about for hours, especially as it's Sunday. What time's the last train back to Breckham Market, Hilary?"

"Eight-thirty. But I'd hate to travel on it—it's a stopping train, and doesn't get in until just before eleven."

"Hmm." Quantrill frowned, wondering what Molly would

say if he didn't turn up until that time of night, having left the house at seven this morning. Perhaps he'd better ring as soon as they reached Liverpool Street to let her know where he was.

And then a happier thought occurred to him. He looked boldly at Hilary. "We may end up having to stay in London overnight," he said, with meaning.

"Really?" There was no doubt that she sounded pleased. An unexpectedly wholehearted smile lit her face, and Quantrill's hopes soared.

"Oh, that *would* be nice," she said. "I could go and stay with my friend Elizabeth, in Putney."

They went from Liverpool Street Station to Highgate by taxi. Hilary, sitting gracefully composed in her corner, took a lively interest in their journey through Islington and Holloway. Quantrill, completely out of his element, ignored the wet grey streets and stared with gloomy fascination at the meter as it clocked up its astronomical fare. The Super would never wear this . . .

Austin Napier QC lived in a house in a tall, late eighteenth-century terrace built of yellow brick that had weathered to a dignified dark grey. The uniformly cream-painted sash windows were handsomely proportioned, the doors surmounted by semi-circular fanlights with delicately varied tracery. Each door had a brass knocker, and having looked in vain for a bell Quantrill rapped the dolphin knocker on Napier's black door.

They waited, in a drizzle of rain. The street was narrow and lined with parked cars, and the combination of this with low cloud and November's early dusk made him feel hemmed in. He missed the open skies of Suffolk, and when Hilary tried to draw his attention to the finer points of the architecture he said—with truth, though he'd never bothered to take more than passing notice of them—that there were terraces just as good in Saintsbury.

He knocked again. As he did so, a taxi drew up. The man who got out, carrying a small suitcase, was unmistakably the one in the newspaper photographs.

Austin Napier paid off his taxi and advanced, frowning, on the detectives. He was high-browed, bespectacled, distinguished-looking, with silvery wings of hair brushed back above his ears and deep lines running from nose to mouth, pulling down the corners of his lips.

"Yes?" he said haughtily.

Quantrill introduced himself and his sergeant. "We're making enquiries concerning your former wife's husband," he added.

"I have no 'former' wife." The barrister's nostrils flared to emphasise the inverted commas. "Marriage is indissoluble."

"The lady is known to us as Felicity Goodrum," said Hilary diplomatically. "May we come in and talk to you?"

The barrister unlocked his front door and walked through, leaving them to follow. "I can give you five minutes," he said, setting down his suitcase in the narrow hall. "You were fortunate to find me. I spent the weekend with my sister in Hampshire, and came back early only because I have a heavy day in court tomorrow."

He led them into the dining room, which looked out on to the street. It was a fashionably dark room, with bottle-green velvet curtains, beef-red walls and a mahogany table. The table was laid at one end with silver for one person, but there were two additional table mats, one on either side of the place setting, as though for temporarily absent members of the family.

Austin Napier did not switch on the lights, nor ask his visitors to sit down, nor take off his dark, slim-fitting city overcoat, though he did undo the buttons. "You have something to tell me that concerns my wife?" he said in his coldly elegant voice.

"Yes." Quantrill pushed his hands into the pockets of his old mackintosh, reflecting that he looked no more out of place in London than Austin Napier must have done in Hampshire. "It does concern Mrs. Goodrum—but more particularly her husband, Jack. He's dead."

The barrister's face showed no trace of emotion; there was no surprise in his voice, but there was, unmistakably, a note of satisfaction. "Is he?" he said. "Is he indeed . . . ?"

"Murdered," said Quantrill. "At his home in Breckham Market, by a 12-bore shotgun fired from a distance of not more than eight yards."

Austin Napier walked to the Adam fireplace and took up a barrister's courtroom stance with his hands slipped beneath his overcoat, as though it were a gown, and held behind his back. "I'm obliged to you for bringing me the news, Chief Inspector. I'm very glad to hear that my wife no longer has an extra-marital attachment. When did the murder take place?"

"On Saturday. Yesterday."

"Ah. And do you know the identity of the murderer?"

"Not yet. But we're going through the usual process of elimination, and it would help if you will give us the address of your sister in Hampshire, please."

Napier shrugged, and dictated the address to Sergeant Lloyd. "I have no objection to being eliminated from your enquiries, of course. I fail to see, though, why you should consider it necessary."

"You made it necessary yourself, Mr. Napier, by expressing your views on marriage," said Quantrill sternly. "I don't mean just now, on the doorstep, but in open court at the time of your divorce. You chose to make your views public, and they were reported in the national newspapers. We can't overlook the fact that you still consider yourself married to the lady who is now Mrs. Goodrum—and that makes you a natural opponent of her second husband."

One hand emerged from behind the barrister's back and took hold of the lapel of the overcoat that was substituting for a gown. "Do I understand that you've been grubbing about in the files of the gutter press?"

"Just making routine enquiries, sir. Tell me, have you ever been to Breckham Market?"

"I believe I've visited the town, briefly."

"As recently as ten days ago?"

"On Wednesday afternoon, November 12th?" added Sergeant Lloyd.

Austin Napier looked from one detective to another. His pale eyes, behind his spectacle lenses, conveyed no expression, but the lines on either side of his mouth deepened in scorn. "More of your routine enquiries . . . ? The twelfth—yes, I believe that was the date of my visit. I happened to be appearing at Ipswich Crown Court that week. I was prosecuting in a case of attempted murder, and the defendant chose to change his plea to guilty. As I was unexpectedly free on the Wednesday, I went to Saxted to see my son. I wanted to take him out to lunch from his school, and to buy him a motor scooter. Then, in the afternoon, I decided to go on to Breckham Market."

"Why?" said Quantrill bluntly.

"Because my wife had recently moved to the town, and I wanted to see where she lived."

"And did you see her?"

"No. That was not the object of my visit. I wanted to know what her circumstances were—to satisfy myself that she was living somewhere near the standard to which I had accustomed her."

"Did you see Jack Goodrum?"

"No. That was not the object of my visit either. I had no interest in the man. I simply found the house, formed my opinion of it, and returned to Ipswich."

"If you had no interest in Jack Goodrum, Mr. Napier," said Sergeant Lloyd, "why did you ask the newsagent where he lived?"

He looked at her with barely concealed disdain. "I should have thought that was obvious, Sergeant. What I really wanted to know was where *my wife* lived. But I had to ask for the address of the man she co-habited with, because the newsagent might not know her as Mrs. Austin Napier."

"Quite probably not," agreed Hilary.

"Then your question is answered." He turned to Quantrill. "I've chosen to give you a full explanation of my movements because I have nothing to hide. But I will add, in the hope of persuading you to waste no more of my time as well as your own, that quite apart from my being in Hampshire yesterday, I have never in my life handled a shotgun."

"Thank you for the information," said Quantrill. "But we didn't come here with the idea that you were in Breckham Market last night, or that you yourself shot Jack Goodrum."

"No?"

"No—we're working on the possibility that the actual gunman was merely the murderer's accomplice, hired for the job." He gestured Hilary towards the door. "Thank you for giving us your time, Mr. Napier. We may be in touch with you again."

The barrister hurried after them, brushing past Hilary to reach the front door first. Holding it shut, he turned to them with his mouth twisted upwards into a semblance of a smile. His pale eyes glistened in the gloom.

"Then let me save you a pointless journey, Chief Inspector, by making myself absolutely clear. I am *not* of a homicidal nature."

"I'm glad to hear it."

"But if I were," the barrister went on, ignoring the interruption, "it would not have been Goodrum who had to die. Oh no—the man's irrelevant. It would have been my wife who had to take the consequences of breaking her marriage vow. And I wouldn't have done it by proxy. No, no—if I'd had to kill her, it would have been with my own hands."

20

The two detectives went back to Liverpool Street Station by bus, and were still in plenty of time to catch the four-thirty to Breckham Market. There was a buffet car on the train, but not even Quantrill could fancy eating a sandwich.

"Austin Napier's a nutter!" he declared, as they drank cardboard-tasting tea.

"We knew that before we came," said Hilary. "It was *why* we came, remember?"

"Can we believe him, d'you think?" Quantrill asked in a respectful tone. Knowing that his sergeant was a qualified nurse, he regarded her as his psychiatric expert. She had often pointed out, at first patiently and then crossly, that she wasn't a doctor, still less a psychiatrist; but he knew she'd read textbooks, and that certainly made her more knowledgeable than he was. "I mean, do you think that if Napier had been a killer he'd have gone for his ex-wife rather than her new husband?"

"I wouldn't take his word that he has no homicidal tendencies, for a start," said Hilary. "From what we've read about their marriage Felicity would seem to be his natural victim— but that doesn't have to mean he'd *kill* her. A man like Austin Napier might prefer a much more subtle way of punishing her. Let's suppose that when he went to Breckham Market ten days ago, he saw the Goodrums together and realised how happy they were. If he *is* homicidal, it might have given him the idea of killing Jack simply as a means of inflicting prolonged suffering on Felicity."

"Hmm—I can see that Austin Napier would go for something clever," agreed Quantrill. "He told us that Goodrum was irrelevant, so he might well have thought nothing of wiping the man out. Or of having him wiped out. I've no doubt Napier's alibi will stand up, so we can't pursue this one until we find the feller who fired the gun. Meanwhile, it's not a matter of wondering whether anyone else was hostile to Lucky Jack, but of deciding what order to put 'em in. Who's your choice, after Napier?"

Hilary took out her notebook, and looked back at the interview with Felicity Goodrum. "Taking family first, it could be significant that Jack's ex-wife didn't want to be divorced."

"That's true," said Quantrill. "It could be a case of jealousy on her part. The first Mrs. Goodrum would know that Jack was a man who kept shotguns in his house, and sending someone to steal a gun from him and later shoot him with it might have given her some extra satisfaction. We'd better go and see her first thing tomorrow. If that's a non-runner—if it wasn't a domestic murder—then we'll have to start making lists of Goodrum's other enemies."

"Business associates who'd fallen out with him, for whatever reason? And employees who'd been-sacked?" The sergeant made a note, and then pulled a wry face. "Jack Goodrum had been in business for over twenty years. And it was a big business, apparently, employing up to a hundred people at any one time. How far back do we go?"

"Oh, come on, Hilary!" Quantrill chided her gently, liking her all the more for her occasional lapses from efficiency. "You know the answer to that as well as I do."

"Yes, all right, stupid question. We go back as far as we have to. But look—I know I'm only trying to avoid making these horrendously long lists, but Jack Goodrum sold his business something like a couple of years ago. Don't you think that anyone who had a score to settle with him would have done so before now?"

"Not if Goodrum couldn't be found. And if he had reason to think anyone was after him, he'd have kept his head well down."

"Then why should the murder have happened now? Are you suggesting that Jack would have relaxed his guard, after he was married again? Because I can't believe that. Remember how protective he was towards Felicity—?"

Quantrill scratched his jaw in thought. "Either the marriage itself or the move to Breckham Market could have been the deciding factor," he suggested. "And I tell you what, Hilary—if Goodrum *was* trying to keep his head down, he spoiled his own game by running over Clanger Bell and getting his name and address in the newspapers."

"I'd almost forgotten Clanger," said Hilary. "His sister's someone who'll have to go on the list—she might have felt so aggrieved over our failure to pin murder on Jack Goodrum that she decided to take the law into her own hands."

"Miss Bell feels aggrieved, all right," remembered Quantrill. "She was at *My Fair Lady* last night—I tried to avoid speaking to her, but she made a point of telling me that her opinion hasn't changed. If she'd wanted to have Goodrum killed, though, she wouldn't have needed to hire anyone to steal his shotgun for the purpose. There was a gun cabinet in Tower House—I caught a glimpse of it in a corridor when she took us to see Clanger's old room. A heavy, glass-fronted mahogany job, her father's or grandfather's, I suppose, with four shotguns in it. So if she'd wanted a murder done, she could have offered whoever she hired a choice of guns."

"I didn't see the cabinet, I must admit—I suppose I was talking to her at the time." Hilary stifled a yawn; it had been a long day, and the railway carriage was stuffy. "I'm surprised," she added with a drowsy grin, "that you didn't take the opportunity, when you saw the guns, to give Miss Bell a lecture on security."

"Not me," Quantrill protested with mock horror. "I was terrified of her! And she said she was about to sell up, so it seemed pointless to make an issue of it. I say—" aware that he was losing Hilary's attention, he sought to revive it—"would you like another cup of tea?"

"No thanks. I don't know about you, but I," his sergeant added elegantly, "intend to have a kip."

She leaned back in her corner and closed her eyes. Frustrated, Quantrill made his way to the buffet car and tried to console himself with a can of beer.

Hilary dozed uneasily, disturbed by images of violent death. She was not sorry when the train, leaving Stowmarket station, jerked her awake. But when she opened her eyes and saw Douglas Quantrill gazing at her avidly, she promptly closed them again.

One of the hazards of being a woman in what was predominantly a man's world was that senior officers so often seemed to think her sex more significant than her job. Rather than treating her according to her rank, and valuing her according to her efficiency, they reacted to her as a woman. Some were smarmy, some were lecherous; some were coldly hostile, some aggressive. Some, like Douglas, were persistently hopeful. Occasionally, as in her previous job with the county scenes-of-serious-crime team in Yarchester, she had been lucky enough to have a really nice boss who treated her with friendly courtesy. But Harry Colman—who was safely through the male menopause and nearing retirement—had been an exception.

She had, though, become very fond of Douglas Quantrill. She liked working with him, valuing his understanding of Suffolk ways and people, and admiring his dogged pursuit of villainy. And she found his occasional lapses into gloom almost endearing. But she had no intention of establishing a closer relationship with him.

He was attractive, certainly; he carried his weight well, and though the contours of his face were becoming a little blurred they were still undeniably handsome. In other circumstances, Hilary would have been only too happy to meet his eye. But as things were, she didn't propose to reciprocate her chief inspector's interest in her. The only kind of relationship she wanted with Douglas Quantrill was as a colleague and a good friend.

She had hoped that he would realise this, by now. Instead, his approaches were becoming more open. She disliked the situation, embarrassed on her boss's behalf as much as on her own. If he couldn't accept the clear messages she'd already given him, their working partnership would have to be dissolved. And that would be a great pity.

Hilary opened her lids a fraction. Douglas was still gazing at her; not with love—that at least was something to be thankful for—but with calculating hope. She feigned sleep again, instinctively caressing her eternity ring with the thumb of her left hand.

She had nothing at all against affairs, as long as they were of the heart. The memory of Stephen hadn't—after the first numbed months following his death—inhibited desire; but his ring had come to act as a touchstone. Recalling the quality of their love, she had discovered that brief physical relationships had nothing to offer but ultimate emptiness.

As for marriage, the right man—right not only emotionally and physically, but also in his willingness to support her in her career just as she would expect to support him in his—had never appeared. No, that wasn't entirely true: there had been another detective chief inspector, an instructor on a CID refresher course that she'd attended just before coming to

Breckham Market, who had seemed wonderfully, almost incredibly right.

Clive had told her, when he first took her out to dinner, that he was separated from his wife. A divorce was on the way, he'd said. And Hilary had believed what he'd wanted her to believe, because she wanted to believe it too.

It was Clive's calculating lie, his smooth-tongued readiness to dismiss what she eventually discovered was a stable marriage, that Hilary thought more despicable than his actual infidelity. She had despised herself, too, for being so easily conned.

There was no danger of a solid countryman like Douglas Quantrill conning her in the same way; but even he had tried to suggest that there was a permanent rift in his marriage. This was another reason why Hilary had no intention of embarking on an extra-marital affair with him. Whenever he had mentioned his wife and son to her it had almost invariably been with gloom or exasperation, but she had not been deceived. She felt sure that he loved them both. It would be a very good thing, she thought, if only there were some way of making him realise that whatever he might imagine, he would be desolate without them.

She started as something touched her knee. Her eyes flew open and she saw, with a jolt of surprise, that it was his hand.

For a few seconds he left it there, large and strong, radiating the heat of his blood. Against her will, Hilary felt her own blood begin to respond. She looked up, met his bold eye, almost weakened; then she gave her head a slight shake.

"Sorry," he said, withdrawing his hand immediately. His breath was shorter than usual. "Didn't mean to make you jump. We'll be arriving at Breckham Market in a few minutes. Thought I'd better wake you."

"Thanks." Hilary composed herself at a different angle, her legs unobtrusively out of his reach, and forced herself to give him a pleasant, non-committal smile. Undeterred, he continued to stare at her with the look of a man who hadn't been properly fed for twenty years.

"Let's have supper together, Hilary," he urged. "We could go to that new place in Ashthorpe. No one knows us there."

This time, she shook her head decisively. "No thank you. I've got a better idea, Douglas. Why don't we both just go home?"

21

During the absence of Chief Inspector Quantrill and Sergeant Lloyd, the other members of the divisional CID had been following the only lead so far in the hunt for Jack Goodrum's killer. Every pub, bikers' café and snooker hall in and near Breckham Market had been visited, with the object of interviewing every young man who could conceivably answer to the description of "a bit of a punk with one gold ear-stud."

This description had been liberally interpreted by the CID to include those who wore any kind of visible metal adornment, on either their clothing or their skin. The incidental charges that arose ranged from possession of cannabis to riding a motor cycle without a licence, and Breckham CID felt that a useful Sunday's work had been done. But only three of the interviewees could be justifiably suspected as the man who had gone into the Coney and Thistle at lunch time on Saturday November 15th—the day the shotgun was stolen—and asked where he could find Mr. Goodrum.

At an identity parade held on Monday morning, the barmaid failed to identify any one of the three suspects. And as for the actual burglary at The Mount, the CID were still no nearer pinning it on anyone.

Chief Inspector Quantrill gave instructions for the search to be widened. He also enlisted the co-operation of the neighbouring police divisions. His opposite number at Saintsbury, Detective Chief Inspector Tait—recently promoted, so young and so ambitious that he chafed at the current dearth of serious crime in his own division—was eager to come straight over to Breckham Market and give his former boss the benefit of his advice. But Quantrill told him firmly that all he and Sergeant Lloyd needed from the Saintsbury division, thank you very much, was a round-up of semi-punks with gold ear-studs— preferably those who also wore size nine trainers with a ridged sole.

By the time Quantrill and Hilary were free to set off for their interview with the first Mrs. Goodrum, Monday morning was

more than half over. But it was still within school hours, and so
they were surprised to see children wandering about the town
doing some pre-Christmas window-shopping. In the market
place a group of senior boys, most of them properly crash-
helmeted, were on the bikers' favourite pitch opposite the
chippy, revving up their scooters. Quantrill was not only
amazed but furious to see his son among them. Peter, bareheaded and with a look of bliss on his face, was sitting astride a
scooter revving with his mates.

Quantrill did an emergency stop. Abandoning the car to
Hilary he threw off his seat belt, slammed out of the door and
advanced menacingly on his son.

"Peter! What the devil d'you think you're doing?"

The rest of the young riders, some of whom recognised the
Chief Inspector and all of whom recognised trouble, stopped
extracting macho noises from their small engines and put-
putted decorously away. The only other boy unable to escape
was lanky Darren Catchpole, the owner of the Yamaha 125 that
his friend Peter was trying for size.

"Hallo, Mr. Quantrill," said Darren guiltily, switching off the
engine. He too was bareheaded, having taken off his helmet
while he explained the controls. He couldn't think offhand of
any offence he was committing—it couldn't be illegal to allow
someone without a licence just to sit on his bike—but he'd
heard from Peter what a totally unreasonable pig his old man
was.

"We can't help not being in school," Darren added. "It's not
our fault." His helmet, a super model with a full-face tinted
visor, had been snatched out of his hands by Peter and jammed
on as soon as the Chief Inspector appeared. Peter was now
deaf, unintelligible and facially invisible. All right for *him*.

"A hot water pipe leaked, you see," Darren plunged on
desperately. "All the cloakrooms are flooded. We were sent
home as soon as we got there . . ."

Quantrill ignored him. He pointed an angry finger at Peter.
Take that thing off, he mouthed.

Slowly, with sullen resentment, Peter removed his headgear
and returned it to its owner.

"And now get off that bike."

Peter gave his father a furious look, but complied.

"This is your machine, I suppose, Darren?" The Chief
Inspector grilled the youngster, demanding to see his licence
and insurance and checking the tax disc. Then he turned back

to Peter and, with angry deliberation, blistered his son's ears in front of his friend.

"Don't you *ever*," he concluded, "let me catch you on a motor bike again, whether it's on the road or not. You do as you're told, my lad—or old as you are you'll get the biggest hiding of your life!"

Quantrill travelled most of the way towards Ipswich in a silent fume. "Blast the boy . . ." he muttered at intervals. "*Blast* the boy."

Hilary maintained a discreet silence, until she needed to navigate the last few winding rural miles to Jack Goodrum's former home.

On a dull winter's day, Factory Bungalow looked particularly desolate. It had been painted up at some time within the last couple of years, but its immediate surroundings consisted of nothing but rough, rain-sodden grass and scrub. A dead-end concrete road led past it to a group of ex-wartime aircraft hangars, once presumably used for Goodrum's poultry-processing enterprise but now standing abandoned in the November mist.

The door of the bungalow was opened to them by a big, slatternly woman. Although it was well after midday she wore a dressing gown over a nightdress, and bedroom slippers on her feet. Everything about her—her yellow-grey hair, her cheeks, her chins, her voice, her body—sagged. She held a newly opened packet of custard cream biscuits in one hand, and throughout the course of her conversation with the detectives she used the other hand as a semi-automatic conveyor between the packet and her mouth.

She agreed that she was Mrs. Goodrum, Mrs. Doreen Goodrum; she supposed, reluctantly, that the detectives had better step inside. Yes, that's right, she was Jack's first wife . . . Her voice as she said it was as sour as the air in the sketchily cleaned, electrical appliance-crammed living room.

The three of them stood round the table, on which was all the evidence of a permanently on-going makeshift meal. The local newspaper also lay on the table: SUFFOLK MURDER ran the banner headline; *wealthy former businessman shot in front of wife*.

"You were notified yesterday, I believe?" said Quantrill

Doreen Goodrum nodded. Her conveying hand speeded up the transfer of biscuits to her mouth, cramming them in faster than she could chew. At the same time a fat tear rolled out of one eye and down her cheek, and plopped to join the various other stains on the front of her dressing gown.

A half-empty cup of stewed tea stood on the table in front of her. "What about some fresh tea?" said Sergeant Lloyd. "Perhaps one of your daughters—?" She had been watching out for the other members of the family, and now she began to move as she caught a glimpse of a wraith-like girl crossing the narrow corridor beyond the open inner door. "Shall I ask her?"

"No," said Doreen, speaking hurriedly through a mouthful of biscuit. "Tracey won't . . . she's not much good at making tea . . . she's not too well . . ." Then, with relief as she heard the plug being pulled in the bathroom: "Oh, there's my Sharon! She'll do it—won't you, my lovely, eh?"

The girl who emerged into the corridor was, at twenty-three years old, almost as big and ungainly as her mother. Sharon was dressed in what might have been a leisure suit, or there again pyjamas, in bright blue thermal material. She had a lovely head of hair, with natural butter yellow curls, and the uncomplicated expression of a shy eight-year-old; but behind her blue eyes was a shadow of bewilderment.

She had been about to enter the living room, but as soon as she saw the visitors she backed away down the corridor. Her mother, pausing for the first time in her comsumption of biscuits, coaxed her to return.

"You'll make us a cup of tea, won't you, my pet? Fill up the kettle, there's Mum's good girl, and switch it on."

Sharon stood in the doorway, her eyes lowered, swinging her shoulders bashfully. "How many tea-bags, Mum?" she asked in a loud whisper.

"Four—and mind you don't burn yourself on the hot kettle . . ."

Sharon disappeared into the kitchen. Doreen Goodrum turned back to the detectives, her voice hardening. "She wasn't always like that, my Sharon," she said belligerently. "Two years ago she was the same as any other girl—not very clever, I grant you, but happily engaged to be married. And this is what Jack Goodrum—her own father—did to her!"

"How did he do it?" asked Hilary, narrow-eyed, thinking immediately of criminal abuse.

"Why, by leaving us and marrying that other woman! By cheating us out of our rights. Sharon was all set to marry her Dad's sales manager, but when the little runt realised we

wouldn't ever get Jack's money, he left her. Flew off to Spain—
on business, he said—then sent her a telegram the day before
the wedding, calling it off. No wonder the poor child went
nearly out of her mind."

Hilary agreed that Sharon had been ill-used, and kept to
herself the thought that she sounded well rid of the sales
manager. "And what about your other daughter, Mrs. Goodrum? What about Tracey?"

Doreen Goodrum's eyes shifted uneasily to the corridor. She
seemed relieved that it was empty, and that her younger
daughter was declining to put in an appearance. "Trace has
been hard hit too," she said. "Very hard hit. We all have."

Her face suddenly flushed an exhausted red. She slumped
into a chair. Sweat sprang out just below her hairline. She
gasped for air, and wiped the back of her hand across her
forehead. "All that work . . ." she panted. "All them years of
nothing but work, first me and then the girls as well . . . And
what reward have we had for it?"

Her flush began to subside. She dragged a handkerchief
from the pocket of her dressing gown and mopped her face,
then snatched up the packet of biscuits and began to cram
them into her mouth for comfort, continuing the recital of her
grievances through a splutter of crumbs.

"Jack settled some money on us, but there's only just enough
coming in each week to keep the three of us going. Mind you,
his crafty lawyers made it *sound* good. I was being given the
matrimonial home and all its contents, as well as the cash, they
said, and the divorce judge got the idea we were set up in
luxury for life . . . Oh, if only I'd known where to find Jack
Goodrum, this last year, I'd have made him pay for what he's
done to us!"

"Didn't you know where he was living?" said Quantrill.

"Not till yesterday, when I heard he was dead. The old devil
kept his head well down—we weren't the only ones who
wanted to find him, and he knew it."

"But you read the Suffolk newspapers. Didn't you see his
name and address a couple of weeks ago, in the report of an
inquest at Breckham Market?"

"No," said Doreen Goodrum. "I never saw it." She leaned
back in her chair and called out to her elder daughter in the
kitchen: "Can you manage, Sharon? Shall Mum come and help
you with the tea, my lovey?"

"But if you *had* seen it," persisted Quantrill. "If you'd known where Jack was living, what would you have done?"

"I'd have gone after the bastard."

"With a shotgun?"

She snorted. "No chance of that—he'd taken all his guns with him."

"But you could have got hold of one from somewhere, couldn't you? You could have asked someone to get hold of a shotgun for you."

Doreen wiped her forehead again as another hot sweat afflicted her. "Look, I wasn't the only one who wanted to get Jack," she said.

"Name me some of the others, then."

"I dunno their *names*. I had nothing to do with keeping the books. But I know there were some businessmen he cheated—his suppliers, small firms that went bankrupt because he kept them waiting so long for the money he owed them. And he cheated on his taxes, too. The Inland Revenue was after him for years."

"The Inland Revenue doesn't go after people with a shotgun," said Quantrill. "But that's what somebody did to your former husband—and you've just told us how badly you wanted to get him."

Doreen Goodrum lifted her head and looked straight at the Chief Inspector with anguished eyes. "But I wouldn't ever have killed him! All right, if I'd known where he lived, I'd have wanted to go after him. I'd have shown him up in front of his new wife and his neighbours—camped on his doorstep if I had to—to shame him into paying us what he owes us for all them years of work . . . But—but I wouldn't have wanted him *killed*."

Tears began to roll from her eyes and wobble down her cheeks. Great sobs came wrenching up out of her chest. Blindly, she reached for the last of the biscuits.

Sergeant Lloyd, interpreting her tears as a lament for the husband who had left her, offered a word of guarded sympathy. But Doreen immediately stopped sobbing.

"I'm not blubbing *for* the bastard," she said indignantly, snuffling back her tears and wiping her wet cheeks with the palm of her hand. "Now he *is* dead, I hope he burns in hell. That's what he deserves, for all the people he's ruined.

"But the last thing I wanted was for him to *die*. Can't you see that? As long as he was alive, there was a chance that I could get at him and make him give us the money that's our due. But now he's dead, everything will go to that new wife of his. And who's going to take care of his daughters?"

22

The weather had changed from dull to a bone-chilling drizzle. A hot drink would have been welcome, but Chief Inspector Quantrill preferred to leave Factory Bungalow before Sharon Goodrum had finished brewing her pot of tea.

Instead of setting course immediately for Breckham Market, he decided to take a look at the empty factory. He drove past the side of the bungalow, and on up the mud-splashed concrete road that had served first the wartime airfield and then Jack Goodrum's empire. Now, *Industrial site for sale* boards (identifying the property rather than advertising it, since it was surrounded by sugar beet fields) referred prospective buyers to a London agent.

Quantrill got out of the car, dressed for the weather in mackintosh and tweed hat, and made a brisk tour. The former aircraft hangars had obviously been well maintained when they were owned by J.R. Goodrum Ltd., and further modern buildings—an office block and a large processing plant—had been added. There was no doubt that it had been a considerable business, and that one way or another—first in operating it, then in selling out—its owner must have made a packet. And there was growing evidence that much of it had been made at the expense of other people.

"I thought my list of disgruntled ex-employees was going to be long enough," said Hilary when Quantrill returned to the car, his tweed hat fuzzy with droplets of rain. She was too experienced a detective not to be appropriately dressed, but she saw no sense getting wet unless she had to. "But now it looks as though we need to add bankrupted suppliers as well."

"We'll go and talk to Goodrum's accountants about them," said Quantrill. "His first wife's given us a useful line to follow, if we can believe her. But that's the catch, isn't it? I reckon she knows more about his death than she's letting on. For one thing, she takes the local newspaper regularly—there were back numbers lying about the living room—so the chances are that she'd seen the report of the inquest on Clanger Bell's death. If so, then she'll have known where to find her ex-husband. And the way she hated him, I don't see her planning to sit meekly on the doorstep of The Mount trying to shame him into giving her some extra cash."

"But I believe what she said about not wanting him killed," said Hilary, "for the very good reason she gave. His death had obviously come as a shock and a disappointment to her. I agree with you, though, that she may well have something to hide. Perhaps she persuaded someone to do the burglary, and steal the gun. She might then have sent someone else, the following week, to threaten Jack with it. But if so she picked the wrong man for the job, because he turned out to be less interested in getting justice for her than in having his own revenge."

Quantrill drove back down the service road, raising his hand to a tractor driver who was towing a trailer-load of newly lifted sugar beet across the adjoining field.

"Either Doreen Goodrum knows nothing, as she wanted us to believe, or she's deeply involved," he agreed. "She's so angry about the murder that if she's innocent I'm sure she'd have given us at least one name to try. Hullo—" he slowed to a stop as a stout figure in a headscarf, a man's old raincoat, and heavy wellington boots emerged from the back door of Factory Bungalow and came stumbling down the overgrown path to intercept them, waving something in her hand. "Perhaps she's decided to co-operate after all."

"That's Sharon," said Hilary. "I recognise the knees of her pyjamas." She got out of the car, turned up the collar of her trench coat and picked her way across the muddy road to the wire fence that separated it from the Goodrums' piece of rough land.

"Sorry we couldn't stay for tea, Sharon," she said with a friendly smile. "What's that you've got—something for us?"

The girl cast a nervous glance over her shoulder at the bungalow, and then held out a crumpled scrap of paper. "It's from our Trace," she said in her loud whisper. "She wants you to know about Uncle Dave."

Hilary smoothed out the paper. On it was written, in shaky capitals, DAVE WHEELER.

"I see. He's your mother's brother, is he, Sharon?"

"No, I don't think so . . ." Eyes lowered, the girl swung her sturdy shoulders in embarrassment. "Me and Trace called him uncle when we were little. He used to work with Dad, up at the factory. He was ever so nice . . ." Her voice trailed wistfully away.

"And what about him? What is it that Tracey wants us to know about Uncle Dave?" prompted Hilary gently.

"I don't know . . ." The girl looked up for a moment, her blue eyes bewildered; then she returned to her study of the unoccupied toes of her man-sized wellington boots. "He used to bring us presents, sometimes," she said, wistful again.

"Ah—" Hilary thought for a few seconds, then returned to the car. Quantrill had his window down, listening to their conversation. "This may be a profitable use for that large bar of fruit and nut chocolate you keep in your door pocket," she said. "The one you think I don't know about . . ."

"That's my iron rations!" he protested. "Emergencies only. Besides, I doubt you'll get anything out of her."

"It's worth a try. Oh, come on Douglas, hand it over. I'll buy you a replacement."

Chuffed that she'd called him by his first name, he did as Hilary asked. Sharon received the chocolate with evident pleasure. But as he'd suspected, she refused—or was unable— to say where Dave Wheeler lived, or anything else about him. Shyly smiling her thanks, she turned and lumbered towards the bungalow.

Hilary, looking back as they drove away, saw a front window curtain twitch. But whether they were being watched by Tracey, or by Doreen Goodrum, or both; and whether the lead was genuine or they were being craftily misled, she had no means of knowing.

The Chief Inspector, who had been putting his mind to the quickest method of finding out who Dave Wheeler was and where he lived, came up almost immediately with the answer.

"No sense in wasting time trying to get hold of the personnel records of J.R. Goodrum Limited. We'll go straight to the best source of information in any firm—she's bound to live some- where local."

"Who is?"

"The tea lady."

An enquiry at a shop in the village half a mile away sent them to another bungalow, far less lavishly equipped than the Goodrums' but clean and budgerigar-neat. Its occupant, Mrs. Alice Fulcher, a widow who greatly missed the companionship she had had at Goodrums, was delighted to receive her visitors. She had just had an early dinner, she said—there was an emptied mug and a slightly used small plate on the kitchen table, together with two opened packets, one of individual servings of instant soup powder, the other of cream crackers— and she assured them that it would be a pleasure to have someone to drink a cup of coffee with.

Yes, she'd read about Jack Goodrum's death. A shocking business. Mind you, she wasn't entirely surprised, the way Jack had treated everybody, his own poor wife and girls as well—a slave driver if ever there was one. But there was no call for anyone to go and shoot him. Two wrongs would never make a right.

Yes, she'd known Jack most of his life. Knew him when he was a little terror of a boy, knew him when he was a young tearaway, knew him when he first started his poultry process- ing business and hadn't got a penny to pay his bills with. Let the b . . . . . s wait, he used to say. Didn't care for anybody except himself.

And yes, she certainly knew Dave Wheeler. Poor Dave— the last she'd heard of him he was unemployed, his wife had left him, and he was living with his mother in a village the other side of Ipswich. Clayford, that's where he went back to live. He and Jack Goodrum had been mates for years—Dave used to have a small poultry farm in the village here, and they'd often gone out shooting together.

Dave supplied Jack with poultry in the early days, but he was always kept waiting for his money. When Jack eventually persuaded him to give up the smallholding and join him as a partner, Dave thought he was on to a good thing at last. He didn't realise that it was just Jack's way of wiping out one of his debts.

"How long were they in partnership?" said Quantrill.

"Hah!" said Mrs. Fulcher with bright-eyed relish. "*They never were*—not properly, that is. I didn't realise it, and neither did Dave, until they had a big row when the news leaked out that Jack was selling the business. It seems there never was any written partnership agreement—Dave was fool enough to trust Jack to see him right! He'd been working for rock-bottom wages, same as everybody else, because Jack wouldn't allow any trade unions in his factory. And when Jack sold out, Dave discovered that all he was entitled to was his redundancy money."

Having talked herself almost hoarse, Mrs. Fulcher suddenly paused and gave the detectives a worried look over the rim of her coffee cup. "Here—" she said, "I'm not talking out of turn, am I? I couldn't help knowing what went on in the offices—I used to go in and out with my trolley, and they'd carry on with what they were saying regardless. They seemed to think I was just an automatic hot-drinks machine. But don't you go getting the idea that Dave might have shot Jack Goodrum! I'm sure he wouldn't have done that. It wasn't in his nature to be violent."

"But did he threaten Goodrum, in that big row they had?" asked Quantrill.

"Well . . . He said he'd get even with him, one day . . . But what you've got to understand is that just about everybody who worked for Jack hated him. They didn't say so to his face, naturally. He'd have sacked them on the spot. But you should've heard what the production workers reckoned they'd do to him, if ever they got the chance! And I don't mind telling you that some of them were a rough lot . . . Oh, if it's suspects you're looking for, there's plenty to choose from without picking on Dave Wheeler."

Sergeant Lloyd could put off the job no longer. She took out her notebook and started making the long list of former employees, ex-employees and associates who might, with good reason, be suspected of complicity in Jack Goodrum's murder.

23

Disregarding Mrs. Fulcher's opinion, the detectives left her bungalow to go looking, first, for Dave Wheeler.

They found his mother's house, in a red brick terrace built in the late Victorian Station-Road style, in the railway village of Clayford. Their knock at her front door went unanswered. Walking through an entry to the rear of the terrace, they opened the gate of rough, creosoted planks that led into her small back yard, and tried their luck at the kitchen door.

Mrs. Wheeler senior was at home. A good twenty years older than Mrs. Fulcher, with wispy hair and trembling lips, and so unsteady on her pins that she needed to lean on a walking stick, she was still full of fight. She seemed to have a shrewd idea why the detectives were there, and all she was prepared to give them was sufficient space in her kitchen to allow her to shut the door against potentially eavesdropping neighbours.

Her son was out. He'd gone off that morning after a job—somewhere in Colchester, she thought. Or perhaps Chelmsford. He'd had a telephone call, somewhere about midday, and then he'd left to catch the twelve-forty train. He'd said he might be away for a day or two.

Yes, he knew Jack Goodrum had been murdered. She'd seen it in the newspaper and read it out to Dave at breakfast. But that had nothing at all to do with his going away.

She knew it was wicked to say so, but she was glad Jack Goodrum was dead. He'd treated her son shamefully. But they needn't think Dave knew anything about what had happened to Jack, because he didn't. He'd been at home with her when the murder was committed. *Whenever* the murder was committed.

Yes, and he'd been at home all day the previous Saturday as well. And why they were asking she couldn't imagine, but if they must know he took size seven and a half in shoes.

"Does your son own a shotgun, Mrs. Wheeler?" asked Hilary.

"Not that I know of," said the old lady. Her sunken eyes were weak and watery but she stared at the sergeant without a blink.

"He knows how to use one, though," said Quantrill.

"That he doesn't!"

"Oh come now, Mrs. Wheeler—you know that's not true. Your son had a gun licence when he lived at his previous address, and we've heard that he used to go shooting with Jack Goodrum. I think it's likely that he still has his shotgun."

Physically, the old lady was sagging. She needed to rest both hands on the handle of her walking stick to stay upright. But she stood defiant, barring the way beyond her kitchen doormat: "Not in this house, he hasn't."

"What a pity," said Hilary pleasantly. "You see, we've heard that a lot of people had reason to hate Jack Goodrum, and we're anxious to elimate those who know nothing about his murder. If only we could borrow your son's shotgun, we could send it to the forensic lab for a test firing. Then the experts would compare the spent cartridge with the one that was found at the scene of the crime, and that would confirm your son's innocence."

Five minutes later, the detectives were on their way back to Breckham Market with a well-kept shotgun that his mother had fetched from David Anthony Wheeler's bedroom.

"I don't *enjoy* conning suspects' elderly relatives," said the sergeant. "And it seems a particularly mean thing to do when the murder victim was such a bastard to so many people."

"You've changed your tune, Hilary! I thought you had a high opinion of Jack Goodrum's honesty and kindness."

"So I did. But that Jack was the one I met at The Mount: Felicity's husband. It's difficult to believe he was the same pig of a man Doreen was married to—he must have changed completely. But I suppose that's the civilising influence of love."

Quantrill thought it was more likely to be the civilising influence of early retirement and a lot of money, but he didn't say so. He didn't want to provoke her into a lengthy argument. They had at most a twenty-five minute drive ahead of them, on the minor road he had chosen, and he was determined not to waste it. He felt that this was going to be his final chance to establish a more intimate relationship with her.

"Hilary—"

"The sugar beet campaign's still going strong, I see," she said, taking an unusually keen interest in the agricultural scene. "Piles of beet by the roadside, dirty great container lorries ferrying loads of it to the sugar factories, and mud everywhere . . . Well, at least it's stopped raining. That learner-rider must be glad."

They were about to overtake a lad riding an L-plated moped. He must have been at least sixteen to hold a provisional licence, but he seemed very small. He was dressed in jeans and a thin combat jacket, with a spaceman crash helmet that made his head look far too heavy for his body. As they passed him—giving him a wide berth—they saw him wobble. He managed to control his machine and prevent it from going into a slide, but he gave the impression of hanging on to it for dear life.

"Bloody bikes," scowled Quantrill, remembering his encounter with Peter that morning. "D'you wonder I won't let my boy ride one? It's terrifyingly dangerous. A rider can come off so easily, and he has no body protection at all."

"Yes, I realise that," said Hilary. "It must be very worrying for the parents. But—since you've asked me—don't you think you're being a bit inflexible with Peter? It did seem to me this morning that he's going to be a very frustrated young man if he can't ever hope to join his mates."

"Well at least he won't be joining the casualty statistics," Quantrill retorted. "The number of Suffolk sixteen to twenty-three-year-olds who've killed themselves on bikes this year alone is absolutely horrifying. No responsible father ought to allow his son to have one. When Austin Napier—QC, for heaven's sake—told us he'd bought a bike the other week for young Matthew, I thought it was a good demonstration of his complete lack of judgement."

"Oh well, Austin Napier . . ." said Hilary. "Considering that he refuses to recognise his wife's divorce, and that we can't rule him out as her second husband's murderer, what can you expect? But he probably had his own reason for buying the machine. Matthew was taking a bike-riding course at school—his mother told us she was worried about his safety, if you remember—so I suppose his father wanted to try to buy his way into the boy's favour."

"Hmph," said Quantrill. The hurt he had sustained during his major row with Peter had begun to ease, until this morning's incident had aggravated the sore. "I'm damned if *I*'d ever do that."

He glanced at his watch. Although he was driving more slowly than usual, the journey was going too quickly. "Hilary—" he said.

"Is Peter leaving school next summer?"

"Not if I can help it. I want him to stay another year and get some qualifications. Grow up a bit, at least."

"And what then?"

"God knows . . . Hilary—"

"But what's he interested in?"

"Motor bikes. Oh, and the CND; he seems to think that unless we disarm, we'll be overwhelmed by what he calls the nuclear winter."

"Well, it's arguable, isn't it? That sounds very thoughtful and responsible of him—even if you don't agree with it."

"Pah! He doesn't *believe* what he said, he's only using it as an excuse to spend every penny he's got on a bike."

Quantrill slowed the car even more. They were within four miles of Breckham Market, and he knew that this was his last opportunity. The narrow road was enclosed by leafless hedges and the occasional bare, black-tipped ash tree, but he recalled that there was a lay-by just ahead. He pulled in, unclipped his seat belt, and turned to her. Although the words she had used last night on the train had been deliberately discouraging, she had quite definitely responded, if only for a moment, to his touch. She'd met his eyes, and what he had seen there—if only for a moment—encouraged him to persist.

"Look, you know how I—"

"Are you sure you're not underestimating Peter?" she said. "He sounds to me—"

Quantrill exploded. "For God's sake shut up about the wretched boy! And don't start on any other subject, either. You know perfectly well what I want to talk to you about."

"When we're in the middle of a murder investigation?"

"That'll keep for ten minutes. Whoever killed Jack Goodrum had a personal grudge against him—it isn't as though we're expecting any more deaths."

They were both silent for a few moments, Quantrill because he needed to steady himself after his outburst. That had been a fine way to begin propositioning her . . .

This wasn't much of a setting for it, either. The wet November countryside looked dismal, and the passing traffic consisted chiefly of mud-splattered tractors and trailers carting sugar beet from the fields to a nearby collection point. The minor road was greasy, scattered with yellowed beet leaves that had fallen from the trailers. The edges of the road were puddled with dirty rainwater.

Inside the car, Quantrill felt that the atmosphere had begun to thicken. Having at last seized her attention, he was almost too stifled to speak. And now, embarrassingly, the windows had begun to mist up. He started to say something—anything— but she interrupted him once more.

"I think I'd better tell you," she said, briskly winding down a window and letting in a blast of chill air, "that I'm planning to ask for a transfer from Breckham Market."

"But you can't leave!" he protested. "I mean—we work so well together. What shall I do without you?"

"I'm quite sure you'll do just as well as you did before I came," she said.

"But *why* do you want to leave?"

"You know perfectly well why. I like working with you, and I'd hoped to go on doing so—but our working relationship is too close to allow for any personal entanglement. Frankly, it would get in the way of the job."

"Not necessarily," he argued. "We'd probably be able to

concentrate better if we admitted the attraction and did something about it, instead of trying to pretend that it doesn't exist."

"All right, I admit it. But we're not in love with each other, and you're married—and as far as I'm concerned, that's that. I'm not exactly flattered, you know, to be regarded as a married man's potential bit on the side."

"But it wouldn't have to be like that! There *is* such a thing as divorce—"

He'd thought of it often enough. Not of the process of being divorced, but of the end product: of having his freedom. He hadn't anticipated mentioning it to Hilary, and now that the thought had emerged, unrehearsed, he found that it alarmed as much as it excited him. But because she had admitted that she found him attractive, he was recklessly prepared to offer her any inducement. "I could get a divorce," he repeated, hoping that his voice didn't sound as unnatural to her as it did to him.

"But not on my account," she said lightly. She took a duster from the door pocket and cleared the last of the mist from the inside of the windscreen. "Oh, come on, Douglas, let's get back on the job. I really am anxious to nail whoever killed Jack Goodrum. A man who loved and was loved by someone as nice as Felicity can't have been all bad."

Quantrill made no move. The rain had started to drizzle down again, and he gazed at it disconsolately. "So where does that leave us?" he asked. "Are you really going to put in for a transfer?"

"That's up to you—you're the boss. You may prefer it if we split up, after this. If you want me to stay, I will. But only on the understanding that we'll never be any closer than we are now."

"All very well for *you*," he grumbled. "You can't expect me to turn off my feelings, just like that."

"You can direct them somewhere else, though," she said. "Why not pay a bit more attention to your marriage?"

"There's precious little of it left, except the appearance . . ."

"Have you tried the kiss of life?" She gave him a whole-heartedly friendly smile. "It really can work wonders, so I'm told."

Quantrill acknowledged her suggestion with a half-scornful, half-rueful nod. The fact was that he found himself considerably relieved that she hadn't taken him up on his rash proposal. What *would* Molly have said, if he'd had to go home and tell her that he wanted a divorce? What would Alison have thought of him? And what kind of trouble would Peter have got into, without a resident father to keep him under control?

Besides, there were all the practical problems that he hadn't contemplated until this minute. What would it all cost? Where would he have lived while his divorce was going through? And who would have kept him supplied with clean shirts and socks and underpants?

All the same, he was still in the prime of life and he wasn't going to succumb tamely to a life-sentence of grandfatherhood. If Hilary thought him attractive, then other young women must, too. Dammit, they did! There was that witness he'd interviewed a few weeks ago, the smartly dressed blue-eyed businesswoman whose husband was working on an oil rig in the middle of the North Sea. She'd definitely given him a look . . . He hadn't been able to follow it up because he was so set on Hilary at the time, but there was nothing to stop him from going back for another interview. And if Hilary disapproved—or better still, showed any sign of jealousy: good.

Vigourous, resolved, he fastened his seat belt, switched on the engine, and positioned the car to re-enter the narrow road.

A tractor, chugging along in the opposite direction at fifteen miles an hour towing a trailer laden with sugar beet, was causing a temporary traffic hold-up. Behind it crawled a large container lorry, its air brakes snorting impatiently. On Quantrill's side of the road, an approaching car kept him stationary, and prevented the lorry from overtaking the tractor and trailer.

As he waited for the road to clear, half a dozen 2-stroke bikes following each other from the direction of Breckham Market came up behind the container lorry and held back, spluttering like demented motor mowers. All of the riders were young, and the last two were displaying L plates.

Quantrill watched them, glad to see that they had the sense not to try to cut in between the tractor and the approaching car. Then he drew in his breath sharply. "That last one—look at that last one!"

Leaning forward, he wiped the windscreen with his fist. The rider bringing up the rear of the small procession of bikes was helmeted and visored like a medieval knight. It was impossible to identify him visually, but although Quantrill recognised both bike and helmet as the property of Peter's friend Darren

Catchpole, he had a closer acquaintance with the rider's navy blue windcheater and dark red cord trousers.

"It is—it's Peter! *Blast* the boy—"

The approaching car passed them, spraying their bonnet with puddle-water. The road was now clear for the container lorry to overtake the tractor, and for the bikes to follow the lorry. In a minute Peter would be away.

Intent on putting an immediate stop to his son's escapade, Quantrill wrenched open the door of his car. He rose to his full height, shouted the boy's name, and flung out his hand as though by doing so he could physically detain him.

Peter saw his father. Quantrill had no doubt about that. The helmet turned towards him, and for a few seconds the boy's body stiffened.

It was something that Quantrill was going to have to live with for the rest of his life: the fact that Peter saw him, knew that he'd been caught disobeying orders, and knew too that retribution wouldn't be long in coming. Not that Quantrill would have carried out his threat to give his son a good hiding—for God's sake, Peter would have *known* that. The boy had never had more than three or four serious smackings in his life, and the last of those was before puberty. Peter had no reason to be afraid of his father's anger. They'd always been a basically happy family. Yes, all right, Quantrill had bawled the boy out often enough, had been sarcastic with him, had despaired over him . . . but God knew it was only because he loved him.

He stood watching helplessly as his son frantically revved the borrowed machine. The container lorry had overtaken the tractor, and the other bikes had begun to follow, but Peter couldn't wait to fall in at the tail of the small procession. The boy shot away, trying to overtake his mates. His wheels slid on the greasy road. The machine skidded, and fell, flinging its rider under the sugar beet trailer.

As though in slow motion, videoed for perpetual mental replay, Quantrill saw his son slide across the road. He saw the boy's borrowed, ill-fitting helmet bang on the asphalt and come off. He saw Peter disappear under the trailer, and he watched the vehicle bump, as if it had run over some fallen globes of sugar beet, before it came to a stop.

Then Quantrill ran. Arms flailing, heart pounding, his shoes seemingly leaden-soled, he willed himself towards his son. Peter lay sprawled on a blanket of mud and wet beet leaves,

colouring both with his blood. His trouser legs were ripped in
several places, revealing the shocking whiteness of protruding,
jagged bone. His long eyelashes, soot-dark against the sudden
pallor of his face, were closed. But he was still alive. His body
twitched, and every now and then he moaned.

Quantrill dropped on his knees beside his son, holding his
hand and calling his name, in an agony of self-recrimination.
Anything he had ever learned about first aid deserted him, but
almost immediately he was joined by Hilary Lloyd and he
remembered thankfully that she had been a nurse. And that
was all he felt towards her, as she did what she could for Peter:
a great thankfulness for her support. Sick with dread, he knew
that the person who really mattered to him was his son.

"How is he?"

"Not good. Let's hope the ambulance comes soon—we need
to get him on a drip."

"His legs—"

"It's not his legs we need to worry about." She felt the boy's
pulse, and shook her head dubiously.

"Can I—will it hurt him if I hold him?"

"I should, if I were you."

Douglas Quantrill knelt on the muddy road in the rain,
cradling Peter's dark head in his lap. First, he offered frantic,
guilty prayers for the boy's survival. Then, as his son's pulse
grew weaker, he abandoned hope; weeping, he bowed his
head against the onslaught of his own personal nuclear winter.

Then the ambulance arrived.

24

During the first forty-eight hours when Peter Quantrill lay
critically injured in the intensive care unit of Yarchester
General hospital, his father scarcely left his side. Quantrill's
colleagues throughout the county were sympathetically concerned; but the job had to go on, and in DCI Quantrill's
absence the Detective Chief Inspector from the neighbouring
Saintsbury division was sent to Breckham Market to take over
the murder investigation.

In the opinion of county headquarters, this was an ideal solution: Chief Inspector Tait had once worked as Quantrill's sergeant, and therefore knew his way round the town already. In the opinion of the members of Breckham Market CID, however, the solution had no merit at all. They had been thankful to see the back of Martin Tait, a young graduate entrant to the force, on his rapid promotion to Inspector. It had been bad enough when he had subsequently reappeared at intervals in his role as a member of the regional crime squad, but at least Chief Inspector Quantrill had been there to slap him down when he became too effortlessly superior. But now, in charge, he was bound to be insufferable.

"Good to be back!" said Tait, a slight, sharp, impeccably suited, fair-haired man, four years younger than Hilary Lloyd. He looked about Quantrill's office with satisfaction before taking his seat, for the first time, behind the Chief Inspector's desk. "And it's good to see you, Hilary. No promotion yet?"

She ignored the question. She and Tait had once been sergeants together at Yarchester, and she intended to take no gratuitous aggravation from him. "You mustn't expect much of a welcome from any of us, in the circumstances," she said. "We're all very anxious about Mr. Quantrill's son."

"It's a traumatic time for the whole family," Tait agreed seriously. "I saw Doug yesterday evening and he's really anguished, on the quiet. Almost as cut up about it as his wife is. I hadn't expected him to be as distressed as that . . ."

"Perhaps you don't know all the circumstances."

"Oh, I think I do. I'm a close friend of Alison, after all: she got in touch with me immediately, and of course I'm doing everything I can to give the family my support."

In her concern for Douglas Quantrill and his wife, Hilary had temporarily forgotten their daughters. "How *is* Alison?" she asked.

"She's taking it harder than I'd have expected, too," said Tait. "Peter used to tease her a lot, and she always seemed to regard him as nothing but a pest. But now his life's in the balance she's recalling their childhood—apparently she adored him when he was small."

"I think his father did, too . . . I do hope this accident draws the Quantrills together, whatever the outcome. But I'm rather afraid that without Peter, Douglas and Molly would drift apart."

"I shouldn't be surprised," said Tait. "I believe Doug's taken quite a shine to you, Hilary, hasn't he?"

"If he ever did," she said, "it was a long time ago." She handed Tait the bulky folder she was carrying. "Here you are, then, sir: John Reuben Goodrum, deceased."

"Ah!" Tait took it eagerly, then looked at his watch. "Right—the best thing I can do for Doug Quantrill is to get this case wrapped up as soon as possible. Give me a very quick briefing, will you?"

Sergeant Lloyd did so. Breckham Market CID were still working, she added, on the burglary at The Mount and the theft of Jack Goodrum's shotgun, as well as through the long list of his disaffected former employees and associates. Goodrum's unofficial partner, Dave Wheeler, had been a strong suspect and still couldn't be eliminated; but the lab's test-firing had shown that his shotgun hadn't been the murder weapon.

"And what's your own theory?"

"I'm not satisfied that Jack's first wife was telling us the truth. I think she knows something. And though I caught only a glimpse of her younger daughter, Tracey, I'm sure the girl was wearing a nose-stud. I'm going back this morning to find out whether Tracey has a boy friend who's a bit of a punk with a gold stud in one ear—that's the description of the bloke who was in the Coney and Thistle on the day of the burglary, asking where he could find Jack Goodrum."

"I see. Well, don't go out until I've had time to read this through and reach my own conclusion. I may well decide that I want you to concentrate on something else."

Chief Inspector Tait gave the sergeant a dismissive nod, but as she reached the door he called her back. "Oh, Hilary—" He favoured her with a charming smile: "I like your shorter hairstyle. It suits you."

"Thank you."

"Do you still make that excellent coffee . . . ?"

"Frequently," she said, with a very cool smile in return. "But your best bet will be to ask one of the lads to fetch you some from the canteen."

Less than an hour later, Sergeant Lloyd was summoned to the Chief Inspector's office. Tait was leaning back in the swivel chair, his feet up on the desk, a look of satisfaction on his face.

"I'm disappointed in you, Hilary," he reproached her. "In you and Doug Quantrill, both . . . This case has an obvious solution!"

"Has it?" Having been prevented from continuing her enquiries, she had immersed herself in the tedious job of checking and cross-checking statements. And when you were doing that, it was always difficult to see the wood for the trees. She sat down, trying not to let Tait's attitude irritate her; unfortunately, he had a nasty habit of being right. "What have I missed?"

"Didn't you ever ask yourself," he said, "why the theft of the shotgun and the murder were both carried out on a Saturday?"

"Yes. We decided we were looking for someone who lived some distance from Breckham Market, and who was working during the week."

"I see. A reasonable assumption, I suppose. But didn't you ask yourselves why the person who stole the shotgun hadn't stayed to do the murder later that same night?"

Hilary explained, patiently, what their theories had been.

"It didn't occur to you, then," said Tait, swinging his legs off the desk and sitting forward in his chair to emphasise his words, "that the person who stole the shotgun couldn't wait for Goodrum's return to The Mount *because he himself had to get back by a certain time*? And that he had to wait a whole week before returning to Breckham Market for the murder *because Saturday was the only day he could get away from his boarding school*?"

Sergeant Lloyd stared at him. "Felicity's son—Matthew Napier?"

"Of course. He's the one with the overriding motive."

"I don't agree. If he'd loved his own father, and resented his parents' divorce, yes. But he didn't—in fact it was Matthew who suggested Austin Napier to us as a suspect."

Tait gave her a patronising smile. "Don't you see what he was up to? He wanted to draw your attention away from himself—and he succeeded, didn't he?"

"But we've no evidence that he disliked his stepfather. He said Jack Goodrum was very generous to him."

"That might have been so. Goodrum probably tried to buy popularity. But Matthew could still have hated his guts! This is something I can tell you from my own experience, Hilary, because my father died when I was sixteen, and after a decent interval my mother began seeing another man. There was nothing much wrong with the fellow, I suppose. But I couldn't stand the idea of him pawing my mother about."

"Did they marry?"

"Certainly not. I made things so unpleasant for him that he took himself off."

"That was arbitrary of you. Didn't you consider your mother's feelings?"

"Oh, I'd acted in her interests as much as my own. It wasn't even as if the man had any money to recommend him. She didn't particularly care for him, and I think she was quite glad, in the end, that he'd gone."

Hilary made no comment. "Felicity Goodrum loved Jack, though," she said thoughtfully. "I can see that Matthew might have felt excluded and hurt about that. And it could have occurred to him that a murder, besides getting rid of his stepfather, would also provide his mother and himself with all Goodrum's money . . . Yes, all right, Martin, I'll buy the motive. But Matthew Napier is at school at Saxted, twenty miles away. How do you suggest—"

She remembered, and gave herself the answer immediately. "Of course—his father told us that he'd just bought Matthew a motor bike. But it could only be a low-powered one, at his age. Saxted to Breckham Market and back, especially at this time of year, would be too long a journey."

"No it wouldn't, given his motivation. And you'll be interested to hear that I've telephoned his school, and dicovered that Matthew Napier is known to have gone out on his motor bike, alone, on both Saturday 15th and Saturday 22nd. On each occasion he was back in his study bedroom at the required time, 10:30 p.m. But as he's a sixth-former, and is allowed some degree of independence, the school can give us no information about where he went."

Hilary thought about it. "So your theory is that Matthew rode to Breckham Market on the 15th. He'd kept in touch with his mother, so he'd have known that she and Jack planned to be out that day. Then he broke into The Mount to steal one of the shotguns he knew his stepfather kept there. He intended to return the following Saturday and kill Jack, but he disguised his plan by stealing various other items to make it look like an ordinary burglary . . . Yes, that all fits. But *you* didn't see the state the house was left in, Martin. The boy loved his mother, I'm certain of that, and I can't believe that he'd have deliberately offended her by fouling the house while he was about it."

"I can," said Tait.

Sergeant Lloyd took a deep breath. "And there's another

thing," she said obstinately. She knew she was going to lose the argument, because Martin Tait wasn't a man to put forward a theory without having thought it through; but she wasn't going to let him make any unchallenged pronouncements.

"Nothing very bulky was stolen from The Mount," she went on. "But even so, how do you suggest the boy removed it? There was far too much loot for him to have carried away on his bike, as well as the shotgun."

"According to Goodrum's statement after the burglary," said Tait, "the shotgun was in a waterproof carrying bag. His stepson could have hidden it somewhere in the gardens—"

"We *searched* the gardens."

"—somewhere just outside the gardens, and picked it up the following Saturday. As for the rest of the loot: did you think to search the house for it? *Did you think to search the boy's own room?*"

Hilary seethed, quietly. Then she said, "We have no evidence that Matthew Napier knows how to handle a shotgun."

"But I've found out that he's a member of the Saxted College combined cadet force, and that he knows how to fire a rifle. I have no doubt he'd be lethal with a shotgun at a range of eight yards. And then of course," Tait continued, enjoying himself at his former colleague's expense, "Matthew knows his way round the outside of The Mount. He'd have had no trouble in finding the best place to fire the gun from. Oh, and the footprint that was found in the downstairs cloakroom after the burglary— what size was it?"

"You know perfectly well it was a nine . . ."

"Ah yes. The headmaster of Saxted College thought it an odd question for me to ask, but he found out from the matron that Matthew Napier does take a size nine. And as it happens, the boy does possess a pair of training shoes with a ridged composition sole—"

Hilary looked at him. "Do you know something, sir?" she said. "You really are *sickening*."

"So I've heard," said Tait modestly. "But that's how I came to be a Chief Inspector while you're still a sergeant, Sergeant . . ." He laughed, and stood up. "Oh, come on, Hilary, don't be miffed. We're old friends, aren't we? In fact I don't mind telling you that I took quite a shine to you myself, at one time. Get your coat on, love, and come with me to Saxted to pick Matthew Napier up."

"No thanks. I've got too much to do, with the boss away."

"Rubbish, you're just making excuses!" Martin Tait was no taller than Hilary Lloyd, but he contrived to put an indulgent arm round her shoulders and shepherd her to the door. "Come for the ride, and I'll buy you a good lunch afterwards."

"Really, no thank you." She slipped away from his arm, and turned to face him with a firm but pleasant smile. "Yes, you're right: I'm miffed that I didn't spot Matthew Napier as a suspect. But I still intend to stick to my plan to interview Jack Goodrum's daughter Tracey, the one with the nose-stud. Because there has to be some good reason why a bit of a punk with an ear-stud, who's unknown in Breckham Market, should have been in the town on the day the shotgun was stolen, asking where her father lived."

25

By noon the following day, when Chief Inspector Tait and Sergeant Lloyd met again, the weather had changed.

November had started mild and damp, and deteriorated to cold and wet. But now, Breckham Market seemed to have dried out overnight. The low cloud had dispersed, the temperature had fallen sharply, the air had been crisped by frost. The sun was putting in a guest appearance, and Hilary had suggested to Tait that they should make the most of it by walking through the town to lunch at the Coney and Thistle.

But it was not an occasion for celebration. Martin Tait, very much the aspirant county chief constable in brown racing trilby, cashmere scarf and Burberry, was unusually silent. When spoken to, he answered abruptly.

They left divisional headquarters, crossed the main London–Yarchester road, and walked down Market Hill into the narrow streets of the old town. Most other pedestrians looked reasonably cheerful, perked up by the sunshine; but Tait only scowled.

"It was completely logical. Wasn't it?" he demanded at last.

"Completely," confirmed Hilary. "I couldn't fault it, anyway, and you know how hard I tried."

"Matthew Napier's statement was so feeble. He 'didn't like

the school' so he spent both Saturday afternoons 'just riding round on his own.' And he said he spent both evenings on his own at the cinema in Woodbridge. That's one of the flimsiest alibis I've ever heard."

"But you can't call it an alibi, Martin, if it was what the boy actually *did* on those two Saturdays. And there's no point in disputing it, if you've discovered that there isn't enough mileage on the bike since he acquired it to have got him here and back twice. You can't argue with a milometer."

"I most certainly can! They're not difficult to alter if you know how, and if you've got the right tools. And Saxted College prides itself on its craft workshops."

"Even so—"

Martin Tait sighed. "Yes, all right, Hilary. Even so, what's the point in pursuing the boy, when you've discovered that he didn't do the burglary. *And* when we know that his stepfather's shotgun wasn't the murder weapon."

They had reached the market place, which was used as a car-park for the Town Hall on five days a week, and for the parish church of St. Botolph on Sundays. Today however was market day. Vehicles were barred, and the open space had sprung into vigorous commerical life. Stalls piled high with fruit and vegetables were besieged by customers, and the detectives had to edge through the crush to reach the Coney and Thistle.

On their way, Tait paused to greet his former bank manager, now retired, and took the opportunity to restore his own ego by mentioning his recent promotion. Hilary went to a stallholder Douglas Quantrill had introduced her to, the wife of a local market gardener whose parsnips and onions and celery still had fresh earth clinging to them, and bought a bag of crisp russet apples and the makings for a winter salad. Just as she had completed her purchases, Tait came to join her.

There were a couple of old galvanised buckets on the end of the stall, crammed with shaggy garden chrysanthemums. Their rich colours, bronze and yellow and dark red, glowed in the sun. On an impulse, Tait bought a bunch and handed them, their stalks damply paper-wrapped, to Hilary.

"Sorry I was so sickening yesterday," he said.

"Martin, how lovely!" She closed her eyes and sniffed their spicy scent. "Mmm—instant nostalgia . . . Autumn walks in the park opposite our house when I was a child . . . Thank you very much. Let's fight our way into the Coney, and I'll buy you a drink—after all, the theory *I* was pursuing yesterday hasn't really got us any further forward, has it?"

Over hot toast, pâté and wine—and it was pleasant, for once, Hilary reflected, to share that kind of lunch with a colleague of her own generation—they discussed Jack Goodrum's original family. As the sergeant had suspected, Doreen had not told her and Quantrill the truth on their first visit.

When she returned to Factory Bungalow, late the previous morning, Hilary had contrived to catch Doreen's younger daughter Tracey before the girl had a chance to dress and make her escape. Tracey, as Hilary had thought from the brief glimpse she'd had of her, was a bit of a punk: the colour of her spiky hair was unnatural without being conspicuous, and her facial ornament was limited to ear-rings and the one gold stud in her nose. Without doubt—Hilary recognised all the signs—the girl was a drug-user.

All three female Goodrums had, as usual, been in their nightwear. Hilary had insisted that Doreen and Tracey should sit down with her at the living room table, though she agreed that Sharon would be better occupied in making a pot of tea.

But sitting with mother and daughter over the ingredients and the dirty crockery of their permanent meal was one thing; persuading them to talk about Jack Goodrum's death was another. They were obviously unaccustomed to communicating with each other, on this as on any other subject.

Sergeant Lloyd had broken their silence by telling them—without saying how she knew the man's name—that she had visited the home of Jack's one-time partner, Dave Wheeler, and had taken his shotgun for forensic examination. Doreen Goodrum had immediately burst into an angry denunciation of Wheeler.

She'd rung him, she said, a week or two back, to say that she'd found out where Jack was living. Jack had owed both of them, and she'd wanted to meet Dave Wheeler to discuss how best to go about getting their rights. But she'd deliberately kept Jack's whereabouts to herself, because she'd been afraid that Dave might go rushing there on his own account, and so spoil her chances.

And then she'd read in the local paper about the burglary at her ex-husband's house in Breckham Market. She'd been livid. Dave Wheeler had done it, she'd been sure. But when she rang to tell him what she thought of him, he had denied it. He said his old mother had seen in the paper that a shotgun had been stolen—so it couldn't have been him, because he had a shotgun of his own, as Doreen very well knew.

But Doreen hadn't believed his denials. Dave had been crafty, that was all: stealing a gun he didn't need so that he wouldn't be suspected. She had tried to go on discussing their joint plan for tackling Jack, but Dave seemed to have lost interest. There would be police about, after the burglary, he had said, and he for one wasn't going near Jack's place, with or without a shotgun, until the hoo-ha had died down.

And then, having already helped himself to money and jewellery and stuff, without even offering to share it, if Dave hadn't gone back to Breckham Market the following week and taken his final revenge by shooting Jack! It wasn't right, Doreen had protested, mopping her flushed face. It wasn't *fair* . . .

Sipping the tea that Sharon had made—strong, but perfectly acceptable if you didn't notice the imperfectly clean cups— Hilary had revealed that there was no evidence to connect Dave Wheeler with the burglary at The Mount. She had come, she told them, because she believed that Tracey might be able to help her.

Tracey, thin and pale and withdrawn, had kept her eyes down and said nothing until she was asked a direct question, when she answered belligerently. She was smoking ordinary cheap cigarettes, but she held them in shaking fingers.

What if she did have a boy friend who had hair like hers and wore an ear-stud? It was the fashion, wasn't it? No, she didn't know what size shoes he wore. No, she didn't know if he'd ever been to Breckham Market. What would he want to go there for?

Yes, all right, she needed money. Didn't everybody? Yes, she reckoned her Dad owed her. Yes, she knew he'd moved to Breckham Market—she'd heard her Mum phoning Dave Wheeler, so she'd looked through the local paper and found the report of the inquest that mentioned her Dad's name. So what?

No, of course her boy friend hadn't gone to Breckham Market last Saturday and shot her Dad! What'd be the point of that? The mean old sod was no good to them dead. As her mother said, it must've been that cheating Dave Wheeler who shot him. Tracey was glad the police had got on to Dave—she hoped they'd put him away for the rest of his life.

It was then that Hilary had explained how forensic tests had shown that Dave Wheeler's gun was not the murder weapon. That meant, she told Tracey, that the police were still urgently looking for Jack Goodrum's own gun, the one that had been stolen during the burglary.

But the police weren't at the moment interested in the burglary itself, she emphasised. That was a minor matter. It was the murderer they wanted.

They had reason to believe that a man answering the description of Tracey's boy friend had done the burglary. If that was so, and if he wasn't the murderer, it would be in his—and Tracey's—interests, Hilary had told the girl, to hand over her father's gun in order to prove it.

"A very useful tactic," agreed Chief Inspector Tait. "It rarely fails to work."

"Oh yes, it worked. They promptly turned in Jack's own AYA side-by-side 12-bore. But since forensic says that it wasn't the murder weapon either, it doesn't take us anywhere, unfortunately. We've got Tracey's boy friend—not a nice young man— for the burglary, and Tracey herself for handling stolen goods. They'd intended to return to Breckham Market, disguised, and threaten her father into giving them more money, but his murder put a stop to their plans. And as far as *that's* concerned, we're still plodding through the wretchedly long list of people who had good reason to hate Jack Goodrum."

Tait took their empty glasses to the bar, and returned with cups of coffee. "It's the second Mrs. Goodrum's ex-husband who interests me most," he said. "Austin Napier QC . . ."

"He may be a QC," said Hilary, "but he's also unbalanced, as far as his relationship with his ex-wife is concerned."

"That's exactly why he interests me." Tait looked at his watch. "I'll go up to London and try to catch him at his chambers. The three-thirty train should do it—I can't spare the time to go by car, I've a briefcase full of my own Saintsbury work to deal with. What about you, Hilary? Shall you be out on enquiries this afternoon, or in the office?"

She had been admiring her bunch of chrysanthemums, and didn't answer immediately. She sniffed them again, intrigued by their instant evocation of her suburban childhood. Then she said, "They remind me of my family . . . And that reminded me of the poor Quantrills, and what you said about Alison's anxiety for Peter because she'd loved him so much as a child. And *that* reminded me of Eunice Bell and her brother Cuthbert. You remember Clanger, the town drunk, don't you?"

"Yes, of course. I heard he'd been killed in a road accident—he played chicken once too often, I suppose?"

"That was what everyone thought, except his sister. She tried to convince us that he'd been murdered. We didn't entirely disbelieve her, but we simply couldn't prove it. The thing is, though, Martin—the man who drove into Clanger was Jack Goodrum."

"*Really?* Well then, doesn't that suggest that Clanger's sister might have taken a shotgun to Goodrum in retaliation?"

"We've thought of that one, but Douglas knows she was at the Operatic Society's performance of *My Fair Lady* on the night of the murder. No, the point I'm making is that Eunice Bell couldn't suggest a really convincing reason why Goodrum might have wanted Clanger dead. She told us that they'd known each other as boys, and that they got into some kind of mischief for which Jack was thrashed by her father. But she didn't know what the mischief was . . . and I'm beginning to wonder whether it was something more serious than she thought."

"That's an interesting possibility," said Tait. "You mean the boys had shared a secret, all those years ago, and Jack Goodrum was afraid Clanger might blurt it out?"

"Something like that, yes. After all, Jack was newly arrived in the town, and very much in love with his wife. If there was some old scandal that only he and Clanger knew about, Jack wouldn't want to risk having it revived to spoil his marriage."

"Ah—but perhaps Clanger wasn't the only other boy originally involved?"

"That's what I've been thinking. We could be looking for someone who's had no connection with Jack Goodrum for thirty or forty years. Someone who recognised him as soon as he returned to Breckham Market, and took the opportunity to settle a very old score."

26

Although he was interested in Sergeant Lloyd's theory, Chief Inspector Tait declined to give the pursuit of it any priority.

"It's not as though we're having to search for a motive for

Goodrum's murder," he pointed out as they left the Coney.
"Just the opposite—there are so many people who had reason
to hate the man that it's hard to know which lead to follow next.
So unless you can come up rapidly with some proof that he
intended to kill Clanger Bell, I'd rather you didn't waste time
digging about in Goodrum's remote past."

"That's fair," agreed Hilary. "What's niggling at me, you see,
is the fact that there were three such respectable and
convincing witnesses to Clanger Bell's death. It was on their
evidence that the Coroner decided that Jack Goodrum didn't
have a chance of avoiding the collision. I went to interview all
three of them and I couldn't find any real ground for suspicion,
but I'm still not entirely satisfied. Come and see where it
happened."

Hilary darted up Pump Hill, just off the market place, the
narrow street in which Clanger Bell's favourite pub was
situated. The Boot, an inn since the eighteenth century,
displayed its sign in the form of a gilt-painted wooden riding
boot that hung from an iron bracket high above the doorway of
the flint-faced building. The pub was too small to be brought
up to the carpeted and upholstered standards now demanded
by female social drinkers, and so it remained what it had
always been, a male preserve with a doubtful reputation.

Despite that—and the fact that a betting shop had been
strategically placed next door to the Boot—Pump Hill itself
was a perfectly respectable street. It also contained a bank, the
offices of a building society, and a number of small country
town shops; in addition, it provided a useful pedestrian link
between the upper residential part of the town and the market
place. There was nothing suspicious to be read into the
presence on Pump Hill of the three eye-witnesses to Clanger
Bell's death.

Hilary pointed out to Tait where they had been standing:
Mrs. Napthen outside the Trustee Savings Bank near the top
of the street, Mr. Woodrow by the ironmonger's opposite the
Boot, Mr. Pike at the greengrocer's at the bottom. "They were
so conveniently spread out," Hilary said. "And they all
happened to be looking in the right direction at the right time.
Miss Bell thought that suspicious. But the DCI made the point
that everyone who knew Clanger would always stand and
watch, when they saw him emerging from a pub, to see
whether or not he was going to make it across the road."

"I've done it myself," Tait agreed. The detectives moved

back, out of the way of shoppers and pedestrians, into the angle between a sixteenth-century timber-framed building, now an electrical retailer's, and the late eighteenth-century grey brick of the building society. "But these three eye-witnesses," he went on; "after Clanger was knocked down, did they volunteer their information on the spot?"

"Yes, and that seems significant. Some people do rush towards road accidents, a few wanting to help but most of them with a kind of instinctive ghoulishness. Others just as instinctively hurry away, even if—perhaps because—they saw what happened, and they don't want to be involved. But I understand that our three witnesses hung about until the police arrived, and then spoke up without any persuasion."

"Did they? And what have they got in common?" asked Tait. "Are they all local people?"

"Yes, Breckham Market born and bred, so they told me."

"Age?"

"Mrs. Napthen's a widow in her late fifties. The men are both widowers, both retired—Mr. Woodrow's late sixties, Mr. Pike's well into his seventies."

"They're all older than Goodrum, then. And not exactly affluent?"

"Far from it. They're decent, respectable people who've worked hard all their lives, and they're now managing as best they can on their state pensions."

"If they were all brought up in the town, they knew each other, presumably?"

"Not necessarily. They seem to live quiet, rather lonely lives in different parts of the town, keeping themselves to themselves."

Chief Inspector Tait folded his arms and thought silently for a few moments. "But Goodrum might well have known them when he was a butcher's boy . . . What did you ask them?"

"Whether they knew the driver of the vehicle that had knocked Clanger down. All three of them denied it, and repeated what they'd told the Coroner. But now I've thought about it again, I wouldn't be at all surprised if Jack Goodrum had planted them on Pump Hill."

"Try them again, Hilary," said Tait, making a quick decision. "When you went to see them, Goodrum was still alive. Now he's dead, they may be prepared to talk. I'll give you the rest of today to prove that Clanger's death was no accident—if you can't, your theory's a non-runner. All right?"

"Thank you, sir," she said.

* * *

The last time he'd been here, Martin Tait reflected as he stood
on the platform at Breckham Market railway station waiting for
the London train, was with Alison. That was four years ago,
when he was a detective sergeant and she was his chief
inspector's daughter. He'd come to see her off, back to her
London job, and it was here—just about where he was now
standing—that he'd first kissed her, and realised that he was
already half in love with her.

A lot had happened since then. But their relationship had
endured, in an off-on fashion that suited him. He thought he
might well marry Alison, eventually; but he had no intention
of doing so before his next promotion. Superintendent by the
time he was thirty, that was his immediate goal.

True, he ran the risk of losing her by waiting so long. But
Alison had so far shown no serious inclination to desert him for
anyone else, though she'd rejected his suggestion that they
should live together, and had even refused (to his great relief)
the premature offer of marriage he'd made when he thought he
was going to inherit a fortune. The fact that she had turned to
him for comfort and support in the aftermath of her young
brother's accident had convinced Martin that he was secure in
her affections.

He walked briskly to the far end of the platform, executive
briefcase in hand. He was looking forward to his visit to the
Middle Temple, where Austin Napier QC had his chambers.
Though Suffolk-born, Tait was no countryman; he had chosen
to join the county police force only because, as a graduate, he
would shine more brightly among rural policemen than he
would have done in the Met. But he welcomed this opportunity to pit his wits against a London barrister. He didn't doubt
he'd make a better job of it than poor old Doug Quantrill had.

The brightness of the day was fading. From the high,
exposed platform, Tait looked westwards across waste ground
(fields, four years ago; now earmarked for major building
development) to the small town half a mile away, where mist
was beginning to rise from the river and mingle with chimney
smoke. The air was chilly enough for him to be glad of his hat
and scarf.

Turning to retrace his steps he saw, far away up the line, a
dark pinpoint that was the approaching train. At the same time
he noticed an Austin Metro being driven into the station yard

at full lick. A young woman who reminded him of Hilary Lloyd got out and hurried towards the entrance.

It was good to be working with Hilary again, Tait reflected. He liked having a woman sergeant, especially one who was always stylishly dressed as well as efficient. They had a very satisfactory relationship: she knew how to be friendly with him without losing sight of the fact that he was in charge, and that what he said went. Perhaps he could inveigle her over to the Saintsbury division? Doug Quantrill would no doubt be furious, but Hilary herself might well be glad to get away from Alison's father's inarticulate admiration.

The young woman who darted on to the platform, still in a hurry but with hardly a hair of her new short style out of place, was in fact Hilary Lloyd. She looked about her, caught sight of him, and gave him a more-enthusiastic-than-usual greeting.

"I'm so glad I've caught you, Martin! No need to rush off to London—we're on to something here."

Chief Inspector Tait frowned. The train was now well in sight, and *he* intended to be the judge of whether or not he should board it.

"Is it what you thought?" he asked. "Did Goodrum pay his eye-witnesses to be on Pump Hill that afternoon at closing time, when he knew Clanger would be leaving the Boot?"

"In effect," Hilary agreed, "though he did it less crudely than that. So far I've talked to only one of them, Mrs. Napthen. She's very upset about Jack's murder. In her view he was a kind, generous man. He told her, two or three weeks ago, that he'd had the luck to make his fortune, and that he'd sought her out because her family had always been friends and customers of his grandparents. He said he knew that a widow such as herself must find it difficult to make ends meet, and he hoped she'd allow him to pay her electricity bill for her."

The train had pulled in. The diesel engine stood throbbing as carriage doors were opened and passengers began to board. Tait saw no reason, from what Hilary had told him, to postpone his own journey; but he didn't want her to think he was brushing her off. He began to walk up the platform towards the first-class carriages, with the sergeant at his elbow.

"Didn't Mrs. Napthen realise there was something fishy about Goodrum's approach?" he said. "After all, he was a stranger to her, wasn't he?"

"Yes—but don't forget that Breckham Market was much smaller, thirty-odd years ago, and therefore much more of a

community than it is now. Mrs. Napthen remembered Jack
Goodrum as a boy, and she enjoyed talking to him about old
times. She saw no reason to be suspicious."

"Not even when he asked her not to mention to anyone that
he was paying her bill?" said Tait. "I imagine that's what he
said—?"

"Oh yes. He told her that she must be sure to keep warm
during the coming winter, and use as much electricity as she
needed, because he would go on paying her bills. But she
mustn't tell anyone, or even mention that she knew him,
because he couldn't possibly do the same for all his grandfather's old customers. Mrs. Napthen was special, he told her,
because her mother had been such a good friend to his
grandmother."

"Hah!" said Tait. He opened a carriage door and stood with
one foot on the step. Parcels and mail bags were still being
loaded into the guard's van, so he could give Hilary another
minute. "And then he talked her into hanging about on Pump
Hill—?"

"That was on his second visit, when he took her the receipt
for the electricity bill. He didn't actually give her money—I
suppose he thought she might have been too proud to accept
it. Oh, and he went to her house on foot, presumably to give
her neighbours no chance of recognising his Range Rover."

"Crafty devil . . ." said Tait.

"But charming with it," said Hilary. "At least, when he
wanted to be. He offered to take Mrs. Napthen for a ride in his
car, the following afternoon, and said he'd pick her up outside
the Trustee Savings Bank on Pump Hill. While she was
waiting there, she saw Clanger knocked over by a Range
Rover. At first, she didn't realise that Jack was the driver. But
when she recognised him she felt that the least she could do,
as he'd been so good to her, was to wait until the police came
so that she could tell them he was blameless.

"And that's what she still genuinely thinks, Martin—despite
the fact that she remembers having noticed the same Range
Rover just before the accident. It was parked beside the
pavement in Crown Street, across from the top of Pump Hill.
The driver was sitting at the wheel, she said. I tried parking
there just now, and even from my Metro I had a good view
down the hill as far as the door of the Boot. Jack Goodrum
would have been in an ideal position to see Clanger emerge
from the pub, and to set out on a collision course."

"You'd still have had difficulty in proving his intention, if you'd tried to charge him," said Tait. The station staff were slamming carriage doors shut. He swung himself inside, slammed his own door, placed his briefcase at his feet, lowered the window and leaned out to conclude the conversation.

"It's satisfactory, I agree, to know that your suspicions were well-founded—but it doesn't actually get us anywhere, does it? You already knew that Jack Goodrum was a villain. What we're supposed to be doing is finding the man who murdered him."

Still becomingly flushed—probably now, Tait realised, from indignation rather than hurry—Sergeant Lloyd stood her ground and tried to argue with him.

"But because Jack planned Clanger's death so carefully, he must have had a very strong motive for killing him. If we uncover that, we may be able to establish the motive for his own murder."

"Hilary, love . . ." said Tait wearily. He liked keenness in a sergeant, but in his new rank he felt all the sobering responsibility of command. "We don't *need* any more motives, do we? I'm going to London for the express purpose of interviewing the man who had the strongest motive of the lot: insane jealousy of his ex-wife's new husband. In the unlikely event—"

The train gave a sudden jolt forward, and as suddenly stopped. Tait lurched against the door frame, banging his shoulder and almost dislodging his trilby. He made a grab for the hat and adjusted it with dignity.

"Anyway," he said, avoiding the sergeant's amused eyes, "at this stage I don't want you to waste time excavating Clanger Bell's past. *If* I don't succeed with Austin Napier, we'll talk about it again."

Sensing that the train was about to move, he intended this to be his parting word. But nothing happened. For a few awkward moments he felt obliged to remain at the open window, just as Hilary evidently felt obliged to remain on the platform.

"When do you expect to get back?" she enquired politely.

"That depends how long it takes me to break Austin Napier. I may have to stay overnight. But if I do get back at a reasonable time this evening, I'll go round to the Quantrills'. I promised Alison I'd see her tonight if I could."

"Do please give all of them my love," said Hilary soberly.

"Yes, of course," said Tait. Then he thought about it. "Not to

Doug, I won't," he said. "He's very vulnerable at the moment—Molly's in such a state that she doesn't realise that *he* needs support. If I were to give him your love, he'd probably take it too personally . . . How about love to Alison and her mother, and best regards to the old man?"

"Very diplomatic," said Hilary. She looked up at him with a friendly smile. "No wonder they made you a chief inspector."

The train began to move, slowly and this time more smoothly. "Good luck with the Queen's Counsel," she said, standing back.

"I say—" Remembering that he'd given the sergeant no positive instructions, Tait leaned further out of the window to catch her attention: "You're going straight to the office, aren't you?"

"No—I'm going to Tower House," she called back. "I want to talk to Clanger Bell's sister."

"I said *don't*, Sergeant Lloyd!" he snapped. But the train was already carrying him away, and the infuriating woman pretended she couldn't hear.

27

At Tower House, Eunice Bell was supervising the loading of a small removal van. The job was almost finished, but the van was barely one-third full.

She had, after all, decided to leave Breckham Market as soon as possible. With Cuthbert now buried in the family plot in the town cemetery, there was no reason for her to remain in the cold gloomy house any longer. Her solicitor had warned her of the possibility of vandalism if Tower House were left empty, but she had made up her mind to risk it. She couldn't imagine that anyone would want to buy the property as it stood, and her accountant had reassured her that the value of the site alone—nearly two acres of prime building land—would compensate for the value of the house if it were to become uninhabitable.

Having decided on the move, Miss Bell had booked a room for the winter at the Angel in Saintsbury. The few items of furniture she wanted to keep, together with her own china and linen and books and pictures, were going into store until such time as she could find and buy her ideal Georgian town house. The rest of the furniture and the effects of Tower House were going to be disposed of *in situ* by auction; not so much in the expectation of realising money, as with the intention of simply getting rid of the hated things.

The removal van left. As she went indoors to pack her clothes and the personal belongings she would be taking with her in her car, Eunice Bell felt an unaccustomed lightness of the heart. She rejoiced—inwardly, without expression—in the knowledge that she was about to shake off all the grim associations of Tower House: the unhappiness, the fear of punishment, the pain, the adolescent shame. Now at last she could be her own woman, totally independent, free of the past.

"Yes, Miss Lloyd?"

"I've come to apologise to you, Miss Bell."

Hilary had noticed the removal van outside Tower House when she was on her way to the station. It was not so much contrariness that had induced her to disobey Chief Inspector Tait, as the realisation that if Eunice Bell were to leave the house, the evidence of her brother's boyhood association with Jack Goodrum might well be lost.

Miss Bell looked, to Hilary, exactly as she had done at their previous meeting: stiff, self-controlled, severe in navy blue. The Tower House drawing room was even gloomier and colder, more deeply overshadowed by the monkey puzzle tree, than the sergeant remembered it. A difference, however, was that the carpets had been rolled, the heavy mahogany furniture had been lined up, and everything was now labelled with lot numbers.

"I won't attempt to invite you to sit down," said Eunice Bell in her strong, spiny voice, taking up her stand in front of the empty marble fireplace. "I shall be leaving for good tomorrow morning, and I still have all my packing to do."

"I'll try not to keep you, then. I've come to tell you," said Hilary, "that we now have reason to believe that your brother's death wasn't an accident. As you'll appreciate, we can't prove this or make any charges, now that Jack Goodrum's dead. But I wanted you to have the satisfaction of knowing that your suspicions were well-founded. I do apologise, on Mr. Quantrill's behalf as well as my own, for having taken so long to believe you."

Eunice Bell gave a winter smile, and ducked her head in acknowledgement. "Thank you, Miss Lloyd." She paused, then added: "I see from the local newspaper that the Quantrills' son has been badly injured. I had a conversation with the Chief Inspector only last Saturday night at the Town Hall, and I sincerely hope the boy makes a good recovery. Will you please convey that message to Mr. Quantrill?"

Hilary promised that she would, and found herself being ushered out into the echoing, black and white tiled hall. But she declined to be shown the door.

"There is another reason why I came, Miss Bell," she said firmly. "Although we can't charge Jack Goodrum with your brother's murder, we have to find out *why* he did it."

"I told you why, Miss Lloyd. It was in revenge for a thrashing my father gave him."

Hilary shook her head. "I doubt it. Oh, we'd have accepted that, if Jack Goodrum's own death had been from natural causes and all we'd wanted was a note to put on our files. But we're investigating Goodrum's murder—and that involves looking into his past. We know he planned your brother's death very carefully, and that suggests a much stronger motive than revenge for a long-ago thrashing. Wouldn't you agree?"

Eunice Bell inclined her head. "I take your point. You think the two murders might be connected by some past event?"

"Yes. That's why I need to find out all I can about your late brother, Miss Bell. And that's why I've come—to ask, before you move out of this house, if I may search his room?"

"For what?"

The question came at her like a rapier, and Hilary parried it with an apologetic smile. "I'm afraid I shan't know until I find it."

"You saw Cuthbert's room when you were here with Mr. Quantrill," said Miss Bell. "I can assure you that it contains nothing of any significance."

"I don't suppose it does," Hilary agreed. "But then, that room hasn't been used for years, has it? What I'd like to search is the room he actually slept in."

Eunice Bell remained as stiffly composed as ever, but she seemed to have shrivelled in size, as though the coldness of Tower House had finally penetrated her bones. At first she made no reply. Then she said, "Have you a warrant to search my house?"

"No. And I won't try to pretend that I could get one. I've

come to ask for your co-operation, Miss Bell. If you choose to withhold it, that's your legal right, as I'm sure you know. But that would leave us—not just me, but the Chief Inspector and the Superintendent—asking ourselves *why*."

There was another silence. Eunice Bell stood ramrod-straight, her hands folded in front of her. Her bony face remained impassive, but a small patch of red appeared on either cheek-bone.

"Is pride so difficult to recognise?" she asked.

Hilary shook her head. "Pride can sometimes be misplaced, though," she suggested. "Don't forget that your brother was very well known to the police in Breckham Market. He spent a night in the cells several times a year. We were all fond of him—I'm sure you must have noticed a number of policemen at his funeral—but we couldn't avoid knowing that he persistently neglected himself. We never held you to blame for his physical condition, and if his room is equally neglected I shan't consider that your responsibility either."

Eunice Bell's high colour abated a little. She gave a stiffly gracious inclination of her head. Explaining that she had locked her brother's ground-floor room against the auctioneer's men, she went upstairs for the key.

Sergeant Lloyd walked down the tiled hall and into the narrower passage beyond, glancing at the lot-numbered furniture until she found what she was looking for. The heavy glass-fronted mahogany gun cabinet that Douglas Quantrill had noticed on their first visit was now empty. Hilary opened it. The cabinet, lined with green baize, was fitted to hold the four shotguns that the Chief Inspector had seen there before Jack Goodrum's murder. The only means of security was a simple door lock.

"I'm glad to see you've got rid of the guns already," said Hilary as Miss Bell returned. "Mr. Quantrill was concerned about them after our visit. They're dangerous things to leave in a cabinet like this."

"So Mr. Glaze—the auctioneer—pointed out. He took them away last Thursday for safety, and he's going to put them in a specialist sale."

"Were they your father's?"

"My grandfather's. Father didn't shoot, but Grandpapa was a keen shot. I can remember seeing him lovingly cleaning his guns long after he was physically incapable of going out with them."

"They haven't been used for a long time, then?"

"No. Grandpapa tried to interest Cuthbert in shooting at an early age, but my brother was a very gentle boy. He hated—as I did—to see rabbits bowled over and birds brought thumping down from the air."

"My own feelings, exactly," said Hilary. "There's quite enough death about already, without any of us contributing to it voluntarily." She gave the older woman an encouraging smile. "Is that the key to your brother's room?"

Eunice Bell's spots of high colour had returned. She said nothing, but led the way through a studded green baize door that had once separated the kitchen and servants' quarters from the rest of the house.

The dimly lit passage they entered had a clinging, frowsty smell, partly attributable to the rising damp that moistened the cracked floor tiles and tide-marked the walls. At the far end was a stout back door. An old wooden tea-trolley stood beside the door of the last room on the left. On the top shelf of the trolley was an empty tray; on the bottom shelf, a lidded basket labelled with the name of an Ipswich laundry.

"It was Cuthbert's choice," said Eunice Bell defensively, "to move into what used to be the cook-housekeeper's room. When my mother died, almost twenty years ago, my brother and I rearranged our lives. I have my own self-contained rooms on the first floor. Cuthbert wanted to be down here, on the ground floor of the tower, so that he could come and go as he pleased through the back door. Our paths rarely crossed.

"I cooked a meal for both of us each evening and left his food on this trolley, together with his pocket money for the next day. Cuthbert usually remembered to put out his dirty dishes for my daily woman to collect. She would have cleaned his room, of course, but he preferred to keep it locked. He was responsible for changing his own sheets and his personal linen. He didn't do it very often, I'm afraid, but I couldn't supervise him without invading his privacy. And that was something neither of us wanted."

"I understand," said Hilary. "Have you looked round his room since his death? Have you moved anything?"

Eunice Bell allowed one corner of her mouth to twitch in distaste. "I opened the door on the day after he was killed," she said. "One of your uniformed colleagues returned Cuthbert's possessions to me. There was a little money, his briefcase, and the key to this room. As I say, I opened the door.

But I closed it again rapidly—and I really would recommend you not to go in."

"Don't worry, Miss Bell. I've been a policewoman for a long time. I shan't be shocked, I promise you."

Eunice Bell unlocked the door in silence. She opened it just wide enough to enable her to reach in and switch on the electric light, then turned and walked away. Hilary pushed the door wide open.

She had seen and smelled worse living quarters: druggies' squats in Yarchester, vagrants' dossers, the six-bedroomed house that a wealthy eccentric shared with forty-eight cats. Clanger Bell's room, harshly illuminated by a single electric bulb, was less filthy than any of those, though the bed looked as if it hadn't been made for a decade or more, and soiled clothes lay about in ripe heaps.

Even so, Sergeant Lloyd was shaken. What got to her was not the appearance of the room, nor the foreground smell, so much as the atmosphere. As soon as she stepped inside, she felt enclosed in such a mesh of wretchedness, of frustration, of grief and bitterness and despair, that she backed out again, overwhelmed.

It wouldn't be impossible, she reflected as she swallowed hard and quickly closed the door, for her to search Clanger's room on her own, if she had to. But just at the moment she saw no good reason why she should.

The back door was open. Eunice Bell had made a point of letting a blast of cold fresh air into the passage. She stood outside in the gathering November darkness with her back to the house, her head held high, but breathing rather more deeply than usual.

Hilary joined her. "I see what you mean," she said quietly. "But what are you going to do? The room will have to be cleared before you can put the house up for sale."

"I know, and I can't face doing it myself. Still less am I prepared to ask my cleaner—or anyone in Breckham Market— to do the job for me. Pride again, you see, Miss Lloyd. So I've decided to keep the room locked until after the contents of the house have been auctioned. Then I'll send in a professional firm of cleaners from Ipswich or Yarchester. They can drag everything outside and burn it, and then fumigate the place."

"Is there nothing of value among your brother's possessions?"

"If there is, I don't want it."

Hilary nodded. Then she said, "What drove him to such despair, Miss Bell? What made him withdraw from life in this way?"

"Heredity," said Eunice Bell drily. "And now, if you've seen what you want to see—?"

"But I haven't. Look—you mentioned his briefcase. He always carried it with him, didn't he? The station sergeant said it was stuffed with old newspapers, but I would like to search it while I'm here. There's a possibility that it may contain something significant."

"I very much doubt it. Old newspapers, yes; Cuthbert worked in a London merchant bank for a few years when he was a young man, and he liked to make a display of reading and understanding the financial news. But search the briefcase by all means, Miss Lloyd." A ghost of a smile flickered over Eunice Bell's face. "You'll find it just inside his door, to the right—where I dropped it before I retreated."

At Miss Bell's suggestion, Hilary spread out the contents of the case on the mahogany dining-room table, now partially dismantled for the sale. There was nothing in the briefcase except brittle old newspapers, chiefly the *Financial Times*. The dates seemed to be in no particular sequence; no topic was marked or followed through; nothing had been torn out. The papers were between four and twenty years old.

One of the oldest was a copy of the local newspaper, folded at an inside page. The main item of news on the page concerned the search for a missing ten-year-old. He had disappeared a fortnight earlier from his home village near Yarchester after setting out to visit a travelling fair, and no trace of him had so far been found.

On the same page was a feature about four other children who had disappeared from the county without trace. One of them, Terry Gotts aged eight, was a Breckham Market boy. He had disappeared some fifteen years before the date of that particular edition of the paper; and by coincidence, also after setting out from home to visit a travelling fair.

The feature included photographs of all the missing children, with their names printed underneath. But young Terry Gotts' photograph had been deliberately damaged. Someone had taken a ball-point pen, and had scored the photograph with lines that obliterated the boy's features; scored them so fiercely that the point of the pen had made holes in the paper.

28

"Does the name Terry Gotts mean anything to you, Miss Bell?"

Eunice Bell had come down from her quarters carrying a small tray on which was a cup of black China tea. She paused, tray in hand, to consider the question.

"I know an elderly Mrs. Gotts who has a number of adult children, but I don't recall a Terry among them." She put the tray on the table. "I'm afraid I have no lemon to offer you."

"It's good of you to give me tea at all, in the middle of your packing." Hilary re-folded the newspaper so that the feature on missing children was hidden. "This particular Terry disappeared at the age of eight, on an August day thirty-five years ago. There's a mention of the incident in one of these newspapers."

"Oh—then yes, I do remember. Mrs. Gotts was our daily cook-housekeeper at the time. Terry was her youngest child. My mother wouldn't allow her to bring him into the house during the school holidays, but he sometimes played in the back yard. His disappearance was a great tragedy for her."

Sergeant Lloyd searched her own memory. "I've never heard any of my colleagues refer to a missing Breckham Market boy of that name—but then, it was such a long time ago. There'll still be a file on the case, but it's probably been moved to county headquarters. As far as you know, Miss Bell, has anything ever come to light?"

"No," said Eunice Bell. She stood with her hands folded in front of her, her attitude not defensive but severely matter-of-fact. "I was fond of Mrs. Gotts, when I was a girl. She wasn't with us for more than two years at most, but she was good to me. I've kept in touch with her each Christmas, and I should have heard if there had been any news of her son."

"And what about your brother? Was he a friend of Terry Gotts?"

"*Hardly*, Miss Lloyd. For one thing, there was a considerable age difference."

"How old would your brother have been when Terry disappeared?"

"That was the year I was nineteen . . . so Cuthbert would have been seventeen."

Hilary stood up and walked across the room, frowning in thought. "Despite the age difference, wouldn't Cuthbert have known Terry? If the boy played in the back yard during the holidays, mightn't your brother have met him and spoken to him?"

"Quite probably. Yes, he did—he used to be amused by the child's antics."

"And did Terry ever follow Cuthbert? You told us, when I came here with Mr. Quantrill, that Cuthbert used to follow Jack Goodrum about like a puppy. Mightn't Terry have followed Cuthbert—or both of them—in the same way?"

It was Eunice Bell's turn to frown. "I don't understand the significance of your question, Miss Lloyd."

Hilary said nothing. She unfolded the newspaper, revealing the mutilated photograph of Terry Gotts, and placed it flat on the table.

Miss Bell picked up the newspaper so that she could hold it in focus under the wall light. As soon as she saw the deliberate obliteration of the child's features, and realised what it might imply, she drew an audible breath. All trace of colour seemed to drain from her bony face.

"Oh God . . ." she said. Her voice was distressed.

"Do you know something about this, Miss Bell?" said Sergeant Lloyd. "Something about Terry Gotts' disappearance?"

"No." Eunice Bell closed the newspaper decisively, and placed it on the table. "I knew nothing at the time, and I know nothing now. But having seen this, I think I can guess where his body is."

"Where's that?"

"At the Town Hall. You'll need to bring some men, and some strong lights. And probably an oil can."

As Hilary drove her through the lighted streets of the town, Eunice Bell began her explanation with an account of the system that her great-grandfather had devised for supplying water to the Town Hall.

It was only within her lifetime, she said, that mains water had been laid on in Breckham Market. When the Town Hall was built, a well had been sunk in the cellar immediately below the Italianate campanile, which—far from being a delusion of grandeur, or even housing bells—was in fact a water tower. A steam-operated pump had drawn water up from the well and into the tank in the tower.

"When he went on to build this house," Eunice Bell continued, "my great-grandfather used the same system on a smaller scale, with a hand pump. My father employed a full-time gardener when I was a child, and the man spent one whole day each week pumping up the water to fill the tank."

"And where's the connection with your brother?" asked Sergeant Lloyd.

"Cuthbert was fascinated by the system. He would stand for hours watching our gardener pumping. And Grandpapa sometimes took us with him on tours of inspection of the Town Hall. Cuthbert's greatest treat was always to be allowed to go down to the cellar and watch the machinery at work."

"So your brother would have known his way round the building?"

"He would have known how to reach the cellar—and without going through the main doors.

"We were never allowed to go to the Town Hall after Grandpapa died, when I was nine. The town was provided with mains water at about that time, and Cuthbert was terribly anxious to know whether the Town Hall pumping machinery would remain there. He was still talking, years later, about the possibility of getting in to find out by sneaking into the yard at the back of the building and sliding down the coal chute."

"And was the machinery still there?" Sergeant Lloyd stopped her Metro in the market place, just outside the Town Hall. She turned in her seat to look at Eunice Bell. "Is it still there—and is that why we need an oil can?"

"Yes, the machinery's there." Miss Bell, her face grimly white under the street lights, stared straight ahead. "I saw it last Thursday. I had to go to the Town Hall to make arrangements for paying the rates on Tower House, now that I'm leaving. I happened to meet the Chief Executive, who knows my family connection with the building, and he suggested that I might like a final look round. No one seemed to know about the old pumping cellar. They couldn't at first find the keys, but they let me in eventually.

"What I noticed there didn't seem significant at the time. But when you showed me the newspaper photograph, I

realised that Cuthbert might have tried to show off by taking
Jack Goodrum to the cellar. And that Terry Gotts might have
followed them. And that the older boys might have harmed
the child."

Sergeant Lloyd got out of the car and glanced round the
market place. The patrol car support she had radioed for had
not yet arrived. It was 6:45 p.m. The administrative staff who
worked at the Town Hall would have long since gone home,
and though the front steps and the windows of the antechamber were lighted, there was little sign of activity in the
building. Outside, the market day rubbish of cabbage leaves
and squashed oranges had been cleared away. The town centre
would have been quiet, if it were not for the bikers gathered
on their favourite pitch just opposite the chippy, revving their
machines.

Hilary gave a moment's thought to the Quantrill family. As
she had so recently seen young Peter fall from a bike, and
knew how critically ill he was, it seemed at best irrelevant, at
worst prurient, that she should now be picking away at the
details of a thirty-five-year-old incident that had not necessarily
resulted in a death at all.

But then, as Martin Tait had meant to say to her (though
he'd put it more arrogantly), the best thing Douglas Quantrill's
colleagues could do for him was to get on with the job.

"Your theory sounds sadly probable, Miss Bell," she said,
rejoining the older woman in the car. "It would certainly help
to account for your brother's disturbed behaviour, wouldn't it?
And it would also account for Jack Goodrum's anxiety to get
Cuthbert out of the way. But you know how finicky we are
about having evidence . . ."

"I do indeed," said Eunice Bell. "But this time I believe I
have it. When you go into the pumping cellar, you'll find what
I think is my brother's school cap, caught fast in the machinery.
It had a distinctive design, a gold hoop on a blue ground. You'll
be able to identify it because I sewed name tapes on all his
school clothes."

"Your brother's *school* cap? I thought you said that when
Terry disappeared, Cuthbert was seventeen?"

The corner of Miss Bell's mouth twitched a little. "It was
before your time, Miss Lloyd. Things were different, then. My
brother had only just left his boarding school, and he was
accustomed to wearing his cap. My father insisted on it, even

in the holidays. He said it marked Cuthbert out as the son of a gentleman."

"I see . . . Did you know at the time that your brother had lost his cap?"

"Yes, though it seems that he lied about where. It was a very hot August weekend, as I remember—

"Cuthbert came to me in a panic on the Saturday evening, saying that he'd lost his cap at the fair on Castle Meadow. He was never allowed to go to the travelling fairs. He'd told me that morning that he intended to go there with Jack Goodrum, even though he knew he'd get a thrashing if Father found out. Next day, we heard that Terry Gotts was missing. I felt cross with Cuthbert because he seemed more concerned about the loss of his cap than about the missing child."

"Did the police interview your brother about Terry?" asked Hilary.

"They interviewed us all. The Gotts family lived not far from us, and everyone in the area was questioned. Mrs. Gotts gave Terry much more independence than we were ever allowed, and she'd sent him off from home on the Saturday afternoon with sixpence to spend at the fair. He had been seen there with other children of his own age, so there was nothing to connect him with Cuthbert."

"But what did your brother say, when the police questioned him?"

"He said he was at home all day in the garden, with me. That was where he was supposed to be. And it would have been a matter of pride with our parents to confirm that their son had been doing what he was told."

"Didn't you suspect anything, though? When you heard next day that Terry Gotts was missing, didn't it occur to you that your brother might know something about him?"

"Not at all."

Eunice Bell paused. Then she added: "You see, Miss Lloyd, it was in many ways a more innocent age than this. Rightly or wrongly, young people were kept in ignorance. At nineteen, I was so naïve that the very worst fate I could imagine for Terry Gotts was that he had fallen into the river and been swept away."

"I see," said Hilary; though in fact she found it incomprehensible. "But you weren't all *that* naïve, were you, Miss Bell? If you supported your brother's story that he was with you in the garden, then you must have lied to the police."

"Certainly." Eunice Bell looked the sergeant full in the face and gave a near approximation to a smile. "I might have been innocent of physical matters, but I was used to lying on my brother's behalf. I thought of it simply as protecting him. And I did it gladly, because at that time I still loved him."

While two uniformed police constables rigged up emergency lighting in the musty, disused cellar under the tower of the Town Hall, Sergeant Lloyd glanced round with the aid of her torch. It looked a sinister place in the wavering light, looming with a mysterious ironmongery of wheels and pistons and pipes and pulleys and chains. Almost, she thought without thinking, like a medieval torture chamber . . .

She screwed up her eyes for a few moments as the lights came glaring on, then got to work. Miss Bell had explained that the machinery included not only the steam-driven pump, but a hand-operated well-cover hoist. The well in the cellar floor was secured by a heavy cast-iron cover. A ring was attached to the cover, and a chain to the ring. The chain went up and over a pulley suspended from a girder, down to another pulley, and so to a winding drum. It was clear from the dust and rust on the machinery that the hoist had not been used for many years.

The schoolboy's cap, growing mould in places but still identifiable in design, was caught fast by the chains on the drum. When it was released, its fabric was found to be so heavily indented and rust-marked by the pressure of the chains that it had without doubt been there ever since the hoist was last used. In the lining of the cap was a linen tape with the machine-embroidered name C.R.F. BELL.

Two constables oiled the winding gear and hoisted the cover from the well. An unidentifiable, ancient smell rose from it.

Sergeant Lloyd had expected the well to be deep. She had been prepared to ask the fire brigade for a ladder; if necessary to call in a police frogman to search the water. She had certainly expected to have to wait a long time for something—anything—to be found.

But for once, there was no need for the detective to hang about.

The brick-walled well *was* deep: the powerful lights caught a glint of water a very long way down. But just six feet below the top, crossing from wall to wall, was an iron girder. And slumped over it was what looked like a small bundle of tattered sacking, with something stick-like dangling from either end.

It seemed that it was eight-year-old Terry Gotts who had been doing the hanging about, for the past thirty-five years.

29

Although it was nearly midnight when Sergeant Lloyd left the Town Hall, she went straight back to the office. Her mind was too active for sleep.

She would have liked someone to talk to, but the other members of the CID had gone home. When Chief Inspector Tait appeared, just as she was making herself a pot of coffee, she greeted him with pleasure.

"Hallo! Have you just got back from London?"

"No, I've been round at the Quantrills' since ten." He sounded dispirited; his racing trilby had lost its dashing forward tilt. "I saw these lights on my way back to my hotel, and hoped you'd be here."

"How's Peter?"

"Still in intensive care—but at least his condition's stable."

"Thank God for that. Would you like some coffee?"

"Please." He parked his hat and scarf and Burberry. "I've been drinking whisky with Doug, and I need to clear my head."

"How's *he*?"

"Rough. He can't talk to his wife, and he's overwhelmed by guilt-feelings about his relationship with Peter. He seems to hold himself responsible for the boy's accident."

"Poor Douglas. And poor Molly." Hilary shook her head over them, then poured the coffee. "Well—how did you get on with Austin Napier?"

"Don't ask." Tait sat down, uncharacteristically slumped. "Particularly if you're going to tell me that you solved Jack Goodrum's murder while I was away . . ."

"I only wish I had."

"Thank God you didn't, or I'd have looked a complete wally." He gulped his coffee. "Austin Napier's a nutter!" he burst out.

"I rather suspected he might be," said Hilary. It seemed unkind to score off the downcast Chief Inspector by pointing out that she'd told him so before he went.

"I was hoping," Tait continued, "to crack Napier's alibi about staying with his sister in Hampshire last weekend. But his brother-in-law happens to be a fellow barrister, who confirms his story. And when I suggested to Napier that Goodrum's murderer hadn't necessarily fired the shotgun himself, he cross-examined me about whether we'd found the weapon. When I had to admit that we hadn't—yet—he had the arrogance to say that I had no grounds for questioning him. But all the time he was referring to his ex-wife as his wife, and denying the validity of her divorce! And he's a *barrister*, a Queen's Counsel, for heaven's sake! He ought to be disbarred."

Hilary commiserated briskly, and poured him another cup of coffee. "Then where do you suggest we go from here?"

"That depends what you found out while I was away. What have you been doing?"

She told him.

"It will be some time before the body in the well can be positively identified, of course, but apparently it's the right sex and age so there's not much doubt that it's Terry Gotts. The pathologist isn't too hopeful that he can establish the cause of death, after all these years. He found that the boy's hands had been tied together with string, and we discovered a penknife on the floor with a piece of the same string caught in the clasp. The initials JRG were scratched on the handle of the penknife, so it looks as though John Reuben Goodrum was involved with Cuthbert Bell in whatever went on there."

Tait grimaced. "Two adolescents, and one eight-year-old . . . They could have been up to anything. Not that the older boys would necessarily have meant the child any harm, let alone intended to kill him—but whatever happened, Goodrum and Bell were left sharing a very dark secret. And that explains a lot."

The Chief Inspector leaned back in his chair and stretched his arms. "Well, congratulations, Hilary love," he concluded. "You've done a good job. I can't think why you haven't been promoted yet—"

"Thank you, sir," said Sergeant Lloyd wryly. "But I still haven't found out who killed Jack Goodrum. I'd hoped that if we could discover why he wanted Clanger Bell out of the way, we'd get a lead on his own murderer—but that hasn't happened . . ."

Revived, himself again, Tait took advantage of Hilary's preoccupation to put his feet—ankles elegantly crossed—on her desk. "Are you still quite sure it couldn't have been Clanger's sister?"

"No," she said thoughtfully. "No, I'm not sure about Miss Bell at all. While I was at the Town Hall I checked her alibi for Saturday evening, and it's a good one. I'm suspicious of it, but so far I haven't found a way of testing it."

"Wasn't it Doug Quantrill himself who provided her with the alibi?" asked Tait. "Didn't he meet her at some local function?"

"Yes, at the Amateur Operatic performance of *My Fair Lady*. But he's a fine one to offer anybody an alibi for that particular evening! Oh, he went to the Town Hall—but he had no intention of staying to watch the show. He simply established his presence, then sneaked off to the Coney. And knowing he did that, I've begun to wonder whether Eunice Bell mightn't have done the same thing: established her presence, then sneaked out to murder Jack Goodrum."

"And did she? Sneak out, I mean?"

"She could've. It's whether she actually did that I can't discover."

Hilary explained that the Town Hall doorkeeper knew Miss Bell by sight; the Chief Executive had introduced him to her the previous Thursday, saying that she was the builder's great-granddaughter. On the Saturday evening, Miss Bell had spoken to the doorkeeper on her way into the Town Hall for *My Fair Lady*, and had wished him goodnight on the way out.

"He's quite sure that she didn't leave during the course of the show," Hilary said, "and he seems reliable. He doesn't know Chief Inspector Quantrill, but he remembers that a man of Douglas's description went out just as the show started."

"But that's only the front entrance," said Tait. "What about the other doors?"

"All locked, according to the doorkeeper—except of course the two emergency exits. But to reach one of them, Miss Bell would have had to go through the backstage area; and to reach the other she'd have had to go past the room where the interval refreshments were being prepared and served. There would have been people about all the time—and they'd have been members of the Operatic Society, so a non-member would have been noticed. I don't think she could have risked it."

"I'll agree with you about the emergency exits," Tait

conceded. "But I think you're putting far too much reliance on the word of the doorkeeper. How can you possibly be sure that he was watching the front doors throughout the entire evening? Didn't you try to find out—"

"I haven't *finished*," said Hilary. She suddenly became aware of him: "And please take your unsightly feet off my desk."

"I only put them there to annoy you," said Tait provocatively. "Hasn't Doug ever told you that you look more attractive when you're annoyed?" But he grounded his feet. "All right, sorry. Go on."

"The point is," she resumed, "that Eunice Bell knows the building inside out. When she went there last Thursday, the doorkeeper took her down to the cellars, unlocked the one she wanted to see, and left her for a few minutes to look round on her own. That would have given her an opportunity to check the second exit from the cellars. It happens to lead out to the yard at the back of the Town Hall."

"Oh ho." Tait sat up.

"There's a narrow passage under the tower, linking the cellars," Hilary went on. "At the far end of the passage, an iron spiral staircase goes up to a small door. The door isn't locked. There are heavy bolts top and bottom, but I could draw them without too much difficulty. So Eunice Bell could perfectly easily have got out of the Town Hall without being seen, shot Jack Goodrum, and returned in time for the end of the performance. And it seems significant that whoever last used that cellar exit must have been wearing gloves, because we haven't been able to take any prints from either the door or the spiral staircase."

Chief Inspector Tait was sitting forward, alert and thinking hard.

"Yes . . . But where would she have left the shotgun while she was in the Town Hall?"

"I don't see why she couldn't have left it concealed in her car. She could have picked the car up, driven from the town centre to Mount Street, and parked somewhere near The Mount while she did the job. It's a quiet residential area, with a lot of trees that reduce the effectiveness of the street lights—and there's Hobart's Lane, just at the back of The Mount, which has no lighting at all. I don't think anyone who wanted to kill Jack Goodrum would have had too much difficulty in getting a shotgun to and from his garden without being seen."

"And how would Miss Bell have got hold of a gun?"

"No problem. Her grandfather's shotguns were kept in a cabinet at Tower House until last Thursday, when they were removed to be sold. I didn't notice the cabinet, when we went to see her after Clanger's death, but the DCI did. He thought there were four guns in it—but the auctioneer tells me there were only three. It's possible that Douglas was mistaken, of course. He didn't get a close look, and he could have been misled by the four-gun cabinet. But it's also possible that Eunice Bell retained the fourth gun."

"If she did—and if she used it on Goodrum—what do you think she'd have done with it afterwards?"

"I can't imagine." It was tomorrow already, and Hilary felt tiredness creeping up on her. "I don't think Miss Bell would have hidden it on her property because she's selling Tower House and there'd be too much risk of the new owner finding it." She suppressed a yawn. "She's probably taken it miles away and thrown it into a river somewhere, or into the sea. Off the Orwell Bridge, perhaps? Or the end of Yarmouth pier?"

"Now *you*'re being frivolous," said Tait severely. "And I don't agree with you. I think it's possible that Miss Bell might have got rid of the shotgun immediately after the murder, by dumping it locally. I'll have this stretch of the river, and the mere, searched as soon as it's light.

"Alternatively," he went on, rising to his feet and prowling about the room, thinking, "she may be keeping the shotgun concealed among her possessions, with the intention of disposing of it after she's left Breckham Market." He turned abruptly to face Hilary. "Didn't you say that when you called on her this afternoon she'd just sent off a load of furniture?"

Sergeant Lloyd drew a sharp breath, then groaned, vexed with herself. She had spent the last few hours suspecting Eunice Bell, without considering the possible significance of the removal van she had seen outside Tower House.

"Yes," she admitted. "I even saw a large packing case being loaded . . . But if by any chance the gun *is* in store with her furniture, at least it'll keep," she added more positively. "And for the record, I had no reason at the time to disbelieve Miss Bell's alibi."

"But you knew that she had shotguns in the house," Tait pointed out. "And you knew she had a very strong motive for killing Goodrum. Eunice Bell should have been your number one suspect!"

"Well, she wasn't. And I don't agree that she had a strong motive. Yes, she's a proud woman. She told us, after Goodrum had been exonerated from blame for her brother's death, that she felt a deep sense of injustice. But she didn't grieve for Cuthbert. She said she felt nothing but relief that he was dead. And I can't believe that just when she'd at last gained her freedom, she would have risked it by planning and carrying out a murder for his sake. It wasn't as if she felt any personal animosity towards Jack Goodrum. She didn't even know the man."

"Then why are you suspecting her?"

"Simply because I discovered this evening that she *could* have done it. But unless we can disprove some aspect of her alibi, we've got nothing against her. We'd never get a search warrant on the basis of that motive."

"I wouldn't try," said Tait. He put on his Burberry. "And I'm not going to argue with you about motive at this time of night! Let's get some sleep. Tomorrow, you can start finding out whether in fact there had been a fourth shotgun in the cabinet at Tower House."

"Shouldn't be difficult," the sergeant said, half to herself. She flipped through her notebook. "Yes, Eunice Bell talked about someone who did the cleaning for her—"

"*Not* tonight," said the Chief Inspector, reaching across the desk and plucking the notebook from her hands. "You've done a good job today, Hilary, and I'm very glad to have you working with me again. Now *go home*, woman."

He put his hat on his head, tipping it racily forward, and took her coat from its wire hanger on the side of a filing cabinet.

"Yes, all right, I'm going," she said, pushing back her chair. "But only because I intended to, anyway." She slid her arms into the sleeves of the coat as he held it for her. "Thanks. I'll talk to the Operatic Society ticket sellers, too," she went on, "and find out if they noticed where Eunice Bell was sitting for *My Fair Lady* . . ."

Tait sighed. He put an arm across her shoulders and steered her firmly towards the door. "Come on, my fair lady," he said with affectionate exasperation.

"*Martin!*" Hilary stopped abruptly and whirled to face him, her tiredness gone. "That's it—*that's* how we can test Eunice Bell's alibi. It's so simple that we can do it right away, even before we know about the gun. All we have to ask her is *whether she enjoyed the show*."

30

Sergeant Lloyd had guessed that Miss Bell would still be up, despite the fact that it was well after midnight. What she had not anticipated was that the lights outside Tower House would be on, the front door would be open, letting out more light from the hall, and Eunice Bell would be loading suitcases into her car.

Tait stopped his own car in the gateway, blocking it. Hilary followed him as he walked up the shadowed drive between the bare pollarded lime trees. Behind the limes rose the spiny monkey puzzle tree; above and beyond that loomed the dark outline of the Italianate tower from which the house derived its name.

The detectives had almost reached the house before Miss Bell noticed them. Dressed for travelling in a navy loden coat, she was about to lift a final suitcase into the boot of her staid elderly Rover. She glared at the intruders.

"This is a private residence," she said, her breath rising like a dragon's in the cold clear night air. "Is that your car in my gateway? Remove it at once, young man, or I shall call the police."

Hilary stepped forward, apologised for the lateness of their coming, and introduced the Chief Inspector. Eunice Bell ignored him.

"This is not a convenient time for a visit, Miss Lloyd. As you see, I've decided to leave Breckham Market immediately. I have a room reserved at the Angel at Saintsbury. You can get in touch with me there."

"Why the hurry to go?" asked Tait. But before she could reply, or disdain to reply, he sniffed the air. "I can smell petrol," he said.

"No doubt. I had my car filled this evening, and the careless youth let the tank overflow."

"May we come inside the house and talk to you, Miss Bell?" asked Hilary. "There's something we do urgently need to clear up before you leave."

"About my brother and Terry Gotts? The child has been dead for thirty-five years. Surely your questions can wait."

"It's not about Terry Gotts. It's about your grandfather's shotguns. May we come in?"

Eunice Bell made no comment. She led them as far as the lighted portico, but then closed the front door to prevent them going any further. "There's no point in going in," she said. Her face looked unnaturally white, her eye-sockets darkly hollowed—but so did all their faces, under the harsh overhead light. "The furnishings have all been dismantled."

Tait's long nose twitched again. "I can still smell petrol."

Miss Bell raised her left hand, and sniffed the back of it fastidiously. "No, not petrol," she told Hilary. "I decided that I couldn't leave my brother's room as it was, with people coming for the sale, so I've just been fumigating it. I seem to have sprayed some of the stuff on my hands."

"About the shotguns," said the sergeant. "How many were there in the cabinet, Miss Bell?"

"There were three."

"When I first came here with Chief Inspector Quantrill, he saw four."

"No. He saw a four-gun cabinet, and obviously came to the wrong conclusion. Why do you ask?"

"We're looking for the weapon that was used last Saturday evening to kill Jack Goodrum," said Tait.

"Indeed?" said Eunice Bell frostily. "Then you're wasting your time by looking here. There were only three shotguns in my house, and Mr. Glaze the auctioneer will confirm that he removed them for sale last Thursday."

"I suggest that there was a fourth gun," said Tait. "And that it was used to kill Jack Goodrum."

Eunice Bell attempted to shrivel the Chief Inspector with a look. "Are you implying that *I* might have shot the man? That would have been impossible. I spent Saturday evening watching *My Fair Lady* at the Town Hall—as Chief Inspector Quantrill knows."

"Ah yes," said Hilary. "He mentioned that you'd had a chat before the performance. Did you enjoy the show, Miss Bell?"

"Certainly."

"And you sat through the whole of it?"

"Of course."

"Such a pity it had to be interrupted, when Chief Inspector Quantrill was called out because of the murder. What happened, exactly? Did they bring the curtain down and make an announcement, or what?"

For a moment Miss Bell stood rigid. Then she said, "I had a headache, and went out to the cloakroom to take some codeine. I believe the interruption occurred while I was away. I knew none of the people who were sitting near me, so I heard none of the details."

"And how long were you away? Half an hour or more?"

"Certainly not. Five minutes at most."

"So except for those five minutes, you were in the auditorium watching the show?"

"Yes."

"Then that's more than can be said of Chief Inspector Quantrill! He didn't intend to watch it, you know. He pretended he was going to, but he left before it began. That was why the performance had to be interrupted twice, because he didn't respond to the first announcement. But then, you were there, Miss Bell, so you'll know about that. Even if you missed the first interruption, you must have been back in the auditorium for the second, twelve minutes later. What happened, exactly? Did they bring down the curtain and make another announcement?"

Eunice Bell drew her coat more closely about her, and made no reply.

"We'd like to search your car, Miss Bell," said Tait.

She gave him another look. "Not unless you have a warrant."

"Not yet—but meanwhile I'm taking charge of your ignition key." He removed it from the car. "When Sergeant Lloyd was here this afternoon," he added, "you gave her permission to search your brother's room. At the time, she decided not to do so. We'd like to do it now."

"No. I withdraw that permission. As I told you, I've just fumigated the room."

"With *petrol*?" the Chief Inspector said. He picked up a five litre can that was lying on the gravel of the drive half-hidden behind the last of the suitcases, as though ready to be taken away. The can was capped, but empty. "For God's sake, you haven't sprinkled petrol in the room, have you? Don't you realise that you could blow the place up?"

"I'm sure Miss Bell does realise it," said Hilary quietly. "If that's what she's done, then it was for a specific purpose." She turned to the older woman. "It's too late for you to carry it through now. Let us in, please."

Eunice Bell took a proud stand immediately in front of the door. "I refuse to allow you to enter."

"Madam," said Tait, "in these circumstances we don't need your permission. We have reason to suspect that there's a serious fire risk in this building, and we're empowered to investigate it in the interests of public safety." He side-stepped adroitly and barged the door open. "Which way, Hilary?"

"Sorry, Miss Bell—but he's right."

Sergeant Lloyd slipped through the door and ran down the lighted, echoing, bare-tiled hall, past the furniture lined up for sale. She pushed open the green baize door that led to the former servants' quarters. The passage beyond was dark, and smelled unmistakably of petrol. "No lights!" shouted Tait from behind her. "For God's sake don't touch the light switches!"

He took a powerful torch from the pocket of his Burberry and spotlit the end of the kitchen corridor. The smell increased as they neared Clanger Bell's room. In the beam from her own torch, Hilary could see the air thickening and wavering as fumes seeped through the gap under the door.

Her eyes began to sting. She pulled the silk square from the neck of her coat, held it to her face and retreated. "We can't go in there just to look for evidence," she protested, coughing. "It's too dangerous. Let's get outside and call the fire brigade. We can come back when they've made the building safe."

"But it could blow up before they arrive," objected Tait. "I'm not prepared to risk losing the shotgun, now we've come this far. It must be in there—why else should she want to destroy the room? If we don't rescue the gun intact, we shall never be able to prove that Eunice Bell murdered Jack Goodrum."

"Don't be a fool, Martin! It's crazy to think of searching a fume-filled room. Quite apart from the danger of an explosion, you'd damage your lungs. No piece of evidence is worth that."

"I shouldn't need to do any searching," he said. "From what you've told me of the state of Clanger's room, would Miss Bell have wanted to stay there long enough to hide anything? I'll be in and out in a matter of seconds. You clear off and leave this to me."

Sergeant Lloyd elected to remain; someone would have to do something if the young idiot collapsed. She lighted the corridor with her torch as Tait, looking absurdly like a thirties gangster with his hat tilted over his eyes and his scarf tied over the lower part of his face, stood back against the wall and pushed open the door with one hand. The petrol fumes rolled silently out, making both detectives cough.

Then Tait sprang in front of the doorway, thrusting his torch like a handgun. Immediately, muffled but triumphant, he cried, "I *told* you so!"

Forgetting her own strictures, Hilary joined him for a moment at the open door. Nothing in Clanger's dreadful room appeared to have been moved since her afternoon visit, but the nauseating mingled smell of dirt and despair had now been swamped by the reek of petrol. The soiled bedding was sodden with fuel; and on it, at the intended centre of the conflagration, lay a double-barrelled shotgun.

"We'd like you to come to the station with us, please, Miss Bell."

She was sitting behind the wheel of her Rover, watching impassively as Chief Inspector Tait, looking pleased with himself, carried the shotgun out of her house. "May I drive my own car?" she asked.

"Sorry, no." Hilary opened the door. "The car will have to stay where it is for the time being—we're very much afraid of sparking off an explosion."

Miss Bell alighted with dignity. "It was foolhardy of you to go into that room," she remarked as they walked together down the drive.

"That was Chief Inspector Tait. *I* wouldn't have done it, and neither would Chief Inspector Quantrill. It's your bad luck that Mr. Tait is more single-minded than either of us."

"My bad luck?"

"Yes, if the shotgun was used to kill Jack Goodrum. Whoever fired it made the mistake of not picking up the ejected cartridge case, you see. The experts will be able to tell whether or not it came from that gun."

Eunice Bell drew an audible breath, but said nothing. They reached the gateway. Tait was sitting in his car, with the door open, using the radio. Hilary went to open the rear door, but Miss Bell put out a detaining hand, almost—but not quite—touching her.

"I would like to talk to you, Miss Lloyd," she said urgently. "In private. On a personal matter. May we stay out here?"

They walked back a few paces. Eunice Bell halted under a pollarded lime tree, where she was shadowed from the street lights on Victoria Road. "I wouldn't have wanted Chief

Inspector Quantrill to hear this," she said, "and I have no intention of saying it in front of that bumptious young man. Only one other living person knows what I'm going to tell you: Mrs. Gotts."

"Terry's mother?"

"Yes. Our former cook-housekeeper."

"I thought you seemed concerned," said Hilary, "after we'd found the child's body, when I said that I'd be going to talk to Mrs. Gotts tomorrow. Did you think she might tell me your secret?"

"That possibility bothered me, at the time. But now the circumstances have changed, I no longer mind *your* knowing, Miss Lloyd. It's the thought of general publicity, and gossip in Breckham Market and Saintsbury, that I abhor. To avoid that, I would even be prepared to go to the length of admitting that I shot Jack Goodrum."

Hilary blinked with surprise, but managed to express nothing but mild interest. "And did you?"

"I could deny it, of course. But tell me: if I were to deny it, how deeply would you dig? How far back into my private life would you investigate?"

"As deeply as necessary, Miss Bell. As far back as we needed to go."

"And what you found would be brought out in open court?"

"If it were relevant, yes."

Eunice Bell stood with her shoulders braced, her head high. "But if I were to plead guilty?"

"We should still investigate. People have been known," said Hilary, "to confess to murders they didn't commit."

"But perhaps you wouldn't investigate quite so thoroughly? Let's assume, for the sake of argument, that you were able without much difficulty to prove my guilt: would you then be prepared to accept, without looking for any other motive, that I killed Jack Goodrum to avenge the murder of my brother?"

Astonished by the proposition, Hilary gave the only possible answer: "I can't make any deals with you, Miss Bell. I can't make promises."

"I understand that. But I want *you* to understand that I cherish my privacy. Whatever is going to be said in Suffolk about my conduct last Saturday evening, I want there to be no gossip about my past. I didn't tell you the truth, you see, when you first visited me to discuss Cuthbert's death. I mentioned that my father had once thrashed Jack Goodrum, and that I didn't know why. But I did know.

"I was nineteen and I had recently been kissed for the first time, by one of my cousins. I liked him, and it was a pleasant experience. And I *did* know Jack Goodrum, though I told you I didn't. I spent several evenings, that summer, sitting on the wall at the bottom of the garden, talking to him. He was only sixteen, but as big as a man, and I knew that he admired me. And I thought he looked rather like my cousin, from a distance.

"So I decided to invite him over the wall and allow him to kiss me. But he wasn't like my cousin at all. He *smelled*. And when I told him so, and tried to push him away, he raped me."

"Was that why your father thrashed him?" asked Hilary.

"Yes: thrashed him and threatened him and ordered his grandfather the butcher to send him back home to Ipswich. Not that I had told my parents. I was much too frightened of them. I knew that I should be punished . . . as though the rape hadn't been punishment enough . . .

"But Cuthbert had seen what happened and he told Mrs. Gotts, though he wouldn't say who the culprit was until my father beat the information out of him. I had begged Mrs. Gotts not to tell my mother. But Terry had disappeared only the previous week, and she had too many worries of her own, poor woman, to keep my secret."

"Did your father report the rape to the police?" said Hilary.

"There was no question of that. My parents would never allow any scandal to touch the family. So throughout my life I have been able to keep at least my *reputation* intact. And I don't want to lose it now."

"But would it so desperately matter if local people knew about the incident, after all these years?"

It was, Hilary realised almost immediately, an impertinent question. Rape, however traumatic for the victim, might raise no eyebrows in the present social climate, but it must have caused a woman such as Eunice Bell a continuing agony of shame. The older woman's hissingly swift reaction left the sergeant in no doubt about that.

"It matters to *me*, Miss Lloyd."

Then, almost to herself, she added: "But I didn't contemplate killing Jack Goodrum for it, when he first came strutting back to Breckham Market as a self-made man. He was beneath my contempt. It was his killing of Cuthbert that angered me into action. All I wanted at the time, though, was for him to be tried and punished. Just think, Miss Lloyd: had you been more efficient when you first investigated my brother's murder, I would have had no need to kill Jack Goodrum at all . . ."

It was a fair gibe; a justifiable return, Hilary acknowledged, for her own tactlessness. "But you said that your brother's death *wasn't* your motive."

"That is so. What finally determined me was that I happened to see Jack, shortly after Cuthbert's funeral, having lunch at the Angel in Saintsbury with his new wife. She was not at all the type of woman one would expect to marry such an oaf. Her first husband was a barrister, you know.

"We exchanged a word in the cloakroom, and she was charming. Well bred, well mannered, well dressed—a gentlewoman. And throughout lunch, Jack was aping the gentleman! I was astonished by the gallantry he was putting on.

"And the dreadful thing was that she was in love with him! Oh yes, she was completely taken in—I could see it, Miss Lloyd, and I was appalled. How could I allow her, a woman of my own kind, to go on loving and trusting a man I knew to be a rapist and a murderer? I had to do something to stop it. I couldn't let their relationship continue, for her own sake. And I know she'll thank me for it, when she hears the truth about the kind of man she married . . ."

A traffic patrol car arrived in Victoria Road, its powerful blue light punching holes in the night sky, and Chief Inspector Tait went to brief the driver about the Tower House fire hazard. Hilary guided Eunice Bell into the back of Tait's car. The older woman's outburst had left her trembling with cold and emotion, but when the sergeant took off her own coat and attempted to put it round her, Miss Bell rejected it.

Regaining her composure, she looked at her watch. Then she said, in her normal stiff voice: "Is it too much to hope that you will respect my confidences, Miss Lloyd?"

"I can make no promise," repeated Hilary. "But I don't think that particular motive is likely to come to light during our investigations. And as it happens," she added, "Chief Inspector Tait isn't looking for any motive other than your brother's death. He seems to be satisfied that your desire for revenge would have been quite strong enough."

"Does he indeed? Then he's obviously a more estimable young man than I had supposed," said Eunice Bell drily.

The estimable young man came hurrying over to his car. "Let's get out of the way before the fire engine comes," he said, driving off down Victoria Road. "I shall be glad to be clear of that Tower House time bomb—"

There was a sudden *wumph* behind them. The car windows rattled. Tait did an emergency stop. They all looked back, and saw orange tongues of flame licking out of the blown windows of the Italianate tower of Eunice Bell's house.

"What set *that* off?" fumed the Chief Inspector.

"I did," said Eunice Bell. "I left a timing device in my brother's room. How else could I have fired the building without risking my own life?"

"But why didn't you tell us it was there?" protested Hilary. "Once we'd found the shotgun, it was absolutely pointless for you to burn Tower House."

"Do you think so?" Eunice Bell turned away from the spectacle and settled back in her corner, upright, self-contained, and yet unusually relaxed. Her face, illuminated by the lights of the approaching fire engine, had a rare look of complete satisfaction.

31

Chief Inspector Quantrill had been on leave for two weeks.

During the second week, after his son had been declared out of danger, he had sent occasional messages to the office. One message had congratulated the members of Breckham Market CID—and of course Chief Inspector Tait, who had returned to the Saintsbury division, mission accomplished— on having made an arrest in the Jack Goodrum murder case. Another had congratulated Sergeant Lloyd, personally, on having solved the thirty-five-year-old disappearance of Terry Gotts. A third, in the form of a personal note to Hilary Lloyd, was a pressing invitation to call at number 5 Benidorm Avenue early on the Sunday evening immediatley before Quantrill was due to return to work.

Although Hilary had met Molly Quantrill once or twice, she

had never before been invited to their house. What bothered
her about the invitation was that she knew, through the Martin
Tait–Alison Quantrill grapevine, that Molly was expected to
spend that Sunday in Yarchester with Alison, visiting Peter in
hospital. This meant that, in the evening, Douglas would be at
home alone.

Hilary was concerned for him, and even more for Molly.
Their marriage had obviously been unsatisfactory for a long
time, and although their son's near-fatal accident might have
had the effect of drawing them closer together, Martin had said
only the previous week that Douglas was having a particularly
bad time because he couldn't talk to his wife. And the last
thing Hilary wanted was to play any part in the irretrievable
breakdown of their marriage.

She thought up several good excuses for declining the
invitation. But on the other hand, she was still one of his
closest colleagues, still very much his friend—and what kind of
friend would refuse to help fill a worried father's lonely
evening? She decided to go. But she also decided that if
Douglas were to give one hopeful hint of any future development in their personal relationship, she would write an
immediate application for the transfer to Saintsbury that
Martin Tait had suggested.

On a wet evening in early December, Hilary presented herself
warily at the Quantrills' door. It was opened by a Douglas who
looked thinner and older than the man who had been pursuing
her before his son's accident; his eyes were darkly underhung
with evidence of sleeplessness, the lines on his face were much
more deeply scored.

He gave her a slightly shamefaced greeting, avoiding her
eye. Then, taking her coat and dripping umbrella, he added
rather too loudly and brightly—and greatly to her relief—
"We're very glad you could come, aren't we, my dear?"

His wife emerged from the sitting-room. Molly's anxiety
over Peter had clearly made her turn for comfort to food. She
had put on all the weight her husband had lost, and more.
Hilary recalled her as a small, healthily plump woman with
ample evidence of the prettiness she must have had in her
youth, but now she seemed ungainly. Her cheeks were pastry-
pale and her eyes still had the staring appearance of residual
shock.

"How's Peter, Mrs. Quantrill?" Hilary asked immediately.

"Comfortable now, thank you. At least, as comfortable as he can be with both legs in plaster, and all those weights and pulleys . . ." Molly's voice rose, its stability threatened by lurking tears.

"He's a lot better than he *was*, anyway," said Quantrill thankfully. He followed the women into the living-room, and uncorked a bottle of sherry that stood in solitary state on the sideboard in the dining area. Hilary, sitting in an armchair that must have been bought for its appearance as part of a suite rather than for its comfort, saw with private dismay how unsuitable the cramped modern house and its obviously feminine choice of furnishings was for a man of Douglas's size and character. How could Molly expect him to be happy in such a pastel-coloured room, with toning framed prints on the walls and an imitation-log electric fire in the imitation hearth?

"In fact," Douglas continued, taking a stand in front of the fire and seeming more at home now that he had an engraved pewter beer mug in his fist, though he still couldn't look at Hilary, "Peter's so much better that we thought we ought to give him a change from family company. His mates have been asking after him, and as they can't go to Yarchester except at weekends, we decided to let them do the visiting today. They're good lads, and he'll be glad to see them. He needs a bit of cheering up."

"He's going to be lame, you see," said Molly, her voice almost out of control. "Even if his legs mend properly, one will be shorter than the other. And he's had to have a lung removed. He was such a fine, strong boy . . . and now his life's been ruined . . ."

Her husband put down his mug and went to her immediately, sitting beside her, taking her hand, and reassuring her in a way that was so effective that he clearly must have had a great deal of recent practice. Hilary sipped her sweet sherry and glanced at a handy copy of *Woman and Home*; but observing the couple covertly, she saw that it was Molly who would most easily be able to cope with their son's disablement.

Once she had recovered from the shock and the anxiety, and as soon as Peter was safely back at home, Molly would set to with vigour and help the boy adjust to his handicap. Molly would be all right. And there seemed to be no reason why Peter shouldn't in time lead a more or less normal life.

But Douglas, with his lowered eyes and guilt-stricken

face . . . how was he going to come to terms with the
responsibility he had accepted for his son's accident? Did he
intend to tell Molly that when he had seen Peter riding the
borrowed motor bike he had tried, in anger, to make him stop?
And, whether he confessed it to her or not, would their
marriage hold together under the strain?

If it came to that, would Hilary's working relationship with
Douglas still hold? Burdened as he was by the additional guilt
of knowing that he wouldn't have been at the roadside to cause
Peter's accident if he hadn't deliberately parked there, while
on duty, in order to proposition his sergeant, there was little
wonder that he couldn't look her in the eye. But if he couldn't
find some way of doing so during the course of this evening, it
really would be best for both of them, Hilary decided, if she
were to ask for a transfer to Saintsbury.

Molly rapidly recovered her composure. She sat up, and
smoothed her hair with dignity. "I'm sorry about that," she said
to her guest, smiling the apology. "I know it's silly of me to be
upset over Peter's injuries, when he might so easily have been
killed. How we'd have coped with that, as some poor parents
have to, I really don't know . . . We've a lot to be thankful
for, haven't we, Douggie?" She patted his tweed-clad knee.
"Let's have another glass of sherry, dear. After all, we invited
Hilary so that she could join us in a small celebration!"

"So we did," said her husband heartily, rising to fetch the
bottle.

"Molly and I have had some very good news," he told Hilary
as he topped up her glass. "I'd have told you about it a couple
of weeks ago, but what with one thing and another—"

He retreated towards the electric fire, and fortified himself
from his pewter mug. Then he looked directly at Hilary. The
underlying guilt was still there in his face, of course; and
shame, and unhappiness too. But at the same time there was
something that lightened his expression, and made him seem
younger—a look almost of wondering pride.

"It's just a family matter, really," he said. "But because you
and I, Hilary, spend so much of our working time together,
Molly and I wanted you be the first person outside the family
to know. Didn't we, my dear?"

He smiled at his wife. Molly got up eagerly, and stood
beside him. She was still a little shaky, but there was no
mistaking the expectant happiness in her eyes. There was no

mistaking, either, the genuine affection with which Douglas put his arm round her comfortable waist.

"Thanks to our daughter Jennifer," he announced "—not to mention her husband Nigel, of course—Molly and I are looking forward to becoming proud grandparents next year. Congratulate us, Hilary!"

Postscript

2 St. Mary's Terrace
Colchester, Essex
1st January

Dear Sergeant Lloyd,
Now that Matthew and I have established a permanent address, I am at last writing to thank you for the kindness and consideration you showed me after Jack's death. I had hoped to be able to thank you in person. But I went straight to Northamptonshire with my parents after leaving hospital, and then found that I couldn't bear to return to The Mount. My brother and sister-in-law very kindly went to Breckham Market on my behalf to clear the house and arrange for it to be sold.

Matthew and I lived in Colchester before my marriage, and liked the town very much, so we have been fortunate to find this house. It's small but v. attractive (early Victorian). Both house and garden need a great deal of work, so I shall keep myself busy. Matthew's school is not too far away, and he has plans to come and visit me at weekends on his motor cycle, when the weather permits. He seems to have matured a great deal during the past month, and has been a tower of strength in many ways.

I miss Jack so much—
He was such an honest, kind man that I still find it incomprehensible that anyone should have wanted to kill him. My solicitor tells me that Miss Bell has been charged—it appears that she killed Jack in revenge for his having run over her drunken brother. (But no doubt you know a great deal more about this than I do.) The most charitable thing I can think is that she must be out of her mind. As if poor Jack would have *meant* to kill her brother!

One of the things I am hoping to do, when I feel able to socialise again, is to meet and make friends with Jack's daughters. I've written to them, but they haven't so far replied. This is understandable, I suppose. I'm sure they must have loved their father, and so naturally they would have been upset by their parents' divorce. I expect they think of me as the Other Woman and want nothing to do with me, and I would like to try to make amends.

I was astonished to find that Jack had left me absolutely everything in his will. A great deal of money, far more than I shall ever need. Dear Jack—we were so absorbed in each other that I can only suppose he temporarily overlooked the existence of his daughters. Knowing his generosity, I can't for one moment think that he intended to disinherit them. I know that he settled money on them when he was divorced, but I'm quite sure that had he lived he would have topped this up at intervals throughout their lives. So I've arranged with my solicitor for fair portions of their father's estate to be made over to Sharon and Tracey as soon as possible, as Jack would have wished.

I mention this to you because I believe you have met the girls—you told me, when you came to see me in hospital, that you intended to visit them. So, in a way, you know more about Jack's past life than I do! And you are one of the few people who saw us living so happily together in our lovely house at Breckham Market. This is—forgive me—my reason for writing to you at such length. Until I meet the rest of his family, you are really the only person I can talk to about Jack. And I miss him so much.

Sadly, my parents took an immediate dislike to him and refused to believe that we truly loved each other. How wrong they were! In face of their unspoken relief that my marriage was so short-lived, it has been a great comfort to me to recall that you are a witness to the happiness we shared.

With all good wishes.

Yours very sincerely,
Felicity Goodrum

ABOUT THE AUTHOR